Something hits him hard from behind. He hears two quick *pops*—some part of his brain tells him it is gunfire, but it doesn't sound nearly as loud as he'd imagined—and glass breaking. Yoko whips around, screaming.

"I'm shot," he gasps.

"No," says a voice in his ear. "You're not. Not this time."

He realizes then that the thing that hit him was a man, another lurker who must have sprung out of the darkness and tackled him like an American footballer, right before the gunshots started. The pain and breathlessness aren't from bullets in his chest, but because this big man is lying on top of him, covering him with his body. Protecting him. "Who are you?" he grunts.

"A fan," says the voice in his ear. "For forty years, ever since I was a boy. It's an honor to meet you, Mr. Lennon."

John has just enough time to think: that doesn't make sense. *I'm* only forty. Then blue lightning flashes and his mouth floods with acid and his stomach drops ten miles into the earth and all of it—the Dakota, the madman with the gun, Yoko—it all disappears.

—from "But I'm Not the Only One" by Chris Pearson

TIMESHARES

edited by Jean Rabe and Martin H. Greenberg

DAW BOOKS, INC.
DONALD A. WOLLHEIM, FOUNDER
375 Hudson Street, New York, NY 10014

ELIZABETH R. WOLLHEIM
SHEILA E. GILBERT
PUBLISHERS
http://www.dawbooks.com

First Printing, March 2010

1 2 3 4 5 6 7 8 9

DAW TRADEMARK REGISTERED
U.S. PAT. AND TM. OFF. AND FOREIGN COUNTRIES
—MARCA REGISTRADA
HECHO EN U.S.A.

PRINTED IN THE U.S.A.

ACKNOWLEDGMENTS

"A Timely Introduction," copyright © 2010 by Jean Rabe

"The Authentic Touch," copyright © 2010 by Word Fire, Inc.

"Timeless Lisa," copyright © 2010 by Robert E. Vardeman

"Been a Long Time," copyright © 2010 by Matthew P. Mayo

"Unsolved Histories," copyright © 2010 by Greg Cox

"Limited Time Offer," copyright © 2010 by Dean Leggett

"The Shaman," copyright © 2010 by Annie Jones

"A Portrait of Time," copyright © 2010 by Kelly Swails

"But I'm Not the Only One," copyright © 2010 by Chris Pierson

"It's Just a Matter of Time," copyright © 2010 by James M. Ward

"Time Sharing," copyright © 2010 by Jody Lynn Nye

"Two Tickets to Paradise," copyright © 2010 by Vicki Steger

"The World of Null-T," copyright © 2010 by Gene DeWeese

Contents

A Timely Introduction

If it was truly possible to vacation in time, I would visit early America on the off chance I'd meet Benjamin Franklin. I always thought it would be great to share a meal with him and talk about politics and electricity. Maybe fly a kite together. George Washington could join us—I'm still curious about the whole wooden teeth thing. And I'd like to chat with Thomas Jefferson about his recommended authors. After all, Jefferson wrote one of my all-time favorite quotes: "I cannot live without books."

So early America for me.

But just for one of my timely sojourns.

Then there's Rome in the time of Caesar—I could spend a week or two there. I studied Latin in high school and have kept up with it enough that on a good day I just might be able to make it through a marketplace to sample the wines and wares. I've no interest in watching whatever bloody act would be taking place in any arena.

Or maybe I'd go back to see the very first football game ever. I am a football junkie. That would be a seriously delicious kick, especially if I could get a seat on the 50-yard line.

I think I'd even give prehistoric Africa a try, just to see the dinosaurs. Real dinosaurs, not the skeletons on display in museums or the cinematic ones of *Jurassic Park* and the like.

Yeah, now that I'm thinking about it, if I was going to take a vacation in time it would have to be for the dinosaurs.

Up close and personal with a stegosaurus first, then a meet-and-greet with Ben Franklin.

Fortunately for you, the authors in this collection went to all manner of interesting places not on my list— a veritable whirlwind tour across the globe and through the centuries. They opened my eyes to some interesting possibilities.

Allister Timms took a risky vacation during World War I. Robert Vardeman went looking for a costly work of art, Jody Lynn Nye discovered a classic romance, and Vicki Steger found paradise. Greg Cox's traveler found danger, Chris Pierson's found John Lennon, and Michael Stackpole's found Jesus.

Each vacation in this anthology will stir your imagination and make you think about your own possible *Timeshares* journey.

Where would you go?

Or, more precisely, *when* would you go?

Enjoy the trips *Timeshares* offers up in this collection.

Me? After reading all of the tales I'm thinking paradise might not be so bad. Maybe I could take John Lennon and Leonardo da Vinci with me.

—Jean Rabe

The Authentic Touch

Kevin J. Anderson

Kevin J. Anderson is the author of more than one hundred novels, forty-seven of which have appeared on national or international bestseller lists. He has more than twenty million books in print in thirty languages. He has won or been nominated for numerous prestigious awards, including the Nebula Award, the Bram Stoker Award, the SFX Reader's Choice Award, the American Physics Society's Forum Award, and the *New York Times* Notable Book Award.

Mainz, Germany, 1452

All these dirty, crowded medieval towns looked the same to him. He double-checked the small glowing screen on his locator/communicator/emergency signal. Yes, Mainz, Germany. 1452. Right on target.

He was no historian and had no aspirations to become one. To him, historical settings were to be studied on an entertainment screen or read in a novel, not to be experienced firsthand. But a job was a job ... and the job had taken him here.

His name was Bill—"Bill the PR Man." Not a very

memorable name, but his parents had given him little to work with. Bill Smith, not even a middle name. When he'd started his career, talking himself up to various corporations and showing off his skills, Bill had considered changing his name. Maybe something that would leave a more distinctive and powerful impression—"Brom Zanderley"—or stuffy and imposing—"P. Jason Higgenbotham"—but he was *Bill*, and he felt like *Bill*, and so he turned the disadvantage into a focus, making the very simplicity his calling card. Bill, the PR Man.

Honesty, veracity, authenticity. "I want your clientele to remember *you*, not me," he told his customers. The name and that attitude had served him very well.

And now it had taken him across the centuries just to do a simple brochure. But it was perhaps the most important contract job in his career.

In Mainz, he drew a deep breath, driving back the dizziness and the slight nausea that always resulted from traveling through time. For some reason, though no other travelers had mentioned it, Bill always tasted vinegar in the back of his throat during a transport. Other people experienced severe waves of diarrhea for the first hour; given the alternative, he preferred the vinegar taste.

The night was dim, and fog seeped along the streets, but the swirling mists did little to lessen the stench. Once a person traveled back more than a few decades, Bill had found that all historical places carried a definite and oppressive *odor*. Not surprising, considering the lack of hygiene, the garbage and sewage, even dead bodies lying around. He couldn't imagine anyone wanting to *vacation* under conditions like this. But he certainly wouldn't call attention to the unpleasantness in the promotional literature. Rose-colored glasses, soft focus, a bit of license with descriptive language . . . while still keeping that authentic touch.

From a tavern at the other end of the alley he could hear loud Germanic voices singing and arguing. High overhead, a thick-armed woman opened the shutters of a window and poured the contents of a chamber pot down into the street, missing Bill by only a few yards. He hurried away, shouting up at the impolite person, "Watch what you're doing!" But of course she did not understand modern English, and he received a volley of curses right back.

Bill moved out of the alley toward a wider street, getting his bearings. He wore period costume—scratchy fabric, rough and uncomfortable seams. Surreptitiously, he glanced down at the screen of his locator again. The techs had missed the target by two blocks. Not bad, considering the centuries crossed but they would have to fine-tune their skills before large waves of customers signed up for the Timeshares service. It would really ruin a vacation if a customer materialized through time on the wrong side of a cliff . . . or in the middle of a crowded square in colonial New England where people might be inclined to point and cry out, "A witch! A witch!"

Scouts had gone ahead to chart all the locations, as they would for any approved vacation. Bill consulted the photos and saw what he was looking for—a nondescript print shop, although it wasn't exactly called a "print shop" yet. Nobody in 1452 Mainz was going to run down to the corner to make quick copies.

All the cramped businesses on the street were closed up and shuttered for the night. Timeshares headquarters had chosen the late hour intentionally, but night watchmen prowled up and down the streets carrying lanterns, and Bill did not want to bump into the medieval equivalent of a street gang.

Walking along, studying the buildings in the dim light, he compared the doors of the shops to the photo taken by the scouts. It was a very distinctive place. He found the correct door. He paused, looking up at the half-timbered structure, the window box cluttered with dead flowers, water stains and moss on the plaster. Not much to look at. Sooner or later, there would probably be a placard hanging outside, but so far no one knew what Johannes Gutenberg was doing in there and printing that enormous Bible, at forty-two lines per page, was going to take him a while.

The thick iron padlock hanging from the door latch was the height of medieval security, but with a screwdriver, a lock pick, and a little trial and error, Bill easily removed it and slipped inside a darkened workshop that smelled of ink, wood shavings, and cat urine. Now there was one detail the history books hadn't included.

He clicked on his bright and totally anachronistic flashlight so he could look around, then opened his leather satchel to remove the stack of tan, rough-surfaced sheets of papyrus. They were still moist and still smelled a little rotten from the manufacturing process; they had been made only two days ago, back at the Nile Delta in the first century A.D.

Bill had traveled back to ancient Egypt to obtain the actual papyrus—again, for the authentic touch. He had, however, underestimated how difficult it was just to pick up some paper. Since papyrus was a common substance in Egypt at the time, he thought he could just go down to a marketplace and pick up a ream.

Though Bill did not speak the difficult language, the ancient Egyptians along the Nile were accustomed to strange merchants coming from far-off lands. Near the open-air, reed-roofed shop, workers harvested the tall green sedge from the swamp, peeling the stalks to take out the pith, laying down strips, crisscrossing them, pounding them, pressing and drying the sheets, then scraping them smooth with a well-worn seashell.

Bill had paid the papyrus maker well and had received fifty rough-cut sheets, enough for the first printing of the Timeshares brochure. Since the Timeshares Travel Agency advertized authenticity above all things, they couldn't do any less with their promotional materials. He had already told Rolf Jacobsen, the mysterious and wealthy head of the agency, that these brochures must be used for only the most elite potential clients. He didn't intend to go through all this hassle for a second printing.

Even more difficult than obtaining genuine papyrus had been securing the original artwork. It had sounded like a good idea. He'd gone to prehistoric France to track down a Neanderthal tribe, and he had commissioned original drawings from one of the cave painters. Attempting to art-direct a Neanderthal had been a challenge unlike anything else in his career, but Bill had gotten his sketches, daubed and chalked onto flat pieces of slate, which he'd then taken back to the present and the headquarters of Timeshares, where the art could be scanned and incorporated into the brochure layout.

The final materials would also include photos of the time-travel facility, its high-tech interior with spindle-shaped apparatus topped by silvery spheres haloed by crackling static electricity. Rolf Jacobsen wanted it to look sleek, futuristic, high-tech, but in a "Jules Verne" sense rather than a "neon, hard-edged, Hong Kong" sense. So far the interior of Timeshares had undergone numerous face-lifts and retoolings. Bill had no idea what the final interior was going to look like; it might even change weekly. In his opinion, the time-travel device looked more like something out of Dr. Frankenstein's lab than a comforting and safe gadget, but he didn't say anything. His only priority was the sales brochure.

Bill had already written the text: "We're not just a

travel agency—we're a *time* travel agency. We offer excursions into the past and future. Take a vacation wherever and whenever you like."

Inside the dim workshop, Bill studied Gutenberg's clumsy looking printing press, a cumbersome gadget whose design was based on an old wine press. Gutenberg's workers would line up the small wooden letter blocks in the tracks, use an ink roller, and then crank down the press upon each sheet of paper.

The next page of Gutenberg's Bible had been set up for the following day's printing. He took a quick snapshot with his imaging device so that he could reassemble the letters when he was done, though he didn't understand many of the German words or the too-fancy type style. "Quickly, his fingers rattling the wooden blocks by the glow of his flashlight, he slid all the words off into a tray, and then painstakingly mounted his own letters, his own text.

"Afraid of flying? The high cost of gas got you down? Want to *really* get away? Step into our perfectly safe time-travel device and find yourself in exotic historical locations. Adventure and mystery guaranteed, danger definitely possible. It'll be the experience of a lifetime—of anyone's lifetime."

The process of setting the letters was tedious, but authenticity was the most important thing. If Mr. Jacobsen advertized that his clients would experience real history, then the brochure had to be the real thing. Fortunately, all of his promotional text fit onto a single page, even with Gutenberg's large letter blocks.

As payment, in addition to Bill's standard fee, Timeshares had offered him an excursion to anyplace he chose, any time. He could witness the greatest events in history, meet the most important figures in all of human civilization. Instead, Bill had asked for a week in the most luxurious resort in Cancun on the Caribbean coast. He had his priorities.

When he had the appropriate words in place, he used a stiff ink roller to cover the printing surface with pasty ink. When it was ready, and before he could make a mess of things, he placed a sheet of clean papyrus on the flat block beneath the press and cranked down the letters, pushing hard to make a clear impression. Then he unscrewed the press, raised it up, and peeled off his sheet of papyrus.

The rough surface of the reeds made the impression blurry and weak in certain spots, but the letters were readable. With so few sheets of papyrus, he couldn't afford to make many mistakes. Not perfect, but *authentic*. That was what Mr. Jacobsen wanted.

Timeshares clients would coo over the imperfections and would marvel at the difficulties that had been required just to make this flier. However, Bill didn't think that the clients would be quite so forgiving of imperfections when they encountered glitches on their very expensive time-travel vacations. . . .

He balanced the flashlight where it would better illuminate the work area and put another piece of papyrus under the press, rolled the ink over the printing surface, squeezed down the block letters. He had to get through at least fifty sheets.

That Cancun resort was going to feel wonderful when he was done with this.

Bill finished printing the last sheet an hour before dawn. He didn't think Mainz had a good coffee shop nearby, so he would have to return to the present for a good strong cup. Now it was time to put everything back in order in Gutenberg's print shop.

He called up the digitized baseline image he had taken, referring to the biblical words he had disassembled. The verses weren't familiar to him, especially not in old German. He plucked out the letters he had used for the Timeshares brochure and began to realign the sentences and verses on the page. Bill realized he was short on time, and he moved quickly, several times scrambling letters, which forced him to remove the little blocks and reassemble the words.

Outside the shop, he saw light in the street, a figure moving along. The segmented window glass in Gutenberg's workplace was rippled and murky, but a man with a lantern was visible out there. A night watchman. He'd probably seen the glow of the flashlight inside the shop.

Bill had left the padlock dangling open on the door, and now the watchman rattled it, and then shouted, apparently calling for help. Bill nearly panicked, but he hurriedly added the last letters to the verses on that page.

The door creaked open, and the watchmen swung his lantern, illuminating the cluttered workshop. "Sorry, I was just leaving," Bill said, grabbing his stack of papyrus sheets and stuffing them into the leather satchel.

The night watchman yelled something incomprehensible but indisputably German and indisputably furious. Bill shone the flashlight beam in the man's face, blinding him, and grabbed for his locator device. He punched the panic button.

Back in the Timeshares control room, somebody would be watching (unless they were on a cigarette break). From the other end of the cobblestoned street, some of the drunken and surly oafs from the tavern came lurching along to help.

Bill punched the panic button again and again. When the big smelly men crowded the door, pushing their way to Gutenberg's shop, Bill grabbed his flashlight, his locator, and his leather satchel with the printed brochures.

He stepped back, putting the printing press between himself and the angry men.

Then he felt the flashing blue crackle around him, the dizziness and nausea, the taste of vinegar in the back of his throat.

And he found himself surrounded by clean, modern equipment and air that smelled of ozone rather than printing ink and cat piss.

Rolf Jacobsen met him outside of the field area, arms crossed over his chest and a proud look on his face. Once the Timeshares agency began to operate in full swing, Jacobsen planned to be more of a silent partner and not see off all travelers, but Bill knew that Jacobsen had a hunger for attention. Maybe he would come to watch; maybe he wouldn't.

Bill let out a long sigh of relief and held out his leather satchel. "I have your brochures, Mr. Jacobsen. They turned out rather well."

Jacobsen opened the satchel and withdrew one of the papyrus sheets, looking down at the printing, smudged one of the letters with his fingers.

"The ink will need to dry for some time, sir. Be careful."

"We'll digitize and print the other artwork and photos onto these. Authentic and perfect. Exactly what we want." The leader of Timeshares gave a sincere smile. "Our project is just beginning, Bill."

"Thank you, Mr. Jacobsen, but I am glad to be done with this project."

The head of Timeshares had expected nothing else. "We will be happy to recommend your PR firm to many of our sister companies and investors."

"Thank you, sir. I can always use the work. For now, I'd like to change out of these—" he frowned down at his heavy, scratchy clothes "—authentic period garments."

Jacobsen gestured him toward the changing rooms. "Be my guest."

Bill was glad he wouldn't have to go back in time again. He had seen enough of history, and that last trip had been a little hair-raising. He'd been so rushed putting the wooden blocks back onto the page of Gutenberg's Bible. Under such circumstances, perfect accuracy couldn't be expected.

He went off to the changing area where a locker held his real-world clothes. In his hand he still held five of Gutenberg's wooden blocks. In his rush to reassemble the page, he hadn't had time to include the last word on the page, "nicht." Just a little thing, but he didn't know which Bible verse he had unintentionally altered.

Somehow, he had left out the word *not*. "Thou shalt" instead of "Thou shalt not."

Oh well, he wondered if anyone would notice. That was for history to decide.

Timeless Lisa

Robert E. Vardeman

Robert E. Vardeman has written more than seventy science fiction, fantasy, and mystery novels. His most recent title is a novel in the Star Frontiers trilogy, *The Genetic Menace*. In addition to *Timeshares*, Vardeman's short stories can be found in the recently published *Stories from Desert Bob's Reptile Ranch*, which contains two dozen short stories collected from the past thirty years. Branching out into e-books, his work can be found on the iTunes store (at www.zapptek.com/legends) and at Amazon's Kindle store. He currently lives in Albuquerque, New Mexico, with his two cats, Isotope and X-ray. One out of three of them enjoy the high-tech hobby of geocaching. For more info, check out the author's Web site at http://www.CenotaphRoad.com.

"You'll be hit with severe diarrhea, maybe for a week," the time tech said, never looking up as he made his way down the lengthy checklist scrolling on his handheld computer.

"I know," Alexander Carrington said, shifting nervously. The stainless steel walls, ceiling, and cold, cold floor caused him to squint as light was reflected in all directions. Electrodes in every corner of the room focused on the spot where he stood. He wished the tech would turn up the temperature, though the freezing temperature might be required for the time transit. He didn't know, and that bothered him. There was so much he didn't know and everything looked different this time.

"I've taken some A-D." He glanced at the satchel near his feet and felt sweat beading on his upper lip. He fought the urge to swipe it away, fearing he would draw unwanted attention to himself.

"Oh, yeah, right," the tech said, still not looking up. "This is your second trip back. Must be nice. For what Timeshares pays me, I can't afford a cup of fancy designer coffee, much less a month in 1519."

"I'm a Renaissance scholar," Alex said defensively. He fought the urge to clamp his eyes closed to prevent staring at his satchel. He could be thrown in jail for a long time if the tech found what was concealed in the false bottom. He would get an even longer sentence if he was caught on the way back with the real contraband.

"Yeah, see that. How come an Italian scholar is going to France?"

Crunch time. Alex had to sound convincing and unassuming. He had to lie through his teeth, yet it wasn't a real lie.

"Leonardo da Vinci moved to France before his death. I need to document his last days and maybe even hear his last words. For posterity."

"Yeah, for posterity." The tech heaved a sigh and finally said, looking up, "You know the drill, but I have to go through it all. Or you can just sign here. Says you know about time disjunctions, the need for inertial masses to balance back and forth—doesn't matter what, just that they do—and how you shouldn't screw with major events."

"What about minor ones?"

The tech shrugged. "Mr. Jacobsen is working that over with a team of physicists. Real top level stuff, but right now we haven't noticed any time waves coming up against our secure little future shore. That's the way one of them put it. I think it's bullshit—excuse my French—because any change in the past would be incorporated into what we think is history. How'd we ever know?"

"Yes, how would we?"

"What'd you do?"

"What?" Alex glanced guiltily at his satchel with the exquisitely contrived copy of the *Mona Lisa* in it. Other than age, there was no way to tell the difference with a single glance—or even with a detailed analysis. If he had figured out the temporal loop properly, substituting his copy for the original would mean the one currently hanging in the Musée du Louvre was this copy—*his* copy. He blinked as he realized he should have marked the copy in some way to identify it. If he was successful, the mark would have shown up when he studied the Louvre painting, and nobody would have been the wiser. His copy would be the one the world thought was original. But he hadn't and now it was too late. The last time he had studied the *Mona Lisa* in the Louvre, he had seen no special distinguishing mark such as he would have put on, so he didn't dare put one on now. Or when he reached 1519.

"Before? What did you do on your first excursion? I don't get a chance to talk to returnees. I only see that you're off safely."

"Yes, a woman . . ." Alex fought to keep from blurting out his plan to switch the paintings. Would this dolt even care?

"That must have been Jenna. She handles the scholarly types when you guys return. Billy Ray and Jacob get the rest and hear the hot stories. Lucky stiffs."

"I thought you meant..." Alex wiped away the sweat, not caring if the time tech noticed his growing apprehension.

"Oh, so you scored back in time. Lemme see. Florence. A hot one? You found a hot Italian babe?"

Alex could only nod. His throat felt as if iron fingers were clamped around it and he couldn't swallow. He looked again at his satchel. It hadn't moved.

"You gotta tell me. Do they, you know, shave?"

"What?" Alex had not expected that question.

"Women shave their armpits and down there now, you know. Of course you do. I mean, back then? Did they?"

"Eyebrows," Alex said, stunned he was answering. "They shaved the eyebrows. She was an elegant, charming noble lady."

"Eyebrows? Go figure," the time tech said, shaking his head. "What was her name?"

Alex Carrington felt as if he had been transported back in time again to see the wife of the silk and cloth merchant Francesco del Giocondo. She had been married to a pig who had no concept of how to treat a woman of her intelligence and grace.

"Lisa," he said before he realized the name had slipped from his lips again. "She was one of Leonardo's models."

"So you boffed her, huh? You didn't knock her up or anything, did you?"

"No, of course not," Alex said too hastily. "What a thing to accuse me of." He tried to keep the fright from his words by covering them with mock outrage. If his calculations were accurate, Lisa's fourth child was his.

Francesco had been on a business trip to Genoa, leaving her alone in their veritable palace with no one to speak to, other than servants and Leonardo when he came to paint her. It had been easy accompanying the great artist and even easier striking up a friendship with a lonely, lovely woman.

His accent had intrigued her, and he had immediately accepted her offer to improve his Italian. She had been so skilled in so many things that it was a shame her husband ignored her so, probably for a mistress half the woman Lisa was.

"Well, since you're going back to 1519 and France instead of Italy in 1503, you know about the potential for temporal divarication." The tech saw him floundering and added, "We don't want to deal with having two of you present at the same instant. That's something else the physics types are working on."

"What'd happen if I met myself?"

"It's complicated. You build up a huge temporal energy charge returning in time. It's not real energy, not like from a battery, but that's the easiest way to think about it if you don't have a dozen PhDs in math and stuff. Mostly, Mr. J doesn't think there's a problem, but we need to experiment some before letting customers try it."

Bleakness gripped Alex. He wouldn't see his beloved La Gioconda again, nor was he likely to see their child, Camilla. Alex put his hands to his temples as a headache began raging.

"You all right? We can postpone the transit."

"I'm just excited," Alex lied. "There's too much to think about. All that temporal theory."

"Don't let it get you down. I don't. Just enjoy your excursion. You have the remote?" The time tech nodded when Alex fumbled it out from under his period blouse.

His hands shook. "Same as before. You have exactly one month and you'll be automatically returned to this very spot. If you don't press the blue button once a day, you'll be returned. There's a countdown timer on the screen now—that's different from your first trip."

"And the red panic button returns me right away," Alex said.

"You trying to take my job?" The time tech grinned broadly. "Don't catch some STD that antibiotics won't cure and have fun."

Alex would have protested such a comment if he hadn't been worried about his real intentions. *Don't draw attention to yourself,* he told himself over and over.

"Pick up your bag and clutch it to your chest," the tech said, stepping back. "The temporal field takes about thirty seconds to build, and then you'll be in France for thirty days unless you want to come back sooner."

Alex nodded.

"Your only worry will be about how to pay for the excursion. On the behalf of Timeshares, enjoy yourself!"

Alex's knees buckled. Tiny electric tingles built up on the tip of his nose, his fingers, every spot of his body with pronounced curvatures. He tried to cry out as his innards twisted around and then he clamped his hand over his mouth. He was no longer in the stainless steel room with its faint antiseptic smell. Earthy odors assaulted him as the ground turned to mud. He stumbled forward, barely catching himself in time to prevent being entirely submerged in a large puddle.

He looked around, searching for anyone who might have witnessed his strange eruption into 1519 and declare him a witch. Cows lowed in a nearby field and two men argued some distance away. He cocked his head to one side, and then smiled. They spoke French.

He didn't understand French very well but could get by with his Italian—the Italian Lisa had coached him in so lovingly.

He burst out laughing. He'd have to be careful trying to use *all* the phrases she had taught him, as much by demonstration as lecture.

It took only minutes for him to realize Timeshares had dropped him some distance from his intended destination. It took him six days to walk to Clos Lucé, which was neighbor to the palace of King Françoise in Amboise. The gentry proved amenable to a solitary traveler asking directions in broken French. When he eventually found a man hurrying along dressed in Neapolitan style, muttering to himself in Italian, Alex knew he would finally complete his mission.

"Pardon, good sir!" he called in Italian. The man stared blankly at him. "I am looking for Master Leonardo."

"Leonardo? What's your business with him?"

He bit his lower lip. The man had answered in a vernacular, indicating he was of lower class than suggested by his clothing.

"I'd like to see him," Alex said. "I have come a long way and . . . and I hear he is in poor health."

"You might say that. He's dead."

Timeshares had missed the exact moment. Alex had wanted to see Leonardo on his deathbed and record his words, but the primary reason for his second trip back was still possible.

"What of his assistant?"

"Salai's cleaning out the studio. A bunch o' crap there. Leonardo left him more work than ever, and that's sayin' something."

"For you, if you take me to Salai." Alex drew out a small silver coin and turned it enough to reflect the bright sun into the man's eyes. It was only a replica, but counterfeiting wasn't much of a crime when the fake coin cost more than the real one.

"I know Salai. He's not worth so much." The man looked furtively around, and then stepped closer. "Is there more?" He pointed at the coin.

"This is all I have. I . . ." Alex's mind raced. He swallowed and added, "I must collect what Leonardo owed me. If Salai is his executor, he is the one to whom I must present my petition."

"He owes you? How much?"

"Enough to make it worth my while to give this to anyone showing me the way to his quarters."

"He's in Leonardo's old studio." The man looked around again, judging how easy it would be to slit this foreigner's throat and simply take the coin.

"Naples," Alex said. "You're from Naples. I know influential people in Naples who would be very angry if anything happened to me. You have family there?"

"How'd you know I was from Naples?" The man stepped back, eyeing Alex with more interest now.

"The cut of your clothing, your wretched accent," Alex said. "The way you think to steal my money."

"What's wrong with my clothing?"

Alex held the coin in his left palm and slowly closed his hand. As the man reached, Alex grabbed him by the collar and lifted him onto his toes. Alex was barely five-foot-ten, but he towered six inches over his captive Neapolitan. The man twisted around, unable to step away. Alex slowly opened his palm. The coin vanished like mist in the morning sun. He lowered his catch.

"There. There's the old studio," the man said, pointing to a building not fifty feet away. With that the man scurried away, looking back twice before vanishing down an alley.

Alex took a deep breath, then hurriedly found the

narrow, cool passageway to the stairs leading to the studio's second story. He rapped sharply, heard mumbled complaints inside, then the door opened.

"Hello, Salai," he said, recognizing the man although he was fifteen years older.

"You, I remember you. Alejandro! From Florence. But how can it be? You are as I remember, yet it has been so many years!"

"Life has been good to me," Alex said, following his rehearsed script. He had aged less than six months since he had seen Salai, but it had been fifteen years for Leonardo's assistant. "The truth is, I have found a curative, a *pulvilio* brought from the New World."

"So something good has come from all the money spent finding a heathen-infested land," Salai said, shrugging. "I am glad for you. Come in, my old friend." Salai hesitated, and then grinned. "Come in, my young friend. It is I who has aged."

"I had hoped to arrive in time to speak with Master Leonardo, but I heard the sad news as soon as I reached French borders."

"He was an old man and ready to go. In spite of his curiosity and need to see the next sunrise—"

"So he could paint it," Alex cut in.

"No, so he could have his breakfast. What did he care of landscapes?"

"He put in a delightful one behind *La Gioconda*." Alex barely trusted himself. His voice choked with emotion, but Salai thought it was for Leonardo's passing.

"Such a background, such imagination. Icy mountains and rivers and valleys." Salai shook his head. "So many times he reworked that poor painting."

"When he did it originally, Lisa's hair was in a bun. He humanized her with loosely flowing hair. Her hair was as fine as spun gold."

"You and her, you had a thing for her, eh?" Salai shook his head. "Who didn't? Except the master, of course."

"He still captured her exquisite sexuality perfectly," Alex said. Trying to follow his carefully planned speech, he said as nonchalantly as possible, "Is the painting here? Could I see it?"

"Oh, it is somewhere. I don't know where. I have so little time to vacate this studio. Now that the king's grant has been revoked, there is no money to keep up the master's property."

"You were given the painting, though."

Salai looked sharply at Alex, his long, hooked nose lifted slightly. The leathery, wrinkled face turned impassive.

"How is it that you, just arrived in France, know this?"

The question flustered Alex. He had jumped the gun and deviated from his carefully planned script, and now he had aroused Salai's suspicions.

"I . . . it only makes sense that you, his foremost assistant and trusted companion, would receive such a masterpiece for your services."

"Masterpiece? Ha. Leonardo fiddled with it for years. You said he changed her hair, but how do you know that?"

"I heard . . ." Alex began.

"He took the money but was never satisfied. Del Giocondo stopped asking. We never saw the woman again."

"Her daughter Camilla joined a convent," Alex muttered. *His and Lisa's daughter*.

"I did not know." Salai shrugged and half turned. He fell silent, as if expecting some response from Alex that wasn't forthcoming. Finally, he sighed and said, "I must return to my work. This studio must be vacated. Leonardo was a man of many vices and did not leave a great legacy to me."

"Other than his work."

"Who wants it? No one. Bah!" Salai threw up his hands and turned his back entirely on Alex.

"I could help. I mean, what would you like done that I may aid you?"

"Nothing. Get out. Go! I have no more time for you. I ought to burn the building down. It would be easier."

"Don't joke!"

"Who is joking? No one wants his paintings or the scrawled notebooks. Oh, the king has expressed some desire for a painting or two. I might sell some of the larger work."

"For four thousand ecus," Alex muttered. This was the amount Salai's heirs had garnered from the king years in the future for the *Mona Lisa*.

"Such a princely sum," Salai grumbled. "Go now. Go. I have no more time, no time at all."

Alex reluctantly left, taking care to memorize the number of steps he took, the direction, and the location of all the flimsy locks and doors.

That night, total darkness his henchman, masked by rising storm winds whipping through the city streets, he returned to the studio to find the painting of his beloved. He crept silently through the dusty room, poking around. He had a small flashlight but used it sparingly to avoid being seen. Explaining such an anachronistic device would be difficult in a time of auto-da-fé and inquisitions. Alex had to laugh as he said softly, "I can always tell them it is one of Leonardo's inventions. Why not? He sketched everything else from helicopters to still uninvented gadgets."

Alex methodically worked his way through the paintings, seeing some he recognized as masterpieces that would in future centuries hang with honor in a dozen different museums. But when his flashlight began to dim, he shook it as if that would bring the batteries back to life.

All he accomplished was smashing the lens against the edge of a desk. The LEDs were knocked askew when the lens broke and then the flashlight went dark. He started to fling it angrily, and then remembered his instructions. If Timeshares had logged this in his possession—and they undoubtedly had—he had to return with it, broken or not. He carefully picked up the broken plastic lens and tucked it away into his satchel. Feeling around in the closed room was like returning to the womb. The air was close and almost liquid in his nostrils and no light— what little of it there was—penetrated from the outer world. This was not a time of light pollution.

As he reached out, his fingers found the edge of the table that had broken his flashlight. Dust swept under his hand as he quickly examined the surface. A smile blossomed into full, delighted laughter when he found a candle. Returning to his satchel, he fumbled about until he found the small lighter he had brought. It had served him well as he had been forced to camp on the way to Clos Lucé. Now the tiny blue-white flame touched the candle wick and bathed the room in smoky, pale dancing light.

He coughed from the cloud of rising fumes, then stopped and stared. On the table next to the candle lay a stack of sketches he eagerly grabbed and held up.

"My Gioconda!" Alex riffled through the drawings, lingering with every succeeding one that showed more detail, greater care in composition, the changes, everything that made the full painting so accomplished. He had the preliminary sketches Leonardo had done for the *Mona Lisa*.

He went through the drawings again, studying each more closely. He reached out so his fingertip lightly brushed her lovely face—only a sketch but more than his memory of her. The cheap paper crackled at his touch. His finger came away sooty from the charcoal on the top one. Subsequent ones were done in quick, sure strokes—pen and ink. The years showed in the style and how Leonardo had progressed as a painter, almost hesitant about his ability at the beginning to a confident, bold painter totally in control of his work. These sketches would bring a fortune at auction.

But Alex could never part with them. They were glimpses of his lover. He carefully placed them in his satchel's hidden compartment. They were a windfall but he still needed to . . .

He looked up to a frame leaning against the wall. He yanked a cover free and his eyes went wide. The poplar backing facing him was familiar. With shaking hands he turned the painting around and stared into La Gioconda's eyes. Her smile was for him alone.

He had found it.

For long minutes he was transfixed. Transfigured. He returned to the days—the nights!—he had spent in her embrace, every loving kiss remembered, the fleeting touch, the shared intimacy of one soul mate with another.

At first his hands trembled too much for him to properly take the painting and replace his fake with the original. Alex settled himself with a deep breath, and then began the substitution. The wood backing felt identical to him. In the shifting candlelight, he saw how closely the brush strokes had been computer duplicated.

He tucked the original safely in the large, flat satchel. Working with more assurance now, he turned the fake toward the wall and placed the cloth covering over it.

No one would ever know the substitution had been made. Through the years, down the centuries, his fake would be authenticated. And why not? The provenance was complete. No one could possibly know or expect a duplicate of such painstaking skill had replaced the irreplaceable.

Alex reached inside his blouse for the time controller. He had been in France long enough. He experienced a moment of regret that he had not been able to speak with Leonardo on his deathbed to record the history's greatest painter's last words, but this was nothing compared with the trophy he carried back. He started to press the red button that would signal Timeshares when he heard noises.

Fumbling, he ripped his blouse. He spun around, sure he had been caught as the studio door slammed open and crashed into the wall. A gust of wind from the storm outside blew him back a step, causing him to knock over the candle.

In a flash of heat that scorched his back, the cloth over the bogus *Mona Lisa* exploded into flame. Alex grabbed for it, but a new explosion of fire drove him back. He watched in horror as fire devoured the bogus painting he had just placed so carefully. He staggered away as new waves of heat scorched his arm. Clutching the satchel holding the real painting, he made his way through the conflagration to the open door.

"What is this? What has happened?" Salai grabbed him in both arms, arms like matchsticks and yet strong and protective, as he was pulled out into the stormy night.

At his back he felt the heat from Leonardo's studio going up in flames. Against his blistered face hammered fat, cold raindrops.

"You saved my painting," Salai said. "But why this

one? This is not what I would have risked my life to save."

Alex looked over his shoulder and saw that Salai had discovered the original *Mona Lisa*. It had tumbled from the satchel to the street.

"No," he croaked. "Mine." He wasn't going to allow Salai to keep what he had risked so much to obtain. His lover's picture!

Then he sucked cleansing air into his lungs and blood rushed back to his brain. He could not take the painting from Salai. History would change if the *Mona Lisa* were absent from the world of art and culture. Careers would never be made detailing the smile, the background, renovating it and hanging it in the foremost museum in the world. Salai had to keep the original now that the fake had been destroyed in the raging fire.

In the distance fire bells rang and horses' hooves clattered on the cobblestone as volunteer firefighters rushed to quell the blaze. Alex knew he had only seconds. He stood, ripped open his blouse to expose the time controller with its mocking red button, then he lunged for the painting. To hell with history! He had to possess her!

He crashed to the ground as Salai stepped back and beckoned, "Night watch! Here, come here! This man is a thief! An arsonist! He tries to steal my artwork!"

A half dozen armed men rushed toward them. His chance at gaining the painting had passed.

"He stole my painting. He ... he started the fire to cover his theft!" Salai pointed accusingly at Alex.

With a wild grab, Alex pulled the satchel close. Masses had to balance. Then his finger crushed down on the red emergency recall button. For a ghastly instant, Alex thought nothing was happening. The night watchmen grabbed his arms and pulled him upright—and he kept rising. He rose and tumbled and fell hard to a cold floor amid a cascade of fiery sparks, ashes and dirt.

"Goddamn," came the angry outburst. "You didn't come back with the same mass you left with. Now I have to clean up all the dirt."

Stunned, Alex sat up on the floor and look around him. Tiny fires consumed bits of wood from Leonardo's studio. The dirt and ash came from his surroundings. Panicked, he looked around, worrying that a watchman might have lost a hand in the temporal translation. He sank back, clinging to his satchel.

"I failed," he sobbed. Then he gained control of himself. He had failed to retrieve the painting but he had the sketches. In his satchel were all of Leonardo's sketches of his precious La Gioconda. It wasn't the same but it would have to do.

He huddled on the floor, barely aware of Timeshares technicians standing around him.

"Get the camera rolling, Billy Ray. Is it rolling? Good."

"Camera?" Alex looked up into stern faces. "There's no reason for that. You saved me. I panicked and hit the button and didn't have the proper mass and—"

"It's just part of the return debriefing Jacob and I do," Billy Ray said. Alex wasn't so sure from the tone. "You look a mess. We need to find out what happened."

"I didn't mean to unbalance the mass. I . . . I panicked and hit the button."

"That's why we call it a panic button," the other tech said, his tone friendlier. "What happened?"

Alex stumbled through a story he made up as he spoke. He tried to keep to the truth as much as possible but he couldn't tell them he had tried to steal the *Mona Lisa* and had started a fire that might have burned down an entire town. He forced himself to keep from looking at his satchel with the sketches in it. Those were all he had.

"Why are you asking me all these questions? You didn't before. I time traveled before and you didn't debrief me."

"It's like this, Dr. Carrington," Billy Ray said. "The bond you posted for the excursion turned out to be ... irregular."

"We're sure that it's only a mistake," Jacob cut in, "but we need to get the financing squared away as quickly as possible."

"The grant money—"

"Nonexistent. You made it all up and somehow got it past our financial department."

"I'll make it right. I have resources."

"We're checking on that."

Alex sat cross-legged on the floor in the stainless steel chamber. In his current present only minutes had passed. He had been returned to a time only slightly removed from when he had left to prevent more time anomalies. That meant Timeshares hadn't yet plumbed the depths of his financial legerdemain. When they did, he would go to jail for fraud. Forgery. A lot of other crimes he only vaguely understood that had been listed in the contract he had signed.

If they found the sketches, he was in real trouble.

"I need to rest. We can straighten out the misunderstanding tomorrow. I'm a tenured professor and the university will back me on the research project, even if there is some glitch with the grant authorization." He found refuge in academic bureaucratese and this easy professional sounding spiel caused the time techs to look at one another and back off.

"Jacob," Billy Ray said, indicating they should leave Alex. The instant they left, he was on his feet and out an emergency door leading into the depths of the building. Within minutes after he found the main lobby, he was summoning a cab in front of the glass-fronted Timeshares laboratory. He gripped the satchel fiercely.

He wanted to paw through the contents to open the false bottom but waited until he caught a cab and was a block from the company office. One clause had been specific and he had gone back in time with the intent to violate it—no artifact gathering. He might tell them they were his sketches. They were idiots. How would they know he hadn't done the finely wrought preliminary sketches from the world's most famous work of art?

"Take me to Sotheby's," he called to the driver. The quicker he got the money situation settled, the less likely they were to inquire about his trip. It would be a relief for Timeshares, collecting their money. He was buying their silence. That was it, but he needed money *now* to stifle inquiry.

It was best that he sold the sketches immediately, all except one or two for his own collection. If fate denied him the painting, then he could take some solace in the sketches made early in the sittings, the ones closest to the Lisa he loved so well.

The cab squealed to a halt in front of the auction house on York at Seventy-second Street. He paid with the handful of coins left from his excursion before the cabbie could protest. Alex knew he was a mess, dressed in torn, sooty sixteenth-century clothing, but time was of the essence. He was certain any one of Leonardo's sketches would more than pay for his trip. Perhaps he only had to sell one and could keep the rest.

"To commemorate my love," he said, getting an odd look from the guard at the door as the cabbie shouted at him from the street. The guard took a step forward but Alex seized the upper hand, saying, "I have just recovered sketches done by Leonardo da Vinci that I wish to sell."

The guard hesitated. He was probably no art lover but had heard of Leonardo. He motioned for Alex to stay where he was and then spoke softly into a microphone pinned to his left epaulet. A second discussion took place, a long one.

"I'll come back," Alex said uneasily. The cabbie yammered into a radio, telling his supervisor a fare had stiffed him.

"That's okay, sir. I got permission to escort you to an interview room. What do you have to sell?"

"I'll discuss that with an art expert."

"Painting?"

"Charcoal sketches. Pen and ink." Alex frowned as this information was relayed. He waited long seconds and was on the point of bolting and running when the guard punched in the cipher code and escorted him in.

He started to enter the main lobby, but the guard directed him down a corridor leading parallel to the outer wall. The guard strode briskly, occasionally glancing over his shoulder to be certain Alex was following.

"In here, sir."

Alex stepped in. The guard closed the door behind him. The click of the lock made him jump, but he was in the room with two well-dressed men. One stood in the right rear corner and the other was already seated at a long polished cherrywood conference table.

"We are most anxious to see what you have brought us," the elder of the pair said without preamble.

Alex dropped his satchel on the floor beside him, then worked open the secret compartment cradling the precious sketches. He placed them on the table in a long line. Thirteen sketches. He hadn't known how many there were until now. He realized he ought to have held back the best of the lot, but it wouldn't hurt to get an appraisal. Simply showing the sketches did not oblige him to sell.

"What are these?" The man drew out a jeweler's loupe and bent over to examine the sketch closest.

"You tell me," Alex said, "what the original sketches for the *Mona Lisa* are worth."

"This is extraordinary. Period paper, assured lines mimicking da Vinci, well-crafted forgeries."

"Forgery?" Alex shot to his feet and leaned forward. "These are the original sketches." He held his temper in check or he would have blurted that he knew they were authentic.

"It is a crime to attempt to sell art forgeries. I assure you, Sotheby's will prosecute to the fullest extent of the law."

"These are legitimate. Leonardo did them himself!"

"Not of the *Mona Lisa*. Even a first year art history student knows there were no sketches of his masterpiece."

Alex started to protest, then clamped his mouth shut. There weren't any because *he* had stolen them. Salai had little interest in the painting or the work that had gone into it, so he would never mention the sketches, thinking they were lost in the fire.

"A word of advice. If you attempt art fraud, age the paper. This is new. Well, only a few years old."

"Fifteen. Less," Alex said, realizing another flaw in his scheme. Actual sketches would have aged over centuries, not years.

"Sir." The man at the corner of the room stepped forward and held out a PDA. The appraiser dropped his loupe into his jacket pocket and sighed.

"There's another arrest warrant out for you, Dr. Carrington."

"How'd—" He felt faint and collapsed into the chair.

Cameras had recorded him from every angle. Even if he had come dressed in proper business attire, they would have run facial recognitions on him. Somewhere, in some database, his picture would pop up. He had never tried to live as an anonymous hermit.

"It seems you swindled some company or other out of a considerable amount of money in return for their services."

"Timeshares," he said. "That proves these are real. I didn't pay Timeshares and they're—"

"Dr. Carrington, be quiet. Every word is being recorded and can be used against you. Art fraud and simple swindling will only get you a few years in jail. Relic temporal relocation is a crime with a twenty-year mandatory sentence."

The man with the PDA punched in a few numbers and said, "The police have arrived."

The outer door unlatched and two uniformed officers crowded in to arrest him. Alex gathered the sketches of the lovely La Gioconda and smiled ruefully. At least he would have them to put on the wall of his jail cell—if they allowed him to keep the evidence against him.

Been a Long Time

Matthew P. Mayo

Matthew P. Mayo's novels include the westerns
Winters' War; *Wrong Town*; and *Hot Lead, Cold
Heart*. His latest nonfiction book is *Cowboys,
Mountain Men, and Grizzly Bears: The Fifty Grittiest
Moments in the History of the Wild West*. Matthew
has had short stories and poetry published in a
variety of anthologies, and he edited the popu-
lar anthology *Where Legends Ride: New Tales of the
Old West*. He and his wife, photographer Jennifer
Smith-Mayo, divide their time between the coast
of Maine and the mountains of Montana. Drop
by for a cup of joe at www.matthewmayo.com.

It happened so long ago I mostly have forgotten the
why, let alone the how or the who.

Or maybe it happened today.

I don't really know. But I'll tell you what, I can't for
a second forget that I'm not where I'm supposed to
be. Every minute of the day I feel as though I've been
caught shuffling along the main street of some dusty little
poke of a town with my drawers down around my boots,
horses flicking their ears and swishing their tails, and me
with my whatsit wagging, and up on the boardwalk there

are mothers grabbing their kids' faces and pulling them
into shops and here comes the sheriff again . . .

Or at least that's what it's like until I wake up. And
every time I wake up I'm in some louse-crawly bed by
some busted-pane window overlooking that same dusty
main street. And on the floor is a cracked porcelain
thunder pot, crawling with flies and stinking.

I drop back to the shuck pillow and sigh. I've been
here so many times before. The *here* is always this
town—today's town, yesterday's town, tomorrow's
town, all the same. You see, from day to day I can't recall
much of anything. The only thing I really have are slugs
of memories that seem solid, waiting for me to build on.
But once my attention settles on 'em, they're gone. So
really, I have nothing.

I started trying to figure it out by keeping a diary.
Thought I'd write in it every day, that was the idea. I
must have bought it in the mercantile. Actually, I may
have bought it this morning. I can't be sure. Anyway,
I figured I'd finally licked it, knew just what needed
doing then, and that I'd be able to find my way home—
wherever that was. So I jotted down what I know: It
is high summer, mid-July, 1871, Territory of Colorado,
town of Lodestone.

But the next day, might have been this morning, the
pages and pages I'd written about that day were gone, all
those words and thoughts and pencil scratches—gone.
The pages were clean like there never were words there.
The only thing I had was the *memory* of having spent
all that time writing in the damn diary to begin with,
and even that was fuzzy, as if I'd been on a three-day
spree. Which makes me wonder if I only *think* I remember writing it all down. You see how it is with me? Don't
know if I'm coming, going, or if I'm anywhere at all.

*   *   *

I don't think that people actually recognize me from any previous visits, but I do think they sense that something's off about me. Like the smell of a dog when he walks in and settles down by your chair. Somehow you just know that rascal's been up to something. Then you find out he was seen carryin' off your neighbor's prize hen.

But it's more than a fresh-blood smell, it's that feeling of wrongness rising off the little savage like a bad idea. That's what I think folks sense off me. And I can tell they feel that way even though I've been in town but a few hours. Hell, sometimes it's only a matter of minutes before I get the looks. That's when I think I might be better off alone.

Each morning I vow to saddle up and set off early for the hills to do some prospecting, some fishing in the streams, but somehow the day always gets away from me and I never quite make it out of town. I'll wake up the next morning and I'm right back in a nasty ol' shuck bed. And that's the way it's been for as long as I can remember—which admittedly ain't too far back.

At least the name I have sticks with me, probably because it's an easy thing to pull from one day to the next. It's not my real name, of course, I know that much. I can't remember the real one, but this one'll do. I chose it because of the two letters someone sewed onto each piece of clothing I'm wearing. Inside the shank of each boot, in the collars of my shirt and vest, in the waist of my trousers, the beat and battered topper I wear on my head, someone embroidered a "T. S." on everything. Wasn't me who did it, because I can't sew worth a bean and these letters look like they were done by a professional.

A Chinese laundryman asked me my name once when I'd had my duds laundered in some little mining town that, come to think on it, looked a lot like this town. Couldn't have been that long ago because I still remember it. Maybe it was today, just after breakfast. Anyways, where was I? Oh yeah, the laundryman.

He'd tapped the black initials on the shirt with a fingertip, his finger going up and down like a little bird pecking for information. First thing I know I said, "Tim Shaw. Mr. Tim Shaw," and that's who I've been since, Tim Shaw. I say it fast and it feels right somehow, like it means something, and that one day the meaning'll come to me. So I've been dragging that name with me from day to day like an old satchel I can't open, but with something I know is good inside.

Sometimes when I'm telling it to a riled-up sheriff or a livery owner or a saloon floozie, I know for certain it's not my name. I get a feeling, like when I bite a fresh apple and it's crisp and the tang of it sets off a memory. Same thing happened to me earlier today, with a beef stew and four plump dumplings bubbling at the mercantile.

"Oh, but don't that smell good," I said to the old lady counting out scoops of coarse meal into cloth sacks.

She stopped long enough to measure me up and down over those little nose glasses of hers. "It's my husband's dinner."

I'm afraid I took another peek into the pot. I couldn't help it, sitting as it was right there in the middle of the little store, on top of the potbelly stove. The dumplings were even taking on that sheen, like sweat on a pretty girl's face when she's been asked to dance by every lad in town and she hasn't said no all evening. I tell you that stew was a sight.

"Oh, all right." The old lady's voice startled me.

I looked up from staring at the heavenly stew, and I felt my face go red like a struck thumb. "Ma'am?"

"The stew." She'd come out from behind the counter

with a bowl, a spoon, and a ladle. "Worth two-bits to you?"

"Why, yes ma'am. But your husband ..."

She'd already plunged in the ladle and lifted out two of the most heavenly dumplings oozing underneath with dark gravy. I even saw a nub or two of carrot poking up.

"He's always late anyhow. And I've et."

I barely heard her. By the time the warm, butter-strong scent reached my nose I had my coin purse in my palm and had pinched out more than what she'd asked. And let me tell you it was worth it at twice the price. Ten times ... because it helped me remember something.

While I was eating that stew I recalled something important. What the stew had to do with it, I've no idea. But I've thought on it all day, and now that it is night and I expect I'll fade off into sleep or whatever it is that I do, I'll lose the memory by tomorrow. Or maybe tomorrow will be a little bit more of today. Maybe I'll have a two-day run of it this time. Or a week. And that's what keeps getting me out of bed. What if this time it all lasts? What if a memory sticks and I'm allowed to live instead of just exist?

So, what I remembered was this: a woman's arm—the wrist and hand with a dusting of lightish honey-colored red hair, a slice of sunlight laid across it prettier than if she'd draped a diamond bracelet on there. I could tell it was a woman's wrist because of that soft knob of bone that's visible even on a chunky girl and that ain't never the same on a man, no sir. But this girl was slender. And just above that prettiest of sights, a white sleeve ended, not tight and wrapped in frills or lace, but looser like a coat.

I took another spoonful of stew, so hot it burned my tongue and I didn't care, didn't even stop, afraid that it might break the spell and I'd lose that sliver of a memory. It wasn't so much the picture in my mind of the hand, the wrist, the sleeve end, but the feeling behind it. You see, I knew that woman. I'm sure of it. Not like you'll come to know a soiled dove for a few minutes, and not like you come to know your own mother or sister or wife. But somehow I knew who she was, just the same. I guess it was a feeling of familiarity that I was so excited about because nothing has seemed so familiar for such a long time. If it did, I don't recall it anymore.

So I kept my eyes closed and stood right there in the little store and slurped on that stew like it was life-giving nectar from that first garden in the Bible. While I was giving thought to that wrist and coat cuff, I ever so gently nudged my mind's eyes to wander up that sleeve, not tight on the arm like a dress might be, but more like a coat. And then there was a shoulder. I held the spoon in my mouth, the vision I was having just kept going … and with no warning at all, I saw a face, the face of a woman, hair shortish, tucked around an ear, and spectacles, too. Big ones the likes of which I've never seen, and rimmed in thick, clear frames.

Her hair was reddish brown, darker than the light hair on her wrist. And I could see an earring, small and glinting like it was a jewel. And her face was precious, easily the prettiest woman who has ever lived, more of the fine light hairs there on her cheek. She held still, like a painting. And then two things happened at once.

That old woman who'd served me squawked like an early-morning crow will do outside your window, and the pretty woman in my mind cut her eyes in my direction and almost smiled.

"Are you having a fit? Cause if'n you are, then you can get out of here and right quick, too. I don't hold with anyone who can't keep control of himself."

I ignored the old stick of a woman for as long as I could, and tried to keep the vision there before me. The pretty woman in my mind had moved, had looked right at me. That never happened before. Or at least not recently. But what's more, I saw a flash of gold from down lower on her, like a brooch, maybe. But no, it wasn't at the throat, lovely as that was. It was lower, and to the side. A pin of some sort? No. And the white garment itself was not right, not like something a woman would wear. Nor were the spectacles. But what was it that I missed? There was something else, I just know it. The gold thing down below. I—

"That's it. I knew you were a madman the second I clapped eyes on you. Get out of my store right now! Right now before I call for the sheriff!"

I opened my eyes, the spoon still clamped in my teeth. But the pretty woman was gone, replaced by the shouting old biddy in the store. I set the bowl of warm stew on the counter with the spoon beside it. The dumplings stared at me like the pasty cheeks of a dead child. I wasn't hungry anymore. Just tired. I walked out of the shop, the old woman's voice following me until the door cut it off.

I made my way along the boardwalk for a minute, watched by a few folks. I didn't care. I had too much to think about to pay them any heed. Then I walked straight into a chunky bald man in arm garters and a striped shirt. He was sweeping his precious few feet of boardwalk.

"Hey, mister." He stared at me like I'd said boo in church. "Look out where you're headed."

Not even possible, friend, I thought. "Sorry," I said.

"I'll forget it—if you need a haircut or a bit of doctoring . . ."

"What?"

The man shook his head and stepped back inside his shop. "Nothing. I was trying to drum up business. I ain't had coin enough for a drink all week."

I stared at him for a moment, the last of the haziness of the stew-dream leaving me. "Did you say you're a doctor?"

"Close as you'll find around these parts. I've even studied back east. Course, out here a man can't do just one thing. That's why I also cut hair, pull teeth, clean ears, and lend a hand at the *Gazette*."

I stepped into the empty shop after him and pulled off my hat. "I can use a haircut."

"Hell, for a dime I'll cut 'em all." He laughed way too long at his own joke. I tried to join in.

"Have a seat," he said, and waved me into the chair, talking the entire time.

I only half heard him. My mind was still on that woman in my memory. On her coat and the thing I didn't see but I know was there. I closed my eyes while he snipped and fiddled with my hair. I could have cared less what he did with it. Vain I'm not.

"Doc ..."

The man stopped snipping for a second and cleared his throat. I reckon he felt flattered to be called that. "In your professional training, have you ever had any experience working with people who were, well ... off their nut?" I tapped my head and squinted at him in the reflection before me.

He lowered the scissors and comb and looked at me in the mirror. "What?"

"You know—am I crazy?"

"Mister," he said, resuming my haircut. "If you're crazy, then you'd do well to keep it to yourself. People around here don't much like anything that's different."

Outside, a mule skinner's wagon raised a fresh cloud

of dust as it rumbled past. The doc reached out with one leg and toed his door shut. He went back to work on my hair.

I sighed. This way I live feels normal to me because it's been going on for so long. Or has it? I guess I'm either full-bore crazy or not at all. I choose to think I'm not. Small comfort. It's as if I've been forgotten. I bet that the woman in the memory could tell me everything I wish I knew. I didn't know much about her, but I couldn't get rid of her, either. She was lodged in my gizzard like a hunk of cheap steak that I can't swallow or bring back up. Stuck, that's what she is, and me, too.

"There. Never have I seen such a fine tonsorial treatment." The doc stood behind me, hands resting on his girthy middle, looking at my head in the mirror the way a farmer might a prize cabbage. I pushed up out of the chair and rummaged in my vest pocket for money. Then something in the corner, hanging from a peg, caught my eye. I tossed the coins on the little counter and snatched the thing down. It was a white coat.

"What's this?" I said, stretching out the sleeves and admiring it as if it were the latest fashion I might like to buy.

"That's my doctorin' coat. We all got one when we graduated from the Kingsley Medical Program in Providence, Rhode Island."

"You ever known any women doctors?"

He snorted a laugh that tailed off like a sneeze. "Mister, you *are* off your rocker." He took the coat from me and draped it over his arm, smoothed it.

"There wasn't anything there." I nodded at the coat and pointed to the side of my own chest. "On the coat, I mean."

"What would you expect to see? A badge? I'm a doctor, not a lawman."

But that was all I heard. I think he kept talking, and I know he called for the sheriff, because a few minutes later a man with a star marched me down the street, prodding me with his pistol and telling me he didn't have time for troublemakers in his town. I didn't care much. As long as the cell was empty it would give me the time I needed to think. And time was the one thing I guess I had more of than anything else. Besides, they could hold me there overnight but I wouldn't wake up there, that much I knew.

The door squawked and clanked shut behind me and I made my way to the bunk. No one was in the cell with me. I leaned back against the log wall and concentrated on the woman in the white coat.

Then I had a thought: what if I've been doing the same thing forever? What if this is all there is or ever will be to my life? What if I'm being forced somehow to be the same person doing the same things, thinking the same thoughts, over and over, and a thousand more overs besides?

It's as if I'm caught in something that keeps spinning and can't stop. And the worst of it is that I have a strong hunch that it never will stop. Like a pup that's caught his tail and keeps on spinning with that thing in his teeth. Except even dogs will grow bored and chase a rabbit instead. That's what bothers me the most—knowing that if I can't ever gain an edge on this thing, I won't ever grow older, and that means I won't ever die. And I guess that even writing in my little diary won't help me because whatever I write, whatever I learn, will all disappear come tomorrow, and I'll be back where I am right now.

All of that is truly bad, worse than a main-street showdown with a sore loser at five card stud, because at least with him you stand a chance of dyin'. And wouldn't that be a blessed relief. But I don't believe I'm quite there yet. There's still some figuring left to do on this problem.

No, the worst part is that the only thing that keeps me doing this day after day after day, for what could well be thousands or by now millions of years (or is it just one day so far?) is that I still have hope. But what if hope should leave me? I guess then I could kill myself. I snapped my eyes open and sat up again, my knuckles pushing into the rough blanket. But what if I come to find out that death is not even possible?

The cell's grown darker now; the deputy is snoring lightly in the front room. Soon it will be night and I'll drift off, and then wake up in a hotel in an uncomfortable shuck bed with a lumpy pillow, a thunder pot on the floor beside my flopped boots. It ain't much, but it's something, I reckon.

I stretch out full length on the plank cot and try to relax. Before too long I think of the woman in the coat, the woman with short red-brown hair, big glasses, and the gold name tag on her chest that reads: DR. JENNIFER KAPLAN, with TIMESHARES in smaller letters underneath.

I almost open my eyes to . . . do what? Write it down in the diary? Has that ever done any good? I relax and watch her face, and even as she speaks I seem to recall what it is she's telling me. So much information to remember, I think to myself, right before I am once again lost in her words. Once again.

Her smile stretches wide and she says, "No sir, Mr. Barr, there's no need to worry. I can assure you everything has been repaired and tested, and it's perfectly safe now. You'll have the ideal trip." She looks me up and down, leans closer, and says, in a whisper, "You look just like a real cowboy." She winks, the smile again, then louder, "This journey to the Old West will be the trip of a lifetime for you, Mr. Barr. You'll wish you never have to leave. Timeshares guarantees it. Now just relax while we perform our last minute checks."

Her face disappears, a steel door clunks shut, the bright ceiling lights dim. I can just make out faces staring at me through a glass window set into the wall by the door. She is there, standing beside others, a man and a woman, also in white coats. Above the table where I'm strapped down there are metal rods pulsing with lights, others tipped with points, cables and wire coiled all around me. Everything in here seems to be making a sound, each piece rising to a pitch all its own, then something buzzes, lights on the wall above the window flash from red to green. She is still smiling. Then something explodes.

It sounds like a safe door being ripped off its hinges by too big a charge of dynamite. Arms of blue light reach toward me. I cannot move. Something else rips apart and I hear a woman's screams as if from far away, from behind thick glass. She shrieks, "No, not again! You said it was fixed—"

A man shouts, "Get him out of there! Now!"

I try to scream, try to howl loud enough to tell them yes, yes, get me out of here. I try to wake the deputy snoring in his tipped back chair in the next room.

I try, over and over, I try . . .

Unsolved Histories

Greg Cox

Greg Cox is a *New York Times* bestselling author of numerous books and short stories. He has written the official novelizations of such films as *Daredevil*, *Ghost Rider*, and the *Underworld* trilogy. In addition, he has written books and stories based on such popular series as *Alias*, *Buffy the Vampire Slayer*, *CSI*, *Farscape*, *The 4400*, *Roswell*, *Star Trek*, *Terminator*, *Xena*, and *Zorro*, as well as various DC and Marvel comics. He recently won a Scribe Award from the International Association of Media Tie-In Writers. He has traced Jack the Ripper's path through Whitechapel, but only in the twentieth century.

His official Web site is www.gregcox-author.com.

The damp, foggy weather reminded her of Seattle. The gaslights and hansom cabs did not.

"Welcome to the West End of London, heart of the city's flourishing theater district," the tour guide announced. Kenneth Ramsey's bristling red muttonchops and thick walrus mustache fit the era perfectly, as did his formal black attire, white tie, and top hat. A gilded watch chain dangled from his vest pocket. His plummy

British accent certainly sounded authentic. "Home to Henry Irving, Ellen Terry, Oscar Wilde, and other luminaries of the Victorian stage."

His lips barely moved as he subvocalized into the miniaturized microphone concealed in his impeccably knotted silk tie. His spiel was instantly transmitted to tiny receivers discreetly hidden in the ears of the small party of time tourists surrounding him on the sidewalk in front of the legendary Lyceum Theatre. Eager theatergoers dressed to the nines milled past them, necessitating such technological legerdemain. It wouldn't do for the natives of this bygone age to overhear them.

Pretty slick, Celeste thought. Timeshares seemed to have thought of everything. Her earpiece itched, however, and she resisted an urge to fiddle with it. She also felt slightly queasy, apparently a routine side effect of temporal dislocation. Ramsey had assured her the time-sickness would pass. *It had better. I have big plans for this evening, and they don't involve me puking all over the nineteenth century.*

She contemplated her fellow tourists, who included a middle-aged couple from Ohio, their bored-looking teenage son, and a somewhat nerdy-looking young man wearing a deerstalker cap in emulation of his idol, Sherlock Holmes. All were dressed in formal period attire, provided by Timeshares for a nominal fee. Their package deal included three nights in Victorian England, including meals, accommodations in a luxury hotel, and entertainment. Even as a group excursion, it was a pricy trip, but if everything went according to her plan, it would pay off big time.

Or so Celeste hoped.

For now, though, she just needed to play along and pretend to be merely another time-traveling sightseer. A slender woman pushing forty, she found her elabo-

rate Victorian getup less comfortable than her usual
sweatpants and T-shirt. Along with the others, she took
in the deliciously old-time atmosphere, gawking openly
like out of towners. Horse-drawn carriages disgorged a
steady stream of elegantly bedecked gentlemen and ladies who braved the drizzly autumn weather for a night
at the theater. Flower girls, straight out of *My Fair Lady*,
hawked posies to their betters. Liveried coachmen held
open doors. Mist fogged the spacious avenue, adding
a nostalgic haze to the scene. The lambent glow of the
gaslights shone through fog like fairy nimbuses. Tower-
ing marble columns supported the Lyceum's imposing
portico. A hubbub of voices competed with the *clop clop*
of the horse's hooves. A stocky bearded Irishman stood
atop the steps leading to the Lyceum's grand entrance,
fulsomely greeting each dignitary. Celeste realized with
a start that it was Bram Stoker, the theater's acting manager. Had he written *Dracula* yet? No, that was still nine
years away....

"I can't believe it," half of the married couple murmured in awe. What was his name again? Brian? Ryan?
He hesitantly touched the base of a nearby streetlight,
as though expecting it to pop like a soap bubble upon
contact. "It's so real."

"It is real," Ramsey insisted. "This is no theme park
or VR simulation. It's actually November 8, 1888." He
rapped a marble column with his knuckles. "You're
really in London during the reign of Queen Victoria,
when the sun never set on the British Empire." The fading light belied his words. "Metaphorically speaking, of
course."

The fanboy in the deerstalker hat raised his hand.
"Aren't the Jack the Ripper murders going on now?"
Watery eyes gleamed with excitement. "I know it's not

on the itinerary, but any chance we can squeeze in a trip to Whitechapel?"

"I'm afraid not, Mr. Moskowitz," Ramsey replied. "The East End of London is too dangerous at this point in history. Never mind the Ripper; nineteenth-century Whitechapel is a lawless slum where violent crime is commonplace. Maybe someday, if there's sufficient demand, Timeshares can figure out a way to ensure our clientele's safety on such an excursion. But for now liability and insurance issues preclude any detours to the bad part of town."

"Oh," Moskowitz said, obviously disappointed. The teenager, whom had visibly perked up at the mention of the grisly murders, slipped back into sullen adolescence. Moskowitz dabbed at a runny nose with a monogrammed silk handkerchief. "Darn allergies," he muttered. "This fog is wreaking havoc with my sinuses." He blew his nose loudly. "You sure we can't sneak in just a peek at the Ripper's hunting grounds? I promise not to sue anybody."

"Sorry," Ramsey demurred. "It's out of my hands."

Celeste repressed a sigh of relief. She had her own plans regarding the Ripper, and she didn't want any amateur sleuths or murder buffs horning in on them. There was too much at stake. *Namely, my career.*

The tour guide went back to hyping tonight's activities. "Still, if it's chills and thrills you're after, I think we can oblige you with some of the fictional variety." He gestured grandly at the ornate theater. "Tonight we have front row seats to *Jekyll and Hyde*, starring the great Victorian actor Richard Mansfield. This celebrated production, based on Robert Louis Stevenson's immortal classic, has been playing to sold-out audiences for months now. Believe me, it took no little effort to secure some tickets, but at Timeshares we spare no expense to make your vacations literally historic."

And charge an arm and a leg for it, too, Celeste thought. But it would be worth the expense if she succeeded in what she had *really* signed onto this tour for. Forget Richard Mansfield, *Jekyll and Hyde*, and the rest of this whole "Gaslight & Greasepaint" enterprise. She was out to solve one of history's greatest unsolved mysteries.

Who was Jack the Ripper?

The show, and Mansfield's performance, proved entertaining enough. Despite her impatience to get down to business, she had almost been disappointed when the cast took their final curtain calls.

Almost.

Big Ben tolled midnight as she gratefully shed her cumbersome Victorian finery in the privacy of the hotel room Timeshares had booked for her at the Carlton. In theory, the rest of the tour party had retired for the night in anticipation of tomorrow's busy itinerary, which included a matinee showing of Gilbert and Sullivan's *Yeoman of the Guard* with the original cast. With any luck, she'd know the Ripper's identity by then and be fast on her way to fame and fortune.

Corset, bustle, stays, and petticoats hit the floor. On went the men's attire she had stowed in a hidden compartment in her luggage. A dark Ulster coat helped disguise her already boyish figure. She tucked her short blond curls under a bowler hat. Chances were it would be easier—not to mention safer—to navigate the sordid back alleys of Whitechapel as a man. And the trousers would be lot easier to run in if something went amiss. Ramsey had not been exaggerating when he'd described the East End as the most dangerous part of London, and she was heading right into its most murderous depths.

Did she really want to do this?

Now that the moment was at hand, second thoughts assailed her. Maybe this wasn't such a bright idea. Her timesickness had passed, just as Ramsey had promised, but her stomach was still tied up in knots. She shivered at the prospect of venturing out into the foggy night on her own.

What other choice do I have? Sales of her true-crime books had been slipping for years now; royalties and downloads were drying up. Not that it was her fault. Could she help it if there were no truly great murder mysteries in her own time, when most any crime could be solved by matching DNA samples? Where was the drama in that? There were times she wanted to travel back in time just to kick Watson and Crick in their double helixes.

Thank heaven there were still great crimes—and great criminals—lurking in the past. Jack the Ripper was her ticket back to the top of the bestseller list, provided Timeshares didn't get wind of what she was up to and pull the plug on tonight's expedition. Fortunately, she had been able to book the tour under her real name, Celeste Jordan, instead of her pen name, Jordan Pinkerton, so as to avoid raising any red flags with the time-travel agency. If all went well, she could return to the twenty-first century with the Ripper's true identity and no one would be the wiser—until her new book went on sale.

It was the perfect scheme, as long as she didn't lose her nerve.

"No guts, no glory." She had come too far, geographically and chronologically, to turn back now. Tucking an umbrella under her arm, she took a moment to inspect her disguise in a full-length mirror. "Not bad." In the murky gaslight and fog, she would probably pass as a man. "Whitechapel, here I come."

* * *

The East End was even worse than she had imagined. Only a short carriage ride had separated her ritzy accommodations from Whitechapel, yet she might as well as have taken a starship to another world. Celeste had memorized every book ever written about the Ripper and knew just how bad this neighborhood was supposed to be in Queen Victoria's time, but it was one thing to read about the squalid conditions online, in the comfort of her air-conditioned condo in Seattle, and something else altogether to experience it for real.

A clammy fog, reeking of smoke and fouler odors, wafted through a daunting labyrinth of grimy streets and alleys. Hundreds of thousands of the city's poorest and most desperate inhabitants were crowded into a pestilential slum where disease, crime, poverty, and ignorance blighted the lives of anyone unlucky enough to live here. Immigrant families were crammed into overcrowded tenements and sweatshops. Doss-houses offered flea-infested cots to homeless wretches for just a few pennies a night. Raucous laughter, tinny music, and angry voices poured out of the pubs and brothels that proliferated on nearly every block. Gin was mother's milk in these parts, anesthetizing the hopeless populace from the brutish reality of their short, miserable lives. A sickening effluvia filled the gutters. The swirling miasma left every surface greasy to the touch. Celeste gagged on the smell.

How could people live like this?

A door banged open behind her, and a drunken brawl spilled into the streets. Celeste scurried away, her heart pounding louder than Big Ben. She clutched her bumbershoot to her chest. All at once, she regretted leaving her emergency locator beacon back at the hotel. It had seemed like a good idea at the time, though; the last thing she wanted was for Timeshares to yank her back to her own era before she was finished here. What if Ramsey or someone else noticed that she wasn't where she belonged?

You don't need the locator, she thought. *You know what you're doing.*

Nevertheless, as she hurried through the dimly lit maze of streets and alleys, doubts chased after her. Maybe she should have gone for Lizzie Borden instead? Fall River, Massachusetts, would have been cleaner and a lot less intimidating. But how would she have explained to Timeshares why she wanted to visit Fall River in the summer of 1892? Their lawyers would surely have vetoed any attempt to get the real scoop on an ax murderer. . . .

Nope, Jack the Ripper it was. *I'll be fine,* she thought, *as long as I stick to the plan.*

"Oi, guvnor! 'Ow's about it?"

Celeste nearly jumped out of her skin as a filthy figure suddenly accosted her from the shadows. The light from a pub's frosted-glass window exposed a haggard woman wearing a ratty shawl over a rumpled brown frock that smelled like it hadn't been washed since the Queen's Jubilee the year before. Greasy black hair, liberally streaked with gray, was piled beneath a dilapidated straw bonnet. Sunken eyes winked at her. A toothless smile made Celeste's skin crawl. The woman's breath reeked of gin.

"Er, no, thank you." Celeste recoiled from the grotesque apparition, who was obviously one of the countless prostitutes infesting Whitechapel in this era. According to her research, the East End was home to at least twelve hundred so-called daughters of joy. It was upon women like this, selling themselves for shillings just to stay alive, that the Ripper had preyed. Celeste hadn't expected to have to fend one off herself.

Apparently, there were drawbacks to disguising herself as a man.

She tried to hurry away, but the rancid hooker would not take no for an answer. "Don't be like that, laddie." The harlot blocked her path. "Old Nellie knows what you need." Rheumy eyes squinted at Celeste. "Only a shilling for a pretty young boy like yourself."

"Leave me alone, please," Celeste pleaded, lowering her voice to sound more masculine. She wasn't into girls herself, but even if she had swung that way, she wouldn't have been remotely tempted by Nellie's offer. The decrepit old bag was about as sexy as a leper. Celeste tightened her grip on her umbrella. "I'm not interested . . . really!"

"Half a shilling!" Nellie persisted. "A bargain."

Lifting her skirts, she grabbed at Celeste's trousers.

"Don't touch me!" Celeste yelped. Panicked, she poked Nellie in the gut with the point of her bumbershoot. Nervous fingers pressed a button concealed in the grip, activating the high-voltage stun baton built into the umbrella. A bright blue spark jolted Nellie, who dropped onto the cobblestones, twitching and convulsing, before curling up into a fetal position. A low moan escaped her lips.

Yikes! Celeste yanked back the umbrella. Guilt stabbed her as she contemplated the downed prostitute. She had brought the stun umbrella with her for her own protection, but maybe she had overreacted a little. *I didn't want to zap her, but she wouldn't leave me alone!*

Thankfully, Nellie still appeared to be breathing. Celeste glanced around nervously, afraid that someone might have seen her stun the old woman. Bobbies and plainclothesmen were swarming Whitechapel these days in hopes of snaring the elusive Ripper, but nobody seemed to have observed her encounter with Nellie. She doubted that the woman's sprawled form would attract much attention either. What was one more inebriated whore passed out in the street?

Nevertheless, she made tracks toward Dorset Street, leaving Nellie behind. A bobby at the corner nodded as she passed. Celeste felt a little safer knowing that the police were out in force tonight, even though their attempts to catch the Ripper were doomed to failure. Scotland Yard had been hunting Jack since August, but at least four women had been butchered nonetheless. Despite their best efforts, the police were no closer to solving the mystery than they had been when the murders began.

But Celeste had an advantage over the frustrated coppers. She knew exactly when and where the Ripper was going to strike next.

Miller's Court was an enclosed yard just off Dorset Street, accessible via an arched gateway. Mary Jane Kelly, the Ripper's last known victim, lodged in a one-room apartment on the ground floor of a rooming house that catered almost exclusively to prostitutes. Whitewashed brick walls hemmed in Miller's Court, which looked more like an alley than a court. A broken window was left over from an ugly fight between Mary and the man she lived with, Joseph Barnett, who had moved out more than a week ago, perhaps because Mary had starting working the streets again. A thin muslin curtain hid the interior of the room from view. A number by the door identified the address as number 13. The unlucky number would certainly prove so for Mary Kelly. The Ripper had taken his time with her . . .

The infamous locale looked just as Celeste had imagined it. Miller's Court had been (would be?) demolished in 1920 and renovated several times since. Celeste still remembered how disappointed she'd been when she had first visited this neighborhood in her own time; it had been all office buildings, parking garages, and warehouses. A modern loading dock had been built over the site of Mary Jane Kelly's grisly demise. All traces of the gaslight horror had been swept away and gentrified out of existence.

But not here, not now. Celeste had hardly been able to contain her excitement when she'd discovered that the "Gaslight & Greasepaint" tour coincided with one of the Ripper murders. Talk about a lucky break! She had been prepared to sneak away from the tour and hole up somewhere, maybe for days, until the closest convenient killing came along, but, as it turned out, the timing couldn't have better. It was almost as though Timeshares had gone out of its way to make things easy for her.

She made a mental note to thank them in the acknowledgments.

Big Ben tolled one A.M. in the distance. Celeste breathed a sigh of relief. In theory, she should be in plenty of time to catch Jack the Ripper in the act. The coroner had placed Mary Kelly's time of death at around four in the morning, but having little faith in nineteenth-century forensics, Celeste had allowed herself plenty of leeway, just in case the murder had taken place earlier than anyone had realized. She secreted herself in a shadowy doorway facing the entrance to number 13 and popped in a pair of night vision contact lenses. The lenses gave the scene an unearthly green glow, but they would allow her to observe the proceedings unseen. Miller's Court was dark and unlit, making it ideal for both her and Jack the Ripper.

The rain started up again, and she took shelter beneath the doorframe. The winter chill began to seep into her bones, and she hugged herself to keep warm. She was in for a long, cold vigil, but she couldn't complain. Mary Jane Kelly was going to have a worse night.

Much worse.

At the moment, the doomed prostitute was still alive. Smoke rose from the chimney of number 13. Candlelight escaped the broken window. Celeste could hear Mary singing inside her pitiful hovel, sounding tipsy and off-key. An Irish accent betrayed her roots in County Limerick. Celeste couldn't quite make out the words, but Mary's neighbors would later testify that she had been singing "A Violet I Plucked from My Mother's Grave" well after midnight.

She was only twenty-four years old.

A man's voice joined in the singing, and a chill went down Celeste's spine as she realized that Mary might already be entertaining her killer. Jack the Ripper was only a few yards away, on the other side of a bolted wooden door.

Who are you? Celeste wondered. Her brain ran through the usual list of suspects. Sir William Gull, the Queen's physician? The celebrated painter Walter Sickert? Montague Druitt, the suicidal lawyer? Francis Tumblety, the quack American physician? John Pizer, a.k.a. "Leather Apron"? Prince Albert Victor, the Queen's grandson? More than a century of Ripperology had produced a plethora of theories and suspects, but no definitive answers.

She fought a temptation to try peek through the window. It was too early; she couldn't risk scaring the Ripper away or, worse, putting herself in danger. What if she didn't recognize his face? It was possible the Ripper was someone completely unknown to history whose face would mean nothing to her. Better to trail him home after he was done with Mary and get an actual name and address before heading back to her own century. Hell, maybe she could even snag a sample of his DNA later on ...

Mary's song was cut off abruptly. A strangled cry briefly disturbed the night.

Celeste flinched. She tried not to think about what was happening inside number 13 right now. *This is all ancient history,* she reminded herself. *Mary Jane Kelly was murdered over a century before I was born.* Celeste was here to observe history, not change it. Who knew what kind of butterfly effect she might set off if she tried to intervene on Mary's behalf? *I could return to a future in which Charles Manson was the first man on the moon, or maybe I was never born ...*

Mary's murder, and subsequent mutilation, had to happen. It was part of history.

"Rest in peace," Celeste whispered. "It will be over soon."

Long hours passed as she huddled in the doorway, waiting for the Ripper to complete his savage work. Because the final murder had taken place indoors, and not out in the open, Jack had been free to indulge his bloodthirsty predilections as never before, and he had taken full advantage of that opportunity. By now, Mary Jane Kelly was in pieces.

Don't think about it, Celeste thought. Instead, like countless Ripperologists before her, she wondered why the murders had apparently stopped after tonight. What had become of the Ripper afterward? Had he died of natural causes, committed suicide, been imprisoned on other charges, confined to a lunatic asylum, moved away from London, or simply retired? Was Scotland Yard truly clueless, or had there been some sort of official cover-up?

She couldn't wait to find out.

Her vigil was briefly interrupted around three in the

morning when an older woman entered Miller's Court, calling on one of Mary's neighbors. The woman glanced uneasily at the darkened doorway where Celeste was lurking before hurrying inside.

Ohmigod, Celeste realized. *That was Sarah Lewis.* At the inquest, Lewis would later testify that she glimpsed a suspicious figure loitering outside Mary Kelly's flat in the wee hours of the morning. All at once, Celeste understood whom that mysterious figure was. *Me. I'm the one Sarah Lewis saw. I've been part of history all along— and I never knew it!*

This proved it. She was doing the right thing. The revelation strengthened her resolve to stick it out, despite the wet, miserable conditions.

I was always meant to be here. It's my destiny to expose Jack the Ripper—over a hundred years from now.

Finally, about five in the morning, her patience was rewarded. Jack the Ripper slipped out of number 13, closing the door behind him. Celeste glimpsed a furtive figure wearing a heavy Inverness coat and carrying a leather bag. The brim of a felt hat obscured his face, much to her frustration. She held her breath, retreating as far as she could into the murky doorway. This was the tricky part: she needed to shadow the Ripper back to his lair to find out who he really was. Maybe even steal a piece of his mail.

Wonder if he keeps a diary—or trophies of his kills? She would love to get her hands on those!

The Ripper exited Miller's Court, turning left onto Dorset Street. Celeste hurried to follow him, but she had only gone a few steps before she was grabbed roughly from behind. A gloved hand was clasped over her mouth. The cold edge of a knife pressed against her throat.

"Drop the umbrella!" a harsh voice whispered into her ear. "Or I'll rip you to bits."

Celeste froze in fear. *Who?*

"The umbrella!" the voice urged her again. The knife pricked her jugular.

The rigged bumbershoot clattered to the ground, leaving her unarmed. Celeste remembered the emergency locator button she had left behind at the Carlton and kicked herself for her recklessness. Was she about to become the victim of a random nineteenth century street crime?

It's not fair, she thought. *I'm not even born yet!*

Her assailant shoved her toward number 13. Was it just her imagination, or did his voice sound vaguely familiar? "Inside!"

The door was unlocked. The mugger hustled Celeste into the apartment. She braced herself for the horror she knew was waiting.

Mary Jane Kelly's cheaply furnished room now resembled a slaughterhouse. Most of the murdered woman rested on her unmade bed, but choice bits were displayed on a rickety wooden table a few inches away. Her clothes were neatly folded atop a chair. A crimson flood soaked the sheets and floorboards. A blazing fireplace consumed various articles of clothing. Celeste had seen grainy black-and-white crime photos of the butchery, but that barely prepared her for the nauseating sight and stench of the bloody spectacle. Her gorge rose.

What kind of person could . . . dissect . . . another human being like this?

A strong hand shoved her into the corner. "Don't even think about screaming," the man warned, "unless you wanted to end up like her."

Gasping, Celeste spun around to confront her attacker. In the flickering light of the fire, it took her a second to recognize him.

"Ramsey?"

The tour guide stood only a few feet away from her, brandishing an eight-inch hunting knife. Like her, he had discarded his formal attire for less ostentatious period attire: an Inverness coat and felt hat. Perspiration dotted his face.

An overwhelming sense of relief washed over her. "Thank God!" she exclaimed, clutching her chest. "You really had me going there. For a second, I almost thought you were Jack the Ripper himself!"

"I am Jack the Ripper, you stupid cow!" Spittle sprayed from his lips. He viciously slashed the air between them, driving her back into the corner. "Or should I call you 'Jordan Pinkerton'?" He sneered at her startled expression. "Yes, I know who you are. I recognized you right away from the author photo on your books. I've read them all, you know. And I knew exactly what you were up to the minute you showed up for the tour." He snorted derisively. "Like you were really interested in Richard Mansfield or Gilbert and Sullivan!"

She blinked in confusion. "I don't understand. I just saw Jack the Ripper leave, right before you grabbed me."

"That was me all right," Ramsey said. "From the last time I was here. One of the singular advantages of time travel. You can visit the same time twice. Be in two places at once. Take an actual trip down memory lane."

Celeste tried to keep up. "Jack the Ripper is a time traveler, too?"

"Astounding, isn't it?" He grinned devilishly. "I was always obsessed with the case, ever since I was a kid. I read every book and Web site, saw every movie. You obviously don't remember me, but I actually saw you speak at that Ripperology conference in Glasgow a few years back. You even gave me your autograph!"

She remembered the conference, but not the man. "You're a fan?"

"Of Jack the Ripper," he insisted. "Not you. Would you believe I used to dream about being the Ripper? Almost every night. I would wake up panting in excitement. Then, when I got this gig with Timeshares, the proverbial lightbulb went off over my head. I didn't have to be just a spectator to history. I could make my dreams come true!"

Was he serious? Celeste struggled to make sense of what he was saying. "But who was Jack before you? Sickert? Druitt?"

"No one! You're still not getting it. You can't hold onto that old-fashioned linear thinking where time travel is concerned." He gestured grandly at the dingy brick walls surrounding them. "This is November 9, 1888. I was always here. It always happened this way." Bloodshot eyes gleamed with madness. "That's the sublime paradox of it all. I inspired myself!"

He's insane, Celeste realized. Her momentary relief gave way to renewed terror. Had too many trips through time warped Ramsey's brain chemistry? The waiver she had signed had mentioned minor unpredictable side effects ...

"How do you think the Ripper avoided getting caught?" he gloated. "I always knew where the bobbies and undercover cops *weren't* going to be, where history said it would be safe to strike." He fished his locator button from his vest pocket. "Plus, of course, I always had my ace in the hole. If ever I found myself cornered, I just zapped myself back to the future before I could get nabbed!"

She eyed the locator button avidly. If only she could get hold of it, just for a second!

"I think I understand," she humored him. "So what now? What happens next?"

"You're the murder expert. What do you think?" He

leered at her. "You're doing me a favor, actually. I had run out of Ripper victims. To be honest, I'm seriously considering putting in for a transfer to the 1960s and starting over as the Zodiac Killer. You can be my swan song as the Ripper."

Celeste gulped. "But I'm not a prostitute."

"No, you're a money-grubbing writer who cashes in on murder and bloodshed." He stepped forward, backing her up against the blood-soaked bed. "Close enough."

"Wait!" Celeste appealed frantically to his vanity. "You don't want to kill me. I can make you famous, reveal your identity to the world." She nodded at the door. "You can just disappear into the nineteenth century, knowing that someday the entire world will remember your name."

He laughed in her face. "Nice try, but no dice. You reveal my identity and I'm just another boring slasher to be psychoanalyzed and dissected by hack writers like you. Don't you see? It's the *mystery* of Jack the Ripper that will keep people fascinated for generations to come. That what's make him a legend. What makes *me* a legend."

She tried another tack. "But you can't kill me. You'd be changing history. Mary Jane Kelly died alone!"

"Not anymore." He shrugged. "So there's one more body found at Miller's Court, a mystery woman for people to puzzle over for the next hundred years or so. It just adds a new wrinkle to the story." His knife gleamed in the firelight. "By the time I'm done with you, not even the future will recognize you ..."

He raised the knife.

A loud sneeze, coming from under the bed, startled them both.

"What the hell?" Ramsey faltered, looking away from Celeste just for a moment.

She saw her opportunity and took it. A spinning kick

knocked the blade from his grip. The knife skidded across the floor several feet away.

"Hey!" His befuddled expression was a joy to behold. "You can't do that!"

Celeste followed up the kick with a roundhouse punch to his jaw. "Here's the thing, dummy. You're not facing a tipsy nineteenth-century whore this time. I've studied kickboxing, Krav Maga, and taken way too many self-defense courses!"

"Nosy bitch!" Ramsey dived for the knife, but Celeste was faster. She leaped past him and snatched up the fireplace poker. He lunged for her only to get smacked in the arm by the swinging poker. Bone shattered audibly and he dropped to his knees, whimpering in pain. A second blow across the back of his head left him sprawled face down on the floor. Not taking any chances, she prodded him with the poker to make sure he wasn't going to be getting up again anytime soon.

"That's for Mary Jane Kelly," she gasped. "And Polly Nichols, Liz Stride, Catherine Eddowes, and Annie Chapman!"

Ramsey seemed to be out cold, but she held onto the poker just in case. She had seen too many horror movies to turn her back on the downed monster. Crouching beside the prone Ripper, she claimed his locator button. A second sneeze reminded her that they were not alone. She peered curiously at the bed. "Hello?"

"I–is it safe?" a feeble voice stammered.

Celeste stood up. "I think so. Who is that?"

To her surprise, Bernard Moskowitz crawled out from beneath the flimsy wooden bedstead. His Sherlock Holmes outfit was a study in scarlet. His scrawny face was white as a sheet.

"You?" she blurted in surprise. The other tourist was

supposed to be safely tucked away at the Carlton. *Just like me.*

"I ... I couldn't resist," he confessed. "I just had to find out who Jack the Ripper was." His shell-shocked gaze fell upon the morsels of flesh laid out atop the table. He looked away from the carved-up carcass upon the bed. "Oh God ..."

Celeste realized that the poor kid had been under the bed the whole time. *Guess we both had the same idea.*

Thank heaven.

A pocket watch informed her that it was nearly five-thirty. In approximately five hours, one Thomas Bowyer would be dropping by to hit Mary up for thirty-five shillings of overdue rent money. He was in for the shock of his life, but Celeste wasn't inclined to stick around to see.

"You ready to get out of here?" she asked Moskowitz.

He nodded weakly. "Please."

She pressed the locator button.

"My sincere apologies for this unfortunate business." Rolf Jacobsen, founder and president of Timeshares, sat across from her. "But I'm sure you understand how we would like to keep this embarrassing incident our little secret." He slid a notarized document across the top of his antique mahogany desk, which had once belonged to Thomas Alva Edison. "Mr. Moskowitz has already signed this confidentiality agreement in exchange for a free pass to the time and location of his choosing." He flashed Celeste an oily smile. "I believe he's requested a tryst with Mata Hari ..."

"Uh-uh." Celeste didn't even look at the proffered document. "You're not going to buy me off so easily. That maniac could have killed me!"

"Again, my apologies." He handed her a fountain pen.

"Clearly, we need to do a more thorough psychological screening of our employees, both before and after their trips to the past." He shrugged. "It's possible we underestimated the long-term cognitive effects of regular temporal dislocation, but I assure you that we are already putting new procedures in place to ensure that such an aberration never happens again."

"An 'aberration,' is that what you call it?" Celeste was offended by the blandly corporate euphemism. "At least five women were killed and mutilated."

"Those tragedies are a matter of historical record," he pointed out. "We couldn't have prevented them if we wanted to."

"Even though one of your tour guides was responsible?" A horrible suspicion gripped her. "You knew, didn't you? You suspected that Ramsey was the Ripper, but you kept on sending him back to 1888!"

Jacobsen was unruffled by her accusation. "History is history, Ms. Jordan. What happened happens." He pressed the confidentiality agreement on her again. "Now then, how can we convince you to leave this unpleasantness where it belongs—in the past?"

"Don't even try." She got up to go. "I already have everything I need. I know the true identity of Jack the Ripper. That's a gold mine."

"More like a single nugget." Jacobsen gestured for her to sit down again. "Don't be too hasty, Ms. Jordan. You're obviously a shrewd woman . . . and a fine author." He called up one of her books on the monitor of his computer. "Perhaps we can come to a different sort of arrangement."

She eyed him warily. "Like what?"

He tore up the confidentiality agreement. "Suppose you forgo the Ripper in exchange for unlimited access to a host of equally famous mysteries: D. B. Cooper, the

Lindbergh kidnapping, the Black Dahlia, the Princes in the Tower ..."

"Lizzie Borden?"

"Of course. That's a perfect example." He leaned forward conspiratorially. "As a matter of fact, we've been thinking of licensing a line of publishing spin-offs under the Timeshares umbrella. You seem like exactly the kind of ambitious, enterprising author we've been looking for, one who can take full advantage of everything we can offer. Think about it. You would have all of history at your disposal. The possibilities are endless."

"Except Jack the Ripper."

He nodded. "That particular mystery is probably best left unsolved. Do we understand each other?"

Celeste's mind boggled at the prospect. Jacobsen was offering her not just a single bestseller, but a *franchise.* Countless millennia of unsolved histories, from the extinction of the dinosaurs to the heat death of the universe.

"Mr. Jacobsen," she replied, "I think this could be the beginning of a beautiful partnership."

Limited Time Offer

Dean Leggett

Dean Alan Leggett has enjoyed the topic and mystery of time travel since junior high school. While serving in the United States Air Force the debates of time travel paradoxes would last longer than games of Titan. He has since returned to his home state of Wisconsin where he lives with his wonderful wife, Annette. When Dean isn't working in the IT world of virtualization "time shares" he writes about different types of Timeshares.

Peeking through the tiny mailbox window I see an envelope. My heart jumps. Maybe Penny is finally returning my letters. My keychain bangs on the metal and glass wall as old Mrs. Mildred scowls at me from down the hall. My shoulders slump as I see it is just another piece of junk mail. On the back side it reads: "Adventure isn't going to wait for you—act now!" It is hard to believe folks actually fall for this crap.

I stick the fairly thick envelope in my mouth and search through the long string of keys. I swear the key for the deadbolt and the key for the handle are on opposite sides again. How does that keep happening? I never remember moving them around. The rusted hinges give a high-pitched squeak. I slip inside, shutting the door quickly before Mrs. McNosey asks if I have found a new job yet.

I toss the keys on the counter, along with the sole piece of mail, and pull open the fridge. The single light bulb hums at me angrily as I search for anything not yet expired. Damn it! I know I just went to the grocery store Wednesday. How can everything be spoiled already? You would think that by putting the bread in the fridge it would keep longer, but no. Harry's Bakery lives up to its name again. I grab a beer and slam the door.

I crack the edge of the bottle on the counter, sending the cap flying across the room. I grab the sales pitch and head the three steps into the living room and try to relax. The TV stand proudly displays a dust outline. Sipping on my nectar of sanity, I tear open the envelope and read the form letter.

"Mr. Lynch, how would you like to get away from your current life and experience the wonders Timeshares can offer?"

I pause as foam almost shoots out my nose.

"Wouldn't you like to travel back to the lands of your ancestors and meet long-lost relatives? We have a custom travel package ready for you. Stop in for a free consultation and leave your worries at home."

I tipped back to get the last drops.

The letter went on with the sales pitch, but what caught my eye was the last paragraph.

"Open twenty-four hours a day, seven days a week for your convenience, Mr. Lynch. Don't worry about payment arrangements; we have a plan that will work even for you."

I would like to see what type of payment plan they have for me and my overdrawn bank account. I do need to pick up more bread and maybe some cheap beer. I wonder if bottle caps are the type of payment plan they have in mind. I decide to take the bottle cap along—for good luck if nothing else. I wouldn't want the roaches to carry it off.

The Timeshares office is on a small side street just down the block, fittingly enough next to a small all-night diner. The office appears dark, but there is a small light glowing from the back. A flip sign hanging from the inside window reads: OPEN. The diner calls to me louder.

My stomach is rumbling, and the fresh smell of bacon only amplifies my hunger. Surprisingly, there are quite a few folks even at this time of night. It is well past 11 P.M. as I pull open the door and head inside.

The bells announce me. Of the fifteen or so customers, only one seems to take notice. An older man in the back; he smiles and raises a cup. The waitress scowls at him and refills his cup before he brings it back down to the counter. The aroma of the freshly brewed coffee hits me. I take the closest stool I find.

The waitress pours me a cup of coffee and hands me a menu. The scent of frying bacon and an endless selection of breakfast, lunch, and dinner options enthralls me. I don't notice the bells or the tall, dark-haired woman dressed in what appeared to be a Renaissance fair costume until she swings her skirt over on the stool next to me. Her laced corset and ample build makes for quite a sight. Trying to look politely elsewhere, I glance around the diner. I notice not many really seem to pay any attention to her. It is then I notice many of the patrons are dressed very strangely. Older styles of shirts and odd cuts of suit coats are all around.

I decide on a short stack and a side of bacon. I don't know why the waitress bothers to write it down, as she shouts my order as soon as she takes the menu from my fingers. My hands fidget with the salt shaker and I try not to glance too often at the flouncy woman to my right. As if noticing my discomfort, she speaks to me, but I don't catch all of it.

Judging by the look on my face, she repeats herself. "How are you today?"

I do my best to fix my eyes on hers.

"Fine. How are you?" I smile and do my best to act calm. It looks like she could fall out of her dress if she turned wrong.

She gives a heavy sigh and doesn't answer.

Thankfully, my order arrives.

I focus on my meal as if it were my last. If I don't find work soon, it just might be. The bacon is the best I have ever tasted and the cakes sure hit the spot. I pull a ten out of my now empty wallet and give a shout of thanks to the cook. I stumble toward the door.

I intend to head home, but think, what the hell, I might as well give this travel shop a look. If they go to the trouble of being open all night, it couldn't hurt to stop in. If nothing else, it might give me a clue to the assortment of oddly dressed people in the diner. I pull on the door, half expecting it to be locked. It opens easily.

Not wishing to startle anyone, I call, "Hello? Are you still open?"

"Mr. Lynch!" A voice rings out from the back, causing me to jump. "Come in, come in, we were expecting you." A short stocky man in his early sixties comes forward. A few more lights flicker and then pop on. "Have a seat over here while we get your file together." He gestures to a chair in front of an old wooden desk, gathers some papers and a few folders, and sets them on the desk in front of him. "Well, Mr. Lynch it shows here you wish to journey into the past to take some photographs for us."

"I don't think so. I received your flyer offering travel on a budget I could afford. But I can't afford anything."

I stare at him, trying to puzzle out how he knows my name. This whole thing isn't making much sense. I try to get a look at some of the papers hanging out of the folders—no success.

"I used to take photographs for a college newspaper," I tell him. "But that was years ago."

"Oh, so sorry, Lisa hasn't finish sorting your file yet." He flips through some more papers before glancing up. "Here it is. We would like to offer you a free trip near the Sea of Meezee. All we ask in return is for you to take some photos for us. You will be in disguise. We need photos both inside the Chefuncte village and especially inside a certain hut." He pulls out a sheet of paper and hands it to me. "Oh, and you will need to sign this disclaimer."

The form has more than a hundred lines of text in a tiny font. I look it over quickly, noting my name. It has tomorrow's date already filled in. "Why would I sign this and where is this Meezee place?"

"Sorry Mr. Lynch, it isn't a *where*, but more of a *when*. Apparel, footwear, and supplies will be provided." As he speaks, he looks to be checking off some boxes from a form attached to a clipboard. "You already ate; good, good ... Everything seems to be set, just sign and we will get you ready for your journey. Sorry to give you no warning for this, but our regular photographer ... is no longer available. We needed him replaced right now."

I think about just getting up and leaving, but the notion of returning to my empty apartment is just too much. It is time to take a chance. I pick up the pen and sign my name. Glancing at the clock, it reads 12:17. The little man grabs the signed sheet, tucks it into the folder, and waddles back down the hall. He turns back briefly, "Come on Kyle, time to get you on your way."

I spend the next few hours being measured and fitted into various animal pelts. They have a strong but not unpleasant smell. At first, I resist asking, "Why me?" among countless other minor questions. In the end I just stand there. My thoughts of leaving vanish when the dark-haired woman from the diner enters the room. She is out of her corset and wearing a set of animal skins. The skins are mismatched, ranging from fur to bare leather, and stitched with a thick coarse thread. Her multipiece outfit moves with her as she stuffs smaller pieces of hide into a large pack. The native look fits her perfectly; I on the other hand imagine I appear very silly.

She looks at me a few times and smiles.

"I bet this is funny to you," I say. "Why didn't you warn me about this in the diner?"

She walks toward me. "Be happy you didn't get the letter last week. You could have joined me in ole England, and somehow you don't seem like the tights and ruffles type."

Her smile is disarming.

She speaks in a language I don't recognize to the old man. He glances up at me as he responds. "His job is to take photos. Yours, Becca, is to keep him out of trouble and teach him to fit in. You know the drill. I think he will fit in nicely with these folk."

She waits until she has my full attention. "Mr. Lynch, you will be known as Penobscot. Repeat it a few times to yourself so you can get the feel for it. Whenever you hear that name, you will respond. It doesn't matter what you say, they will not understand your language. I will translate for you." Stuffing the last of the leathers into the pack, she flips the thick flap over and ties it shut.

"Well, he isn't as scrawny as he looked before, what with his new clothes. His scraggy red-brown hair will mark him as a Northern, I think."

The old man finishes stitching the leather of my left shoe. "There you go, Mr. Lynch. You are almost ready. I will get your camera, it should be finished charging." With that he turns and heads out of the room. I wondered why all the work on the disguise only to walk in with an anachronistic camera hanging around my neck.

Becca inspects my costume. Still standing on the tailor platform, at least I have a height advantage. "So Becca, you will be my guide, huh? Can I call you Becca? Or do you have a strange name I should use for our cover?" I smile as my heart begins to race. I feel like a spy in a sci-fi movie. Time travel, strange lands, and animal skin clothing from *The Land of the Lost* make for a major change of direction.

Becca takes a step closer and leans into me. The bead work in her hair rattles. "Penobscot, you are about to earn your 'free trip.' You are traveling to a land where cats don't rub against your leg, they gnaw it off. There are bears that stand over fifteen feet tall, and I have seen one crush the skull of a hardened warrior in its jaws. I have seen insects draw the life blood out of rabbits in less than a minute. Travel to the past may not be the picnic you may envision. We are heading to a place where humans were tested and only the worthy survived. The people you will meet during the next few weeks fight daily to feed and protect their families." With that, she turns and heads down the hall.

OK, what am I getting myself into? A free trip to the past to take photos is one thing, but meeting cats that eat legs is something completely different. I look around for my jeans—I'm outta here!

"Mr. Lynch!" The short man sneaks up behind me

while reaching for my boots. He holds a seven-foot high wooden staff, about two inches in diameter, polished smooth with feathers and crystals hanging from thick strings near the top. "Mr. Lynch, pull yourself together! You wanted to get away from your sad, miserable life and go on an adventure. Well, here's your chance. You can follow me, or you can return home and hope you can find another job before they kick you out on the street. Look inside yourself, Mr. Lynch. We are not meant to just trudge through life or sit on our collective asses watching reruns of reality shows. This is your chance. Take it!"

He thrusts the staff at me, causing the crystals to rattle. Knowing the little man is right, I grab the staff proudly. "Count me in! Let's get going, Becca!"

With a wide smile, he explains the various features of the hidden camera staff. "Near the top of the staff there is a clear crystal rod helping to align the camera. You just line up the shot and press on a knot sticking out the side. This is our best technology camera; it can take photographs in near total darkness. With no drain due to flash, the initial charge and internal memory will last for just over four hundred pictures. Anyone can operate it, but only a real photographer like yourself would know how to get the best shots."

They want me to take photos of the day-to-day life and also something rumored to be out of the ordinary. Yeah right! I'm just walking around an ancient world in animal skins carrying a mystic's staff that can take pictures. Seems like everything will be out of the ordinary.

They place my former belongings in a locker and pat me down to make sure I'm not bringing anything else along for the ride. Then he brings over a large jar. He twists the lid off and the pungent smell sets me back. He dips his hands in and rubs them together. Now he starts to rub the stench into my hair. I glance over as Becca unsuccessfully stifles a laugh.

"Hey, why do I get smelly dung wiped in my hair and she gets to keep hers combed with colorful beads decorating it?"

He continues until my hair is fully coated in the goo. "You see, Peno, you are a magician type character from the north. You need to get close to nature to achieve your visions. Beccatelravole is your guide as you travel into the southern lands. She will interpret your visions and provide cover for you. You will not exactly fit in; but that is part of the ruse. Your mannerisms, posture, and voice will be vastly different. She is the one who will bridge the gap. While you shake your staff and look through the crystal, she will explain it to the clans that it is part of your mystical ways. It will help disarm any hostility they may have toward you. The smell in your hair will keep the locals from wanting to get too close."

I shrug. I guess it makes sense. Distracted, Becca approaches and jams a long needle through my leathers.

"Hey! How does this all translate as a vacation for me?"

This brings a stern look and a wag of a finger from the little man. "See here, Mr. Lynch, we didn't promise you a cruise to the Bahamas. We offered you a chance to 'travel back to the lands of your ancestors and meet your long-lost relatives,' and that, Penobscot, is exactly what you are going to do!"

I keep a close eye on Becca as she sets down the needle.

We are taken to a room with multiple large glass capsules. We are secured inside and the covers are lowered. The lights are turned off, and the next thing I know we are in a forest clearing looking up at the stars. It is breathtaking just to see how bright the stars are. The air feels thicker, and the sounds of the night are all around.

"So Becca-tella-ra-volie, I wouldn't have believed any of this yesterday. This is amazing!"

She stands up and secures the pack to her back. "Don't try to pronounce my full name on this trip; we will not be here long enough. Stick to just Becca. Oh, and stay close. We will arrive at the village around sunrise. Try not to gawk too much. Just relax and go with the flow."

She offers me a hand up.

My legs are a bit uneasy and my stomach is starting to churn.

We weave through thick brush before finding a straight, clear path. The stars give enough light so that I can see the path extends almost perfectly straight to both horizons.

"Becca, we really are in the past, aren't we?" I point down the road.

She steps closer. "Yes. Just because modern man paints the past as stone wielding cavemen doesn't mean that is truly how it is. You may not see any cell phones, but that doesn't mean that ancient man wasn't as innovative and exacting. The pyramids were built thousands of years ago, but no one in modern times with modern equipment has ever tried to duplicate them. There are countless wonders all over the past. Most just couldn't survive for thousands of years to be proven true. This is where your pictures will come in handy."

Becca leads us down the path. I start to think of the smell in my hair and those bears she spoke of. I jump at every noise and just about lose it when a small deer darts out about ten feet from us. Becca plods forward.

After a few hours the trees give way to a wooden wall.

Tree trunks stripped of bark and buried into the ground reach almost twenty feet into the air. Every few feet thick ropes are woven in opposite directions, holding them together. When the wooden wall reaches the edge of the road I can make out a small break. The opening is about ten feet across, and a series of smaller logs are crossed and bound with rope. Between the crossed logs, long spears point outward. I look close and note that the spear heads are multifaceted stone bladed tips covered in a yellow green paste.

Several natives are also blocking the way. Seeing us, they turn and call over their shoulders in a language I don't comprehend. A bulky woman strides forward and chatters with Becca, occasionally pointing toward me. I hear my new name repeated a few times in the discussion.

After a moment, everyone relaxes and motions us inside.

Becca leans in. "She wanted to know if you were the magic man I was asked to bring."

We attract a small crowd as the sky turns from pink to a brighter yellow. Light pours in as we walk inside the walled area. I expect a small village, but I'm surprised by this place—it's about the size of a large sports stadium. The oval-shaped tree wall encircles a series of about forty thatched buildings. Becca and I are taken to the large building in the center. Smoke rises slowly from two of the thatch peaks. It is a mystical sight, watching the morning breeze guide the smoke toward the rising sun.

I decide it's time to use my staff, and that I should have gotten a few pictures of the long path. At first I make up nonsensical words as I shake the staff. The crystals rattles and heads turn. I realize I don't have to make up gibberish, English would sound just as confusing.

This is almost fun, and the children seem to enjoy my act. I wonder if Timeshares will let me to keep some of the pictures.

Becca stops me just short of entering the large building.

"This is our real mission. Inside is said to be a dying giant. These people think it is one of the old gods, but we think it's just a species overlooked by time. You know, lost to the ages. I told them you are a follower of this god and need to help him pass on."

"When and where are we exactly, Becca? I know I should have asked this right away, but I was just too caught up in everything. This *giant* isn't one of those short-faced bears you told me about, is it?"

Becca kneels and hands out skins and beads to the local children as she responds. "The giant they speak of is a humanoid creature. They will not let any outsider near it. At this time most of the people in this village know the people from our office well—we've been coming here for a while. That's why we needed someone new, and a photographer at that. We needed an outsider, one with real reddish hair. I rightly assumed they'd think you came from the Anishna to the north. They have been at war with the Anishna for more than a thousand years, and through those years they have learned to respect the supposed magic the Anishna wield."

I look around and finally notice that nearly everyone carries a weapon of sorts, either holding spears or touching hatchetlike tools on their belts. Wonderful. No point in turning back now. I forcefully shake my staff. It makes the older folks flinch and the young ones giggle. I leave Becca behind and follow my guide inside the tent.

It takes a few moments for my eyes to adjust. I move the staff around and take a series of pictures. Most of my shots are directed at the large mound in the center. Firelight dances on the inside of the thatch. I see an outline of a raised straw bed. On top of this is a massive man, likely eight feet tall. His hands are huge; each finger looks to be at least an inch in diameter. I shake my staff to calm my nerves before I realize I may have awakened the giant. I take several more shots and walk closer.

The giant is breathing. He wears only a loincloth and is covered in strange tattoos. I am in awe of this man.

One of the younger boys climbs up the side and offers the giant some water. The giant turns his head to the boy but does not open his eyes. Judging by the blackness around his sockets, he may not have been able to. I take more photos and I start to feel that the giant is near death. His hair is a matted, dirty blond and doesn't fit with the dark hair of the villagers.

I spend the rest of the day meeting various villagers. Becca translates—at least I think she does. With the occasional giggle from the crowd and the blush in Becca's face, I think I am the butt of a few jokes.

The next day, Becca wakes me. "Penobscot, they want you to help the soul cross over."

We rush to the large central building.

The giant is coughing up blood. I wave my staff and in English ask the spirits to take him someplace peaceful.

This is not a time for photos.

That night they take his body to an open fire pit stacked with logs and branches. The giant is set ablaze.

From what I gathered, the villagers found him wandering down one of the roads a few months ago and befriended him. They believed him one of the great giants who pushed back the walls of ice.

The following days fly by. I am saddened when Becca tells me we need to leave. We are given food and water for our trip, and Becca has to drag me away.

We find our way back to the clearing. Becca and I lay in the grass, gazing up at the stars.

"Becca, thank for bringing me on this magnificent journey."

She smiles. "You're not so bad. Maybe you should join the team."

"You mean Timeshares would hire me?"

Becca gives me a serious look. "Sure. You might be asked to risk your life now and again for some good photo opportunities, though."

I am in shock. I have found my dream job. "Do they offer a good employee package? What would they pay me to start?"

Becca looks up at the stars as she answers. "They offer the greatest paycheck anyone could wish for, a re-awakened joy of life." How true those words are.

The return trip is a bit more traumatic. A bright light comes out of the sky and blinds me. I wake up in Time-share's office.

I change back into my modern clothes and meet Becca in the front office. She offers to buy me breakfast. One thing gnaws at me that I need to clear up.

"Becca, you didn't seem too concerned about our crossing paths with the man-eating cats and the huge skull-crushing bears. Were you just trying to scare me? Or did such things exist?"

"This last trip was only about seven thousand years ago. You will not have to worry about those bears until," she pauses to think and glances at a calendar, ". . . a week from next Tuesday. We need you to photograph the first meeting between the Clovis and the Karquees in 12,560 b.c. Those bears surprise us all the time around that area. Just stand tall and wave your magical staff to scare them, and get off a few good photos in the process."

"You really think that will work? Are they scared by the crystals?"

"I doubt it, but it might buy you some time to run away. Just think how cool those photos would be. And don't worry, I'll frame one and put it on my desk to remind me of your heroism."

She opens the door, and we head to Destiny's Diner.

The Shaman

Annie Jones

Annie Jones is the youngest grandma you ever saw and just beginning to write fiction. She has a story in *Terribly Twisted Tales*, and now one in *Timeshares*. She thanks Jean Rabe for sharing her knowledge about writing, which includes everything from soup to nuts and beyond. Annie enjoys working in her yard, digging and planting with hopes that things will grow like they are supposed to according to directions, which is not always the case. She lives in Wisconsin with her husband of many years and one dominating Yorkshire terrier.

"I need a vacation," I said to myself. I'd had a stressful month at my job as supervisor of the perfume counter at one of the local department stores in Columbus, Ohio. I'd been thinking a while about a visit to some of the ancient Indian ruins in the Southwest, perhaps Arizona, inspired by my studies of ancient Southwest history.

So this particular July day as I walked home from work, I spied a travel agency sign that was swinging in the breeze like a hand beckoning from a shaded side street away from the bustle of traffic.

The doorway was hung with those long strings of colored glass beads that were popular back in the sixties. I stuck my head through the beads and they gave a friendly, welcome jingle. There were no computers or telephones that I noticed, just a strange looking little man sitting behind a bare table. His hair was gunmetal gray and hung down to his shoulders. The brown leather vest he wore over a red flannel shirt was ornamented by a string of oddly shaped turquoise beads. His legs were stretched out to their fullest, and I could see brown leather leggings and moccasins beneath the table.

"Come in, traveler." He motioned to me. He looked harmless, so being the trusting soul that I am, I walked in. I was surprised to find the floor covered with about an inch of sand. Nothing like atmosphere, I thought.

"I can tell," he said, "you are looking to take a trip. A trip for a little rest and to find some excitement. Where would you like to go?" He paused. "The Southwest." He answered himself. "Maybe some of the ancient Indian ruins?" His brown wrinkled face looked as if it might crack when he smiled warmly at me.

"How did you know?" I was surprised that he had guessed correctly.

"Oh, sometimes I can tell just by studying a person some. I have a brochure right here, and I know you will enjoy this trip." He pushed a packet to the edge of the table. A gold ring worn smooth by the years gleamed on his finger.

I checked the itinerary, and to my astonishment, the trip was scheduled for today, a little earlier than I had been planning to leave. The brochure, filled with colorful pictures, told me I wanted to go to Verde Valley near Sedona, Arizona.

"Hurry home, pack light, return here within two hours,

and we will send you on your way." He had a strange but familiar singsong voice.

At that particular time, being brain dead from stress at work, it did not strike me as somewhat unusual having plans made out for me on such short order. So I rushed home, packed items I deemed necessary in my backpack, along with a few articles of clothing tucked in—I had plans to replenish my closet in Sedona. In less than two hours, I was back at the travel agency, backpack slung over my shoulder.

"First, we must get a picture of you. Please step into this little nook over here." He guided me to a bright capsulelike container that I had not noticed the first time I went in. He mumbled something about being an "accidental visitor" or "accidental tourist" from the other side.

"Accidental Tourist?" I mused. I'd seen that movie years back.

He mumbled something else about me being his first customer, so to speak.

"Speak of what? Accidental what?"

He didn't answer.

"Just sit right there on the little stool, and we'll get you going, ma'am. Let's see if I've figured out how to use this contraption correctly," he said as he fumbled around with various colored buttons on the capsule. "Oh, and give my regards to the goddess if you should happen to see her."

I was just about to ask him the cost of my vacation and about airline reservations and such—he hadn't even asked my name or to see a credit card. But he shut the door and quick as a blink, I was no longer in the little chamber, or anywhere else in Columbus, but standing in the middle of a narrow dirt road surrounded by mountains of red rock, backpack still slung over my shoulder.

I was startled, angry, frightened—a dozen things at once. Upon gathering my wits, I began following the road with hopes of finding someone who could tell me where I was.

The temp, I was certain, must have been somewhere around 118 degrees. I imagined myself melting right into the ground as I hiked over the rough terrain. After a short distance, I saw a path leading off the road to a grove of trees and decided some shade would be most welcome.

When I had packed my backpack I had actually given myself over to thoughts of survival. In case I happened to wander off the beaten path, I had packed a flashlight, a box of matches, a bottle of aspirin, some packages of peanut butter crackers—the orange kind that kids take to school in their lunch boxes. I also had a neatly folded yellow poncho decorated with leopard spots and six small bottles of Gatorade.

As I sat on the ground, leaning back against a tree, sipping my Gatorade, I saw that at the base of a cliff in the distance was a ruin that must have been deserted for decades.

Suddenly I stopped worrying about how I got here.

Ruins! This was just what I wanted to see.

I walked toward the cliff for a closer look and sensed a foreboding pall descending on the area. Being a lover of ancient Southwest history, my heart was touched as I looked at the small handprints that had patted the clay mud flat to make an outer wall for one of the rooms. The prints were not much bigger than a child's. The walls were in pretty good shape with some crumbling, but years ago someone had lived behind them.

Several of the prints were a little larger than the rest and had an odd indent on the third finger of the right hand. I was certain the prints were the same size as mine.

Reaching up, I placed my hands, fingers spread, into the hardened prints.

"My God, a perfect fit." It was as if a bolt of lightning hit me. I fell, from heat exhaustion or surprise, and I've no idea how long I was out.

As I finally came to, I was aware of people standing around me speaking in a language I did not understand. I concentrated, and after a few moments it sounded as if they might be using an offshoot of Spanish. I speak a few words of that language—I studied it for two years in high school—but the dialect was wholly unfamiliar to me. Still, I managed to make out a few words: "woman," "strange" or "odd," and "pale." All of them were obviously directed toward me. Could they be speaking an Indian language?

I was lying sprawled on the ground with my backpack to the side hanging onto my arm. As I pushed myself up with a moan, a gasp went up from the group, and some of them scurried away into the rooms under the overhanging rocks. Others shied away, but stood their ground. A dog, tail between its legs, barked from some distance back. A little girl, with her finger in her mouth, held onto her mother's hand and gazed at me unafraid. They all wore primitive clothes.

"Where am I? Is this a movie set?" When I spoke, an excited garble of words went flying around the group. "Donde?" I said. Spanish for "where?"

One of the men boldly stepped up and knelt by my side. He didn't look like any tourist, but he somehow looked familiar.

He pointed to me and spread his arms wide. (Where are you from?)

I understood that gesture, but didn't know the words to answer.

"Hola," I said. Maybe he understood Spanish.

"Whole-la?" he responded. He clearly didn't understand.

How could I ask where I was? Maybe I was dreaming all of this. Maybe I was still in the photo booth in the travel agency and had hit my head.

Still, I decided to humor him, figment of my imagination or not. We did much gesturing with hands and nodding of heads and rolling of eyes, trying to make ourselves understood. While all of this was going on, the others began slowly drifting back to stand in a circle around us, but keeping a safe distance in case I made any sudden moves.

By pointing to him, and then to the people, and finally back to myself as I waved my arms to take in the area, I again asked where I was.

"Sin-agua," he said. He flung his arms wide to indicate the area.

"No water? Sinagua?"

"Sin-agua."

The History Channel junkie in me came to the fore and a revelation hit me like a proverbial brick. If I wasn't dreaming, I was with a small group of nameless people who, years after their disappearance, had been called Sin-agua for lack of a better name, but also because of the lack of water in the area. Thus Sinagua—no water. I remembered a two-hour special I'd watched about them last year. They had been extinct for more than a thousand years. They had mysteriously faded into history. How could I be with a people that had simply vanished?

After some decision was reached that I was harmless, two of the women lifted me to my feet and led me into one of the rooms, where it was surprisingly very cool. The wall held a decorative pattern of handprints made by the person who had patted the clay into place. Upon seeing the handprints, I remembered placing my hands in a perfect match.

Hours went by.

That evening the people were amazed that I could take a tiny piece of wood, rub it, and make a flame. They were astounded that I had a yellow magic stick that light would come out of at the mere press of a button, and everyone had to light the flashlight and scream in surprise and laughter.

The peanut butter crackers didn't last long; they were passed around, with each person taking a bite. The Gatorade was sipped out of the plastic bottles with suspicion—until the sweet liquid hit a tongue, then a smile would light up the face.

Days passed.

They honored me by declaring I fulfilled the prophecy that a white goddess who could work magic would come to them. My image was cut into a large flat rock and outlined in black like several other forms painted there.

I found that they were a gentle people of small stature who farmed with very little water. From a river a little distance away, water was carried daily in pottery jars, and to their protest, I insisted in joining in as helper. Channels had been dug to the river for irrigation of their crops. This was a well established, organized little community.

As more days passed, I helped add rooms by using pieces of broken pottery to loosen the earth, mix it with water, and build more inner walls to make a sleeping area for myself.

My class ring became impacted with mud, and I was constantly digging earth from the grooves. The imprint of my ring made it obvious where I worked, and everyone knew which walls I had built. It became somewhat important to them that everyone have a small section of wall with the imprint of the "goddess'" hand, a wall that should stand forever strong against the elements.

The man who had first come to my aid was a shaman—a healer and wise man. Since I had been declared a goddess, I was allowed to help him gather roots and bark, or a scorpion when needed, and other items he used to make his healing salves and potions.

I showed him my bottle of aspirin and animated how they should be taken with water. But he took one out of the palm of my hand and chewed it up. He wrinkled his face at the sour taste and decided water was indeed needed to wash it down. As we gestured and talked, we traded words. He would touch his nose and say "achin," and I would touch my nose and say "nose," and so forth.

As best he could, he explained to me that he was also a shape shifter. He could change himself into another form, from a man to an animal, and could also move himself from one place to another in a wink.

He never demonstrated this art to me. I was skeptical!

He showed an interest in my class ring. His face lit up with delight when I slipped the ring off one day and offered it to him in the palm of my hand. He insisted he must make me a gift in return, as it was the tradition of his people.

The chosen item was his turquoise necklace which had beads that had been cut into unusual shapes and was very valuable to him—definitely more so than my ring was to me. He lifted the necklace over his head and gently placed it in my palm, pushing my fingers closed over it. After he left, I slipped the beads into my pocket.

The next morning, long before the sun had risen, I awoke to a sound of the people rushing around and low urgent whispers. They were preparing to move in a hurry and were grabbing what they could carry in their arms.

"Que?" What? I asked.

"Chindi." I was told in low, frightened tones.

"Chindi?" Not a familiar word.

The shaman rushed into my room and using sign language pointed at himself, then to his eyes. "I will see ..."

He touched me on my shoulder with his index finger then turned his hand sideways and stretched his arm out pointing behind me. "You in the time to come."

He was gone in a blink, and a gray cat ran out the doorway. I didn't see the shaman after that, and I didn't have time to think of what he'd been trying to say to me.

Some of the people had left already, going farther north. Others were still gathering possessions when, with a whoop, what could only be described as devils began pouring into the settlement.

My God, I thought. Chindi ... devil ... Aztec!

I could hardly believe my eyes. Where had they come from? The Aztec nation was extinct, like as the people of the Sinagua area. What had I stumbled upon?

Had I found myself back in time?

Or was I just dreaming?

The women who tried to fight back had their brains bashed out against the rocks. The children died, too. The men, whether or not they fought back, were overpowered and tied together, wrist to wrist.

I hid!

I was cowering inside my room when I remembered my ancient history studies that said that the Aztecs held in reverence a jaguar god. Quickly, I dug my leopard spotted poncho from my backpack, slipped it on, and pulled the hood over my head.

With flashlight in hand, and summoning what bit of bravery I could muster, I spread my arms out to make myself appear as large and threatening as possible, ran out into the center of the compound, and shouted, "Stop right there!"

I stomped my feet and flapped my arms and sang "Yellow Submarine" as loud as I could—all the time waving my lit flashlight.

It had some effect.

The Aztec warriors stood frozen in their tracks as they stared at me, the jaguar woman.

"Be gone, devils!" I shouted in a language none of them understood. A jaguar goddess speaking words from heaven, and whose flashlight batteries had just burned out!

I was hoping they would turn tail and run, but being from a fierce nation, once the initial fright wore off, they quickly realized I was a jaguar god impostor. The leader of the warriors came closer to me with suspicion, not wanting to make any hasty decisions. He reached out and touched my poncho and jerked back as if it had burned his hand.

Once he found he was still alive after touching the plastic, he reached out again, wrapped his big hand around the back of my neck and pushed me toward the living quarters. He wrenched the flashlight out of my hand and flung it into the scrub. As he jammed my face up against the wall and drew back his war club, my hands shot out and landed in two of the handprints. That was the last thing I remembered until I woke to a group of tourists standing around me.

"Give her some air," someone said as they held my head and fanned me with their hand.

"Stand back, I think she must have fainted. Must be this heat."

"She wasn't here a second ago. Where did she come from?"

"Did you see? She just popped up out of nowhere!"

The aches in my body told me I hadn't been dreaming. Somehow I'd been in the past. Well, I was back in the present now, and with a group of concerned sunburned tourists looking down at me.

A park ranger brought water from a nearby refreshment stand and gently removed my poncho.

"Why is she wearing that hot plastic thing out here in the desert?" I heard someone whisper.

"My backpack! Where is my backpack?" I began feeling around, but to no avail. Everyone began searching, but my backpack was nowhere to be found.

Any gear I had was left in the past when the settlement was overrun by Aztecs.

"Are you sure you had a backpack?" The ranger asked. "Are you sure you are okay? Are you driving? Do you need a ride back to Sedona?"

"Sedona? Yes, I do need a ride." A tall man helped me to my feet. After a few minutes, I was fine, no dizziness.

Some of the walls of the ruin were still standing after what certainly had been more than a thousand years, but many had crumbled into dust. The people I had come to know had disappeared, leaving no trace of having been here except for the walls . . . some of which might stand forever because they'd been built by the hands of their goddess.

I walked away from the tourists over to the farthest wall and glanced at the handprints imbedded in the hard clay. Sure enough, there was the imprint of my class ring. I looked at my hand to find that my ring had disappeared, too.

The shaman. I'd given it to him.

Through the many years it has been a mystery discussed by archaeologists as to what must have caused that unusual imprint in the walls. In the end, the historians decided that the ring must have belonged to the chief of the tribe. I knew there were no chiefs in that little band of people, and only I knew the imprint was from my ring.

There, among the pictographs, was my picture hewn out in the flat rock and outlined in faded black. Those childlike lines were a drawing of me.

Tears rolled down my dirty face as I remembered what had happened to my little group of friends. Their abrupt disappearance was due to the Aztecs trekking long miles up from Mexico hunting slave labor to help build their magnificent city or to be offered in a blood-bath. My friends who had escaped to the north were lost to time; even I could not say where they had gone or if they had survived.

I had to make my own arrangements to get back home.

Back in Columbus I went straightaway to the travel agency. I wanted to get a few things straight with that strange little man who obviously sent me to the past instead of taking my photograph. As best I could remember, the little old agent looked a lot like the shaman of the Sinagua.

An accidental tourist?

I walked past the door three times before I realized the storefront had changed. There was no sign waving in the breeze. There were no glass beads hanging across the doorway; they had been replaced with a modern glass and chrome door. The floor beyond was clean and devoid of sand.

I pushed through to the office.

There were two desks cluttered with telephones and computers, with a woman seated behind each desk.

"Can I help you take a trip?" one of them asked.

I shook my head. "Where is the little old man? I saw

him here . . ." When exactly had I seen him? Days ago? Centuries? "A little man with weathered skin."

"Little old man?" She smirked and looked at the other agent, who smiled behind her hand.

"Yes," I insisted. "There was a little old man here who sent me to Sedona, oh, maybe two weeks ago. Wasn't there a little old man? No!"

I just answered my own question.

There was no little old wrinkled man working there, never had been, never would be. He'd found himself forward in time, and then just as likely had found his way back home . . . or somewhere, somewhen else.

I walked back to my apartment. Upon searching through the pockets of the clothes I'd worn when I was transported to ancient Arizona, I jerked my hand as I came across something raspy. I turned the pocket inside out, and to my amazement onto the floor fell a necklace made of tiny turquoise beads cut into odd little shapes.

A Portrait of Time

Kelly Swails

Kelly Swails is a clinical microbiologist by day
and a writer by night. When she's not playing
with bacteria or words, she can be found reading,
watching movies, gaming, exercising, or knitting.
She and her husband Ken live with three cats in
Illinois. If she had the opportunity to go back in
time for a do over, she wouldn't change a thing.
Visit her Web site at www.kellyswails.com.

Gina stood outside her sister's rented townhome.
She shivered in the frigid February air as a tinge of
nausea rippled through her body.

An angry wind that smelled of a neighbor's fire
pushed through her thin houndstooth coat. Wisps of
vapor puffed from her mouth as she blew into her gloved
hands and stomped her feet.

Twenty below, at least. She'd forgotten how cold it
had been. She could have bought a warmer coat but she
hadn't spent a year's salary to be warm. She'd spent it
on this trip. She would stand here in a bikini if it meant
saving her identical twin, Lucy. She had six hours to do
it, Timeshares waivers and warnings be damned.

A storm a few days prior had blanketed the area

with a foot of snow, and now Gina squinted against the daylight glaring off its surface. She checked her watch: eleven thirty. Perfect. The current Gina's plane had just left for a week-long business trip, so there would be no chance she'd run into her past self and cause a time-fracturing paradox.

Gina clutched a plastic grocery bag as she climbed the short flight of stairs. She paused—*come on, Gina, can't do what you came here to do if you don't go inside*—before knocking once and swinging the door open. Warmth slammed into her body—her sister had always kept the thermostat somewhere between inferno and Hades—as her eyes fell onto Lucy's paintings and supplies strewn around the living room. Her voice cracked as she said, "Lucy? You here?"

"What the hell are you doing here?" Lucy called from the kitchen. "I thought you'd be at thirty thousand feet by now."

Tears filled Gina's eyes. Dizziness overcame her, and she couldn't tell if it was from the trip or from hearing Lucy's voice. She managed to croak, "Canceled," as Lucy walked into the living room, wiping her hands on a dishtowel.

"Flight or the whole trip?"

"Flight." A tear spilled from her left eye and ran down her cheek. Gina couldn't breathe as she watched Lucy flick the towel over her shoulder the way she always did.

"That's no reason to cry," Lucy said.

"I know." Gina stared at her sister. Gina wore her brunette hair in a sleek low bun; Lucy let her natural waves frame her face. Gina used the latest Estée Lauder cosmetics while Lucy ran a swipe of mascara over her eyelashes once in a while. Gina had her clothes tailored; Lucy wore Levi's and Chuck Taylors. Where Gina was smooth, Lucy was rough. Where Gina was reserved, Lucy was boisterous. Where Gina was straightlaced, Lucy was free-spirited. Seeing her standing in her living room now, wearing a paint-stained flannel shirt and smudge of flour on her cheek, made Gina feel complete for the first time in five years.

Lucy gave her a quizzical look. "What's with you?"

Gina released the breath she hadn't realized she'd been holding and said, "Nothing. Maybe if you didn't keep your house at two hundred degrees I wouldn't tear up so bad when I came in from the cold." The words slipped from her mouth before she could stop them. She and Lucy'd had the same basic argument ever since they could reach the temperature dial in their childhood home. Having the conversation now felt comfortably absurd. The rational part of her mind said to not waste precious time talking about a few degrees. The emotional side would listen to her sister recite the alphabet all night.

Lucy snorted. "Like you're one to talk. I have to wear a sweatshirt at your house in the summer."

"My thermostat is always kept at the proper temperature," Gina said.

"Sure, for a penguin," Lucy said. She nodded to the sack Gina still held. "What's that?"

"Eggs. Had a hunch you needed some."

"I just started a batch of sugar cookies and realized I was out," Lucy said. She didn't look surprised, and Gina breathed sigh of relief. They'd had moments of apparent intuition where the other was concerned ever since they could walk, and Gina had hoped her sister would think this was nothing more than another instance of that. "But since you're here, I'll make chocolate chip."

"You don't need to make those just for me," Gina said, even though she didn't like sugar cookies.

"I'm not eating a whole batch of these things by myself," Lucy said. "I just need brown sugar and chocolate chips."

"I'll go," Gina said quickly.

"You bet you are," Lucy smiled. "I'm making the cookies for you."

"You were making cookies anyway. I'm going to the store *again* out of the kindness of my heart." Gina gave Lucy a cockeyed smile. It felt great to smirk at her sister. "You know, someday you're going to have to learn take care of yourself, little sister." Gina's voice took on the familiar preaching tone she used so often with Lucy.

"And someday you'll have to learn to live a little, big sister," Lucy finished in the also familiar singsong voice she used with Gina.

Gina hugged Lucy long enough for Lucy to squirm out of her grasp and search her face. "Are you sure you're okay?"

"I am now," Gina said.

After the dough had been sampled and the cookies were baked, Lucy went back to work on her current painting project. Gina settled on the couch to watch her. Lucy's art was influenced by the surrealists like Dali and Ernst; walls had ears, animals were hybrids of three or more species and an inanimate object or two, the colors were bright and distinct. This picture of a woman staring into a full-length mirror and seeing a monster was familiar to Gina—it had hung on her bedroom wall ever since Lucy's death, half finished and full of potential—and now she would get to see Lucy add strokes that weren't a part of the original. She wondered if the painting at home would reflect the changes when she got back. It might not even be on her wall at all. The idea excited

Gina because it would mean that Lucy had been alive to sell it or give it to someone else.

"You don't have to stick around if you've got something else you'd rather do," Lucy said as she mixed paint on her palette.

"There's no place I'd rather be," Gina said.

Lucy shrugged. "I can think of better things to do than watch paint dry, but okay." She spoke like someone assured of her own immortality, or at least whose mortality was a distant, inconsequential concept. She dabbed at the canvas with a brush and a squiggly edge of the mirror frame appeared.

"How do you do that?" Gina said.

"Do what?"

"Make something out of nothing."

"I dunno," Lucy stood back and studied the new addition. "I try not to think about it too much."

Gina moved a stack of blank canvases onto the floor and stretched her legs. She pushed the sleeves of her black turtleneck above her elbows and rubbed her eyes. "Your paintings are so weird."

"I try not to think about that too much either."

"I mean, why does she see a monster in the mirror?"

Another section of frame appeared beneath Lucy's brush. "We all have monsters inside us sometimes."

"You don't." Gina leaned her head back and closed her eyes. Perhaps it was the comfort of being near her sister again that drained all the stress from her body. She listened to Lucy's brush alternating between scraping the palette and swiping the canvas. The rhythm coupled with the warm apartment and a stomach full of fresh cookies lulled Gina to sleep.

After a moment Gina jerked awake. Lucy wasn't standing at the canvas and the room had darkened. She had to have been asleep longer than she'd thought—

the mirror frame in the painting had been finished, its purple squiggles and black shading mocking her. Gina checked her wrist. Three hours had passed.

"Lucy?" No answer. Panic welled in Gina's chest. "You here?" The place felt empty, and she knew Lucy had left. She jumped off the couch and headed for the kitchen, hesitating when spots danced before her eyes. *Great, now I get nauseous.* A note in Lucy's hurried scrawl lay next to the dirty mixing bowl. *Morning, sleepyhead. Since you're going to be here for dinner I'm going to go grab some supplies. Hope you're okay with meatloaf. Be back in fifteen.*

The note had the time it had been written in the upper right-hand corner like their mother had taught them. Gina gasped and threw the slip of paper onto the counter as if she'd been burned. Lucy had written it two hours ago.

Damnit, Lucy. She never kept a lot of food in the house, but it was worse when she was in the middle of a painting. Gina figured Lucy had gone hungry during the blizzard a few days before. Of course, Lucy wouldn't have gone to the store if Gina hadn't been there, probably choosing to snack on some dry cereal for dinner. Even worse, she never would have gone if Gina had been awake to stop her. Guilt pressed onto her chest. Gina only had a few hours to spend with her twin sister. Why did she have to waste them by sleeping? It didn't matter. She grabbed the phone on the wall and dialed Lucy's cell by memory.

The phone rang in her ear several times before the voice mail picked up. *No no no no no no no.* The warnings she'd been given at Timeshares zipped through her mind, the ones about how time had a way of righting itself, that if you changed the past enough to influence great change in the future the universe would reset the correct course. Gina didn't care about the "correct" course. She would *not* allow her sister to die, period. Gina grabbed her coat and ran from the apartment.

Statistics say that most fatal accidents happen within a mile from home, and Lucy's was no exception. The stream that had frozen her to death ran behind her apartment and through her neighborhood to join up with a bigger stream half a mile away. It was the small bridge over this juncture that always got treacherous in the winter.

Gina ran down the street, dodging ice and hopping through the snow where residents hadn't bothered to shovel. Soon her legs burned and cramps ripped through her side as her breath came in gasps. Gina ignored the pain. She could only think about getting to her sister.

I shouldn't have fallen asleep. It doesn't make sense. The doctors at Timeshares had given her a litany of possible side effects, everything from vomiting to diarrhea to weird tastes to phantom smells, but none of them had mentioned anything about sleepiness or fatigue. Not once. Even so, she had made it a point to get extra sleep and take vitamins and hydrate well before the trip. Nothing was going to keep her from saving Lucy. And yet she had slept hard enough not to hear her sister leave. *The universe righting itself.*

At last she ran up the steep embankment that led to the bridge. Her heart stopped as she crested the hill. The thin guardrail that separated the road from the ten foot drop to the water had been torn, the metal twisted and peeled away from the road.

"Lucy! Oh, God, no, this isn't happening, not again. Lucy! LUCY!" Gina sprinted to the bridge, raising her knees high to get through the snowdrifts. Once on the road, her feet caught ice and lost traction. She fell chest-first onto the pavement, knocking all the wind from her lungs. Her eyes watered and her body convulsed as her diaphragm tried to work. Through the blurriness in her vision, she saw Lucy's car sitting nose-first in the stream. Not enough water to fill a car or carry it away, but enough to drown or freeze a person.

Gina didn't hesitate. She flung herself down the embankment and into the stream. Water filled her shoes as chunks of ice banged against her knees. Once she got to the car, Gina saw Lucy turn her head to look at her. *She's alive.*

"Geenie," Lucy said, calling her by their childhood nickname.

"I'm going to get you out of here," Gina said as she tried to wrench the car door open.

"It's stuck," Lucy said, her voice soft and weak. "I'm so tired, Geenie. So tired." She rolled her head back and closed her eyes.

Gina pounded on the car window. "Stay awake," she yelled. "It's important that you stay awake." Her legs were numb from the freezing water. She stumbled over the rocky stream bottom as she walked around and tried the passenger door. She leaned back and used her body weight to leverage the door open, but the impact had jammed this side, too. Gina looked into the car. Lucy's legs were submerged, the contents of her purse floating around her. A packet of soup mix floated by the dashboard. She'd been on her way back from the store, just like last time.

"Did you call nine one one?" Gina said as she pounded on the window. "Lucy! Lucy, wake up! Did you call nine one one yet?"

Lucy's eyes rolled in her head as she shrugged. "Cell's wet. No good." She reclosed her eyes.

Just like last time. "Stay awake!" Gina demanded as she pounded on the door with both fists. After Lucy had died, she'd studied hypothermia and knew if the victim fell asleep, it was all over. She ran over to the driver's side, her body cramping from the cold. If she didn't get out of the water soon, she'd be in danger, too. "Lucy!" Gina cocked her arm across her body. She summoned all her strength and tried to smash the window, hitting it with the back of her arm again and again.

Lucy's eyes fluttered as she touched the window. "I'm glad you came to see me," she said. "I'm glad you're with me at the end."

"Don't talk like that," Gina said, a hysterical edge to her voice. She touched the window by Lucy's hand and imagined she could feel her twin's fingers. "We're going to get you out of here."

"I'm going to paint heaven," Lucy said.

"No you're not, not yet," Gina climbed onto the hood of the car, slipping on the wet metal. She landed on her left hip and elbow, but her body was so numb from the cold that she didn't feel any pain. She stood on the hood and clutched the slippery roof as best she could. "You are not leaving me, Lucy, you're not." Gina kicked the windshield with her right foot, concentrating most of the force on her heel. Her numb legs and the icy hood made it hard to get enough force, and she kept losing her balance. Finally she lay on her back and kicked at the windshield with both feet. Water lapped at the top of her scalp as she kicked again and again.

A crack formed beneath her feet as blue lights swirled around her. She tasted chocolate chip cookies and bile as the nausea spiked in her stomach. *No.* She glanced at her watch. Her time was up. Timeshares was pulling her back. "Not yet!" she yelled, hoping someone in the control room would hear her. "Lucy! No!"

Lucy didn't respond as her fingers slipped away from the glass.

"Lucy!" Gina yelled as flashes of light enveloped her. She closed her eyes against the glare and opened them to find herself lying on the floor of a sterile examination room. Two young men helped her to her feet and stripped off her wet clothes as another wrapped her in a warming blanket. She looked around the room. She was back at Timeshares.

"I've got to go back," Gina said.

"Your time is up, ma'am," one of the men said in a matter-of-fact tone. He sounded like he'd said that sentence a hundred times before.

Gina shivered and her teeth chattered. She felt as though she would never be warm again. Exhaustion overwhelmed her, and she wondered if it was from the traveling or hypothermia. Probably both.

Rolf Jacobsen, the owner of Timeshares, walked through the door. "I see you got a little wet, Miss Warner."

She struggled to keep her eyes open as one of the men wrapped another blanket around her. "You're quick on the uptake," she mumbled.

Rolf gave her a thin smile. "I know what you tried to do."

"What are you talking about?" Gina said as she snapped her head up.

"Rest assured, Miss Warner, that you won't have another opportunity to save Lucy. Consider yourself blacklisted."

Gina stared at Jacobsen's back as he walked away. She felt arms guide her into a prone position and slip a pillow beneath her head. *There has to be a way,* she thought as sleep overcame her.

The next day Gina woke in her own bed. She didn't remember how she'd gotten there, but figured that Jacobsen had had some of his goons bring her home. Lucy's painting hung on the wall opposite her bed, except now the mirror in the picture sported a new purple frame. She slid from underneath the covers and winced. Her body ached everywhere and her skin burned from mild frostbite. She walked across the bedroom on bruised feet and looked at the painting. A fine layer of dust covered the surface.

Gina felt ashamed. Why hadn't she taken better care of Lucy's art? Had she become that complacent about Lucy's death? Pressing her lips into a line, she lifted the canvas from its nail. As she gently brushed the dust away with an old t-shirt, a folded piece of notebook paper tumbled from behind it.

Gina inspected the back. There was a little flap in the corner that the paper must have been tucked into. How had she not noticed that before?

Too stunned after Lucy died to see it, I guess.

She gently propped the canvas against her dresser and unfolded the paper. Lucy's handwriting leaped from the page.

> *Gina,*
> *Somehow you left a voice mail on my cell phone at the same time you were sleeping on my couch. The message said that you've just gotten to your hotel in L.A. and that the flight was fine. And yet you lay sleeping on my couch. So I thought about that.*
> *You came to the apartment with eggs.*
> *You cried when you saw me.*
> *You volunteered to go to the store when I needed more stuff.*
> *As I watch you sleep on my couch I notice a few freckles and a few wrinkles you didn't have yester-*

day. Plus you've started to go gray. You're older. Well, that doesn't surprise me, you are the older sister. But it all adds up. The you on my couch really is older.

My guess is you saved enough money to buy a trip from Timeshares. I can only think of one reason you would do that.

I'm going to the store. If I'm meant to see you again, I will.

I love you.

Lucy

Gina sobbed as tears ran down her face. She touched her fingertips to the words. Lucy had known what Gina had been there to do. Yet she'd left the house anyway. But not before writing a note and hiding it someplace where she knew Gina would someday find it.

Sadness filled Gina's heart as she hung the picture. Even so, she knew she wouldn't try to save Lucy again. She missed her sister and always would, but the emptiness that she had felt for five years was gone.

But I'm Not the Only One

Chris Pierson

Chris Pierson has written eight novels set in the
Dragonlance world, most recently the Taladas trilogy, as well as numerous short stories in assorted
anthologies, *Terribly Twisted Tales* and *Gamer Fantastic* being the latest. He works as a senior world
designer and resident Tolkien freak for The Lord
of the Rings Online at Turbine Games. Born in
Canada, Chris has lived in the Boston area long
enough to become a Red Sox fan but not long
enough to develop the accent. He currently lives
in Jamaica Plain, Massachusetts, with his wife,
Rebekah, and Chloe, the most awesomest baby
girl in the world.

It's warm for December in New York: weather like
two months before. People have been talking about it
all day. Smiling at each other, strange for a city that can
be so mean, particularly as winter is beginning to bare
its teeth. Even at night, people are out without their
coats, laughing as they walk, not caring about any of the
trouble in their city and the world.

It feels safe.

They come out of the studio together, no longer

young but still just as in love as when they first met. It's been a productive evening, polishing up a new song, one of hers. A good day. The new album, the comeback, is selling well, barely a month old, and there's still more new work to be done. After the time he's taken off, he feels more creative, more invigorated than he has since he and the lads called it quits. Ten years gone. A hard decade in a lot of ways, but things are better now than they've been in a long time.

He puts his arm around her as they walk back to the limo, the driver holding open the door, all of them smiling, the sky starry-clear and the breeze warm.

"Where do you want to eat?" she asks.

He shakes his head. "It's late. Let's go home."

She nods, and they get into the limo. The driver pulls out, turns the corner, and heads up Sixth Avenue to the Upper West Side. Central Park slides by on the right, couples walking together, savoring this unexpected jewel of late summer in the dying days of fall. She hugs his arm and leans close, her head on his shoulder. He kisses her hair, loving the way she smells, the weight of her against him.

He leans forward as they stop at a red at 71st Street. "You can let us out at the curb up ahead," he says. "We'll walk from there."

The driver glances back. "Are you sure, sir? It's no trouble for me to pull into the courtyard."

"Don't bother. It's a beautiful night."

Shrugging, the driver pulls over outside the Dakota, near the iron-gated archway of the grand old building. Home. She kisses him, and they get out, head toward the building. He says hello to José, the doorman, who has opened the limo door.

"Lovely evening, sir," José replies.

She goes through the archway first, and someone calls

out to her from the shadows, says hello. She walks by, not breaking pace, not answering, and for a moment he has a strange feeling, a premonition maybe, but it's gone just as fast. He follows her into the darkness, toward the lobby. Sean's upstairs, in bed by now—the boy's five, and it's almost eleven at night—and he just wants to see his beautiful boy, wants to watch him sleep. That and make love with his wife, of course.

Out of the corner of his eye, he sees someone in the shadows, the same one who called out to her. The face is familiar, and he knows where from. He signed the new album for this man earlier that evening, when they left for the Record Plant. There'd been several autograph-seekers and at least one photographer, but this one stood out in his memory. He got that cold feeling again, but made himself keep going toward the front door, Jay the security guy waiting inside to buzz them in.

The man in the shadows calls his name.

Cold all over now, he begins to turn.

Something hits him hard from behind. He hears two quick *pops*—some part of his brain tells him it is gunfire, but it doesn't sound nearly as loud as he'd imagined—and glass breaking. She whips around, screaming. José is yelling too, and then he's on the ground, and the breath's knocked out of him and he can't draw another, and there's a lot of pain.

"I'm shot," he gasps.

"No," says a voice in his ear. "You're not. Not this time."

He realizes then that the thing that hit him was a man, another lurker who must have sprung out of the darkness and tackled him like an American footballer, right before the gunshots started. The pain and breathlessness aren't from bullets in his chest, but because this big man is lying

on top of him, covering him with his body. Protecting him.
"Who are you?" he grunts.

"A fan," says the voice in his ear. "For forty years, ever since I was a boy. It's an honor to meet you, Mr. Lennon."

John has just enough time to think: that doesn't make sense. *I'm* only forty. Then blue lightning flashes and his mouth floods with acid and his stomach drops ten miles into the earth and all of it—the Dakota, the madman with the gun, José, Jay, Yoko—it all disappears.

And then, and then, and then . . .

He's indoors now, lying facedown on white tiles. The man's still on top of him, crushing him flat: he must weigh sixteen stone, at least. After a moment, though, the weight eases off, and John pushes himself up off the floor to look around. Gunfire still echoes in his ears, as does Yoko's screaming, but there's no one else in the room. Just him and the man who tackled him, and what looks like equipment from a science fiction film, perhaps the dreary one Kubrick made or that new one about the alien ripping everyone apart. Only this stuff looks like it's real, not props on a movie set.

Also, there's a shimmer in the air, like you see over New York asphalt in the dead of August, but the air is cool and smells like a thunderstorm. He rubs his eyes, but it doesn't go away.

"Bloody hell," he says, and turns to face his . . . what? Assailant? Savior?

He's a big man, tall and broad-shouldered, a bit of white in his black beard, a bit of skin showing through the hair on his head. Black shirt, blue jeans. There's a trickle of blood in the corner of his mouth, but he's smiling as wide as a man can smile without hurting himself.

"I did it!" he says. "I got you out of there! Up yours, Chapman, you asshole!"

John stares at the man, confused. He's about to ask a question when the lone door out of the room they're in opens and in step three men. Two are dressed head-to-toe in black, with bulky vests and helmets and unpleasant-looking rifles at the ready. The third wears a suit that looks like he's slept in it for a week, and in his hand there's a shiny silver badge.

It isn't an NYPD badge, but John's sure he's police. The men with the rifles aim the guns at the big man, who freezes, suddenly frightened.

"David Stephen Walker," says the man with the badge. Not a question. "You are under arrest for attempted timeline sabotage and pre-mortem abduction, in contravention of Article Six of the Temporal Interference Act. You are also in breach of your Timeshares contract, and your operating license has been revoked."

The big man, Walker, beams like he's been told he just won the lotto. "I don't care," he says. "Do what you want with me, it doesn't matter. Do you know what I've done? I've just saved John Lennon!"

The policeman rolls his eyes. "Big deal," he says. "You're the third this month."

Walker blinks, turning pale.

"What?"

"You heard me," says the cop. "You guys think you're *so* original. Come on. You *really* thought you were the first?"

There is a silence. Walker seems to deflate. He can't think of anything to say.

"Excuse me?" John raises his hand.

The cop's eyes flick toward him. "Yeah?"

"Could someone tell me what in God's name is happening?"

Nick studied the report on the train that morning, on the way to work. Trees slid by outside his window, then a bridge, then the backs of old factories and industrial strip-malls and U-Store-Its. That had all given way to wetlands, thick with loosestrife in bloom, by the time he closed the file on his Reader and shook his head.

Another goddamn Lennon last night. People had no imagination.

He sat quietly for a while, sipping his morning coffee, cream, two sweeteners. He scratched his beard. He glanced at the news on the Reader, but didn't really pay much attention. His mind was already working out the routine for this one. What he'd say to explain. He stared out the windows—suburbs now, whizzing by too fast to pick out individual houses. His stop was coming up.

He sighed, then reached into the inside pocket of his rumpled suit jacket, pulled out his plastic badge, and attached it magnetically to his lapel.

NICOLÁS ORASCO-MENDEZ, it read, next to a four-year-old photo of him, beardless with a fake smile. SR. ORIENTATION CONSULTANT, DEPT. OF ANACHRONISM, MUSIC DIV. The Timeshares company holographic logo shimmered underneath it all.

A tone sounded, announcing an approaching stop, the one before his. The train slowed, halted, got started again. Nick slept his Reader, made sure he had his umbrella, then glanced across the aisle. A small, gray-haired woman sat there: sixty, maybe sixty-five, and reading—a book, actual bound paper, not a Reader.

We Can Work It Out, the title read, and under it: *Six Attempted Beatles Reunions, 1972–1980.*

Nick swore under his breath. That was why so many Lennons lately. Every couple years some joker wrote another book, and even though the surviving two and all their original fans were all older than God, the nostalgia always got people missing John again. George,

too, but that wasn't really Nick's problem. But John . . .
the books, the eternally reissued recordings, the video
games, they all gave people ideas. People who thought
they were smarter than Timeshares' legal department.
And Nick caught the fallout.

The woman glanced up, saw him watching. A dark
line creased between her brows.

"Good book?" Nick asked.

She shrugged and went back to reading.

The tone sounded again. The train started to slow.
Nick got up, grabbed his coffee, and started bracing himself to meet yet another very confused Beatle.

"Time travel," said John, looking across the table. He
adjusted his glasses, ran a hand through his hair. Then he
laughed, shaking his head. "This is a joke, yeah? You're
having me on. I mean, that sort of thing only happens in
terrible movies."

Nick raised his eyebrows. "In your time, yes—as far
as people know, anyway. Not in mine. Here, have a look
at this."

He slid a glossy pamphlet across the old gray table
which had veneer chipped at the corners, coffee rings
here and there. Acoustic tiles and LED bulbs above. A
window looking out on pine trees, gray skies, drizzle. A
bulletin board, bare except for multicolored push-pins
that someone bored had arranged into the shape of a
question mark. A calendar showing a year Nick's current subject found hard to believe. Hell, Nick had trouble believing it was already 2034 himself.

Nick drank water from a paper cup while John Lennon read the Timeshares brochure. "See the pyramids—
while they're being built!" said Lennon. "Travel to
Gettysburg—and watch Lincoln's address! Behold the
Sistine Chapel—with Michelangelo still on the scaf-

fold!" He frowned, and folded the pamphlet up again. "Holiday makers?"

"Premium tourism," Nick said. "My company offers an exclusive service for an affordable price. Go back in time to anyplace you want, any year you want. You'd be surprised how many folks go back to see you and the other three play. The Cavern, Shea Stadium, Budokan."

"Your prices don't look very affordable to me," said John.

Nick shrugged. "Not by 1980 standards. But, well, inflation, you know."

"And this bloke, this Walker. The one who knocked me down. He was one of yours?"

"He was. And he broke his contract, and several federal statutes, by bringing you back." Nick took a deep breath, let it out again. "By saving your life."

Lennon frowned, looked out the window. For a while, the only sound was hiss of rain against the pane.

"So I died, then," John said. "That night, outside the Dakota. That weird fellow shot me . . . and he killed me."

Nick held his gaze, nodded slowly. This was always the hard part, for most of them anyway. The realization that the only reason they still drew breath was that someone had decided to commit a felony.

"I'm sorry," Nick said.

A shadow passed over John's face. He blinked and looked up at the ceiling. It was always this way, with the Lennons. Their reactions never differed. "Oh, Yoko," he said, and his breath hitched. "Oh, Sean."

Nick felt his eyes sting, and he forced himself to stay under control. He'd never broken, not once—at least, not in front of the subjects. Sometimes, in the middle of the night, he woke up crying. It was worse, he knew, in other divisions.

"Look," he said, "I know this is difficult. You can have a moment, if you want."

"No," John said, and chuckled. "No, it's all right. Bit of a shock, you understand."

"If it's any consolation, a large part of the world pretty much lost their minds when they found out. They even interrupted a football game to break the news."

"Good lord."

"And they built a garden in your memory, in Central Park. Called Strawberry Fields."

John laughed. "Well, *that's* original." He shook his head. "You know, when the lads and I were still together, I joked that some lunatic was going to pop me off one day."

Nick nodded. They all brought that up, every time.

The rest of the preliminary interview went smoothly, as it always did. As repetitive as meeting John could sometimes get, he *was* one of the more affable subjects. He wasn't resentful like Kurt Cobain, or depressed like Ian Curtis, or out of his goddamn mind like Keith Moon. Lennon took it all with admirable good humor, considering what he'd been through during—for him at least—the last twelve hours. He even made jokes about it, which was more than most of them ever did. Finally, Nick got through the last of the initial paperwork and set aside his pen. He gazed across the table at that familiar face—the long nose, the round glasses—and raised his eyebrows.

"So," he said. "Do you have any questions of your own?"

"Only half a million," Lennon said. "How long do you have?"

Nick glanced at his Reader to check the time. "Maybe only long enough for the first ten thousand or so. I have another appointment at eleven."

"Oh? Another one of me?"

"No," said Nick. "Mozart."

That stopped John for a moment. He didn't have a quip for that one. "Really."

"Yep. He's one of the more popular ones, in fact. Him, you, Hendrix, Tupac ..."

"Who?"

"He was after your time. You'll meet him, though—there are a couple of him around here right now. The two of you tend to get along quite well, in fact. And you should see Mozart when someone lets him near a synthesizer."

John pursed his lips. "Will I get to meet him too?"

"You'll meet all of them, in time. But with Mozart, there's the language barrier. How's your German?"

"Not as good as yours, I suspect."

"You mentioned Hendrix. Are the others here? Joplin and Morrison? Brian Jones?"

"Joplin and Jones, yes. Morrison was too far gone when he died."

"What do you mean?" John asked.

"Well," Nick said, "it's like this. There are safeguards against bringing people back when you're traveling, for starters. Our designers knew temporal abduction would be a problem, so they engineered the equipment to prevent it from happening so the past didn't get irrevocably changed every other time someone took a trip. But there's a glitch they can't get rid of, one circumstance they've never been able to come up with a block for."

He paused, watched Lennon figure it out.

"Death," John said. "The moment we're supposed to die."

Nick nodded. "The temporal repercussions are fairly small for premortem abduction—too small for our equipment to detect. If you nab someone right when their actions no longer have an effect on the world, you can slip them through. And unfortunately, once word got out on the net, everybody knew."

"Got out on the what?"

"Never mind. You'll find out about that during the acclimation program." Nick waved off John's questions. "Anyway, the trick to all of this, if you're going to kidnap someone from the past, is that they have to be in good shape when they die. No terminal diseases, no old age, and nobody whose condition is so bad they don't survive the trip. The best cases are the sudden ones—accidents, preventable heart attacks, and, well, murders. I'm sorry."

"What for?" Lennon asked. "You weren't the one who should have shot me. So Morrison was in too bad a shape."

"Exactly. Drug-related deaths are touch and go. Some people where the death is because of outright overdose, like Joplin and Hendrix, can survive the abduction. Others, like Morrison and Billie Holliday, where their bodies gave out because of the drugs, no."

"Ah," John replied. He thought a moment. "What about Elvis, then? Can he survive the trip?"

Always they asked this question. Anyone who died in Lennon's time wanted to know.

Nick shrugged. "Well, there's never really been an opportunity."

John blinked, confused. Then his eyes widened.

"Oh," he said. "Good lord. When did people find out?"

"About twenty years ago. He just walked up to a tour group at his grave and said hello. He started recording and performing again the year after that. Kept it up until 2021. They even built him his own theater in Vegas. He's ninety-nine now, retired and living in Memphis. Still says hi to the tours from time to time."

There was a long silence.

"Wow," John said. "What about the lads? Are any of them still alive?"

"Paul and Ringo, yes—though they're both over ninety themselves now, obviously. George died a bit over thirty years ago. Cancer. So he isn't here, I'm afraid."

"Damn. No reunion then, I suppose."

He didn't ask about Yoko. They never did. Somehow, ever since she died, the Johns always knew. He looked out the window a while, the rain streaking the glass.

"What now?" he asked. "Do I ... do I have to go back?"

"God, no," Nick said. "No, no, no. We've already dispatched a team to put in a substitute for you—don't worry, no one died in your place. I'm not sure how it works, exactly, but it involves cloning and the substitute was never alive in the first place. Everything happened like it was supposed to, as far as anyone knows. But you can't go back now, ever."

John drummed his fingers on the table. A fly landed on his knuckle, and he shook it off. "I can't just leave this place either, can I?"

"Not right away. You've got acclimation to go through, but it'll be quicker for you than most. No major psychological work, no rehab. Mainly just history classes covering the last fifty years. Enough so you'll feel comfortable in the present before you move on to the island."

"The ... island?"

Nick met John's gaze, held it. "Here's the thing," he said. "You can't just go into the world proper. Can you imagine how things would be if the world were filled with Gandhis and Martin Luther King Jrs and Joans of Arc? Not to mention Alexander the Great and Hitler ..."

"People bring back *Hitler?*"

"People bring back everyone," Nick said. "We try to

screen out the crazies, but every now and then someone steps back through with Attila the Hun or Genghis
Khan."

John was beginning to look pale. "Jesus Christ."

"Him too. So you can see we need a way to deal with
the abductees without just handing each of you a bus
ticket and a change of clothes and saying good luck. The
company has a facility where abductees can live on an island in the Indian Ocean. The artists' facilities are quite
lovely, I'm told. There are currently nearly two thousand
people there."

"How many of them are me?"

"I'm not sure," Nick said. "Last I counted, there had
been sixty-three John Lennons abducted over the past
nine years."

John grinned. "You know, that's not really what Paul
had in mind when he wrote 'When I'm Sixty-Four.'"

There were, of course, certain things Nick didn't mention. Like how the island hadn't been part of the original plan when abductees started showing up. How the
company board of directors had initially wanted to have
the abductees euthanized—humanely, of course—to
minimize expenses; they were supposed to be dead anyway, weren't they? How a whistle-blower somewhere
in the department had leaked word onto the net, forcing the ethical issue and changing the company's plans
overnight in order to avoid a media firestorm. How the
total cost of buying and equipping the island meant a
travel cost increase of only a few hundred dollars per
back-trip. How they continued to euthanize the more
dangerous abductees anyway, and just kept it off the
books—better that than an island out there full of Mus-
solinis and Neros and Che Guevaras, everyone agreed.

He didn't tell John about the advanced aging, either—

how, for whatever reason, the abductees got five years older for every actual year. He'd find out about that eventually, of course, but experience had taught Nick that those kinds of revelations were best saved for later in the acclimation process.

Most of John's questions were about people, as always. He asked about Stu Sutcliffe, who'd been his friend and had died in Hamburg before the Beatles got big. Yes, Stu had shown up, but just once. Most people now didn't know who he was—and if you were going back for a Beatle, you picked John ninety-nine times out of a hundred, didn't you?

No, no one had ever brought back Brian Epstein. That always upset John.

Were the Kennedys around? Of course. There was a whole political department, in fact. Lincolns and Roosevelts went there too. So did the occasional Garfield or McKinley. Gandhi and Crazy Horse. Reverend King and Malcolm X. Yitzhak Rabin and Princess Diana and Benazir Bhutto. The Kennedys were the hardest, though, because of how John always took it when he first saw Bobby, and found out his little brother hadn't outlived him by much. It was even worse when he saw John-John. Those specific moments were why Nick had transferred out of that department as soon as he made senior pay grade.

What were the other departments? There was one for actors and other performers, where the Marilyn Monroes and Bruce Lees and Lenny Bruces went. There was one for artists, writers, and philosophers, which got the van Goghs and Sylvia Plaths and Camuses. Even a Socrates or two. A lot of psych counseling went on there. There was a high-security one for dangerous subjects—not just Hitler and such, but the occasional serial killer or other madman that some sick person thought it would be fun

to haul out of the timeline; it seemed every six months
or so, some idiot grabbed Jeffrey Dahmer or Vlad the
Impaler. There were *really* serious criminal penalties for
that sort of thing, but it didn't deter everyone.

And then there was the Personal Department.

"What's that?" John asked.

Nick took a deep breath, let it out. "Well, we do a
fair amount of background screening, cross referencing
against intended place-time destinations, but we don't
catch everything. Sometimes people go back for their
own reasons. To find the mother who died in a fall when
they were ten. The estranged brother who had a heart
attack before they could reconcile. The daughter who
drowned in the backyard pool when she was six."

He stopped, letting it hang there. Watching the
stricken look on John's face. A drunk driver had killed
Lennon's mother when he was eighteen—it was in his
dossier. The thought that he could go back and save *her*
hadn't occurred to him . . . until now.

When John finally spoke, his voice was quiet, subdued. "That must be . . . a terrible place to work."

Nick nodded, let the moment pass. He mentioned the
smaller departments for sports figures, for scientists, another to catch the ones who didn't fall into any simple
category—Anne Frank, for instance—and that was it.
John was out of questions or, more likely, thinking about
the Personal Department had drained him of the desire
to ask anything more.

"All right, then," Nick said, and checked the time on
his Reader again. Right on schedule—he'd done enough
Lennon interviews to know, within a minute or two, when
one would end. "That's your prelim done. Let's get you
to your acclimation group, and you can get started."

They went out into the hall, Nick leading the way
while John followed, silent, thoughtful. They passed the

other interview rooms on their way to the elevators. Two were occupied, the first quite crowded because yet another daredevil had decided to grab Buddy Holly, the Big Bopper, *and* Ritchie Valens all in one go while their plane was going down. In the second sat a big bear of a man with white hair and a beard.

"That looks like that bloke from the Grateful Dead," said John.

"It is," Nick said. "You'd remember him younger—he died about fifteen years after you."

When their elevator came, Michael Jackson was on it, but of course John didn't recognize him at all. They eyed each other, and Michael got off on one of the counseling floors. Nick and John rode the rest of the way alone, and headed out onto another floor that looked just like the one where they'd gotten on: beige carpet, gray walls, acoustic tiles, and LED lights.

The only strange thing was the artwork on the walls— paintings by Andy Warhol and Frida Kahlo, photos by Diane Arbus—though none of it had been produced in their lifetimes, of course. One of the nice things about working at Timeshares was the amount of art that was always flying around from men and women whose deaths hadn't stopped their urge to create. Nick even had a Kirchner in his living room, though no gallery would ever accept it as real because it was only two years old. That sort of thing was one of the perks of working in Anachronisms—like all those Versace suits.

"The practice spaces are this way," Nick said, leading John down the hall. "We've got plenty of instruments and recording equipment, and the best pool of bandmates you could ever want. We even have your Ricken- backer around here somewhere—your wife gave it to us a while back, before she passed on."

"Yoko . . . she knew about this place?" John asked.

"She used to come here sometimes, to see you."

"Oh."

Nick went on, not letting him dwell. "Anyway, the guitar's yours—you can play it whenever you want. Assuming one of the other Lennons hasn't grabbed it first, of course. This floor's open day and night, if you want to record anything or just jam."

A muted noise, like the world ending, was rumbling away behind one of the doors, a red light shining above. They paused to crack the door open, Nick smiling.

"I love this band," he said.

The music was so loud, it made them both wince— and this was only the control room, not the actual practice space. They walked past a couple of staff engineers and peered through the glass. A five-piece was cranking out something incredibly grinding and heavy, like a prehistoric beast rumbling through some primeval jungle.

On drums, John Bonham. On bass, John Entwistle. On vocals and rhythm, Joe Strummer. On slide guitar, Robert Johnson. And playing the organ and singing backup . . .

"Good God," said John, "That's *me*."

The other Lennon didn't see him. He just pounded on the keys, glasses off, thundering away with the godfathers of rock and metal, punk and the blues.

"They're damn good," John said after a while.

Nick nodded. "Every now and then, we leak a song from one of the house bands into the market. The revenue from the downloads paid for a fair chunk of the island. Of course, no one's ever figured out *who* these bands are, but the music stands for itself. This bunch calls itself The Afterparty."

He glanced at John and grinned. Lennon had *the look* in his eyes—the same gleam pretty much all the musicians got when they realized what they could do here. He wanted to start a band and get playing *right now*.

"Don't worry," Nick said. "You'll have your chance. And it's even better on the island. There's even an all-Lennon band there, I hear. Named John and the Johns. Come on, let's find your group."

Things got quiet again down the hall. Through a couple crash-bar doors, around a corner, and here were the larger meeting rooms, a few with doors shut. Meetings under way. "You're in room 518, right here," said Nick, stopping outside one door. "Nothing to worry about, no expectations yet. You'll get to know the others in your group, then learn what's happened in the world since you died. Basic stuff first, the end of the Soviet Union, global warming, the net, China's lunar colony. They'll give you a Reader after lunch so you can look stuff up on your own. When class is done, one of the staff will show you to your dorm."

John nodded, bemused. "What about you?"

"I'll be checking in with you tomorrow," Nick said. "And every day till you're acclimated. After that, you'll head to the island."

"When will that be?"

Nick shrugged as if he didn't know, though this was a Lennon and so he did. "Could be three months, could be six, or even a year. Whenever you're ready."

Which would be four and a half months, give or take a couple days. Always was.

"Here's my card," Nick said, and handed one over. "Message me on your Reader if you need to talk. Otherwise, I'll see you at nine tomorrow."

John looked at the card, shifting it to change the rainbow hues of the Timeshares hologram. Then he tucked it into his shirt pocket. He opened the door and walked into a conference room. Georges Bizet was sitting at the long table, with Glenn Miller to his left. Then Patsy Cline. Notorious BIG. Charlie Parker. Selena. And, yes, two other Lennons.

"Hello there," he said. "I'm John."

Nick shut the door and started back up the hall. He was getting off the elevator and heading back to the interview rooms when his Reader rang. He tapped the screen, saw an image of the incoming caller, and picked up.

"I was wondering when you'd phone."

The man on the other end said what he always said.

"Yes, of course," Nick said. "I'll arrange it for tonight."

He hung up, got to the interview room, took a deep breath, and walked in. Sitting at the table was a young man of thirty-five, pale and sickly-looking and bewildered. He was one of the few who, though ill, still survived abduction. Most of the time, anyway.

"Guten Tag, Wolfgang Amadeus," Nick said.

The group breaks up, finally, at six, the sky dark now outside the window, the rain still coming down. They leave, one by one, some going to dinner, others back to their rooms. Bird and Biggie head to the studios to jam. The other Lennons leave without trying to talk to him, which is a relief. He's still not sure how to make conversation with them; it feels too much like going crazy.

The group leader, an enthusiastic young black woman named Erica, is talking with a man in a black hat and string tie, with a patch of hair on his lower lip—another new arrival whose name John can't remember. Stevie something, apparently quite good with a guitar. Erica has promised to take them both to their rooms, to point them toward the cafeteria, and show them the amenities. John just wants to go to bed.

This has been the longest, strangest day of his life.

Or, he supposes, *not* of his life.

Whichever.

He is surprised, then, when there's a knock on the meeting room door and it's Nick Mendez. A bit relieved, too. There's no shortage of familiar faces around here, but Nick's at least doesn't bring to mind an obituary John once read.

"Good evening," John says.

"Hi, John. I'm going to just steal you away, if that's all right with Erica."

Nick looks at her, and she makes a twisting motion with an upraised hand–*whatever you want to do*. "Just make sure he knows his way around the dorm after you're done," she says, and she and Stevie leave.

"What's going on, Nick?" John asks. "I thought you said tomorrow morning."

"Plans have changed," Nick replies. "You have a guest. Come with me."

At once, John has a feeling, like a jolt of electricity running through him. He knows who *someone* is, but he doesn't say anything. Saying it feels too likely to make it untrue. Pushing up his glasses, he follows Nick out into the hall, to the elevators, and back up to the interview rooms.

John's heart hammers in his chest the whole way.

"I didn't know we could have visitors," he says. "Aren't we supposed to be secret from the rest of the world?"

"From the general public," Nick replies. "A few people are allowed in, provided they sign a non-disclosure agreement. Even then, though, security's pretty tight."

They're at the door now, and John is sweating. He swallows. "Go on, then," he says. "Let's see who it is."

Nick opens the door and steps back, saying nothing. John steps in through the door. And Sean turns to greet him.

His Sean. Five years old when this long, long day began. Now he must be almost sixty, nearly twenty years older than John himself. He's wearing the same round, wire-frame glasses. Aside from the gray hair and a bit of Yoko in the eyes, like a ghost, it's like looking in a mirror.

"Hi, Dad," he says.

The tears come, swift and unstoppable. Yielding to them, John goes, at last, to his son.

It's Just a Matter of Time

James M. Ward

James M. Ward on James M. Ward: Obviously, he was born, and not quite as obviously, he has lived a pleasantly long time. He married his high school sweetheart, and she's put up with him for almost forty years. He has three unusually charming sons: Breck, James, and Theon. They in turn have given him five startlingly charming grandchildren: Keely, Miriam, Sophia, Preston, and Teagan. In that same stretch of time he managed to write the first science fiction role-playing game, *Metamorphosis Alpha*; he worked for TSR and did lots of *Dungeon & Dragons* and *After Dungeon & Dragons* things; and designed the best-selling *Spellfire* and *Dragon Ball Z* collectable card games.

He has written all manner of things that he is unusually proud of—the Dragon Lairds board game, the novel *Halcyon Blithe, Midshipwizard*, the My Precious Present card game, and the role-playing game supplement *Of Gods & Monsters*. He's working with a computer company to produce the Panzer General board game.

He reads a lot, greatly enjoys fencing with a rapier when he gets the chance, and constantly gets beat in board games with friends in the area. Currently, he is the managing editor for Troll Lords' *Crusader* magazine, and the go-to guy when his sons need a babysitter.

Jason Nips was possibly the richest man in the world. He'd stopped counting his money a long time ago.

He currently stood in line waiting for his turn into the temporal field like the five other rich tourists. Mr. Nips was the owner of Refresh, a corporation responsible for keeping a youthful look on the faces and hands of the rich. Standing five-foot-eight, Jason didn't look a day over sixty. He was far older, but the products from his company kept him looking younger and fitter than almost any other man his age in the world.

What's the sense of owning one of the largest companies in the world if you couldn't take advantage of it?

Zap!

Another tourist walked into the field dressed as a Roman soldier, and the line grew shorter. In front of him stood a lovely woman in Renaissance garb, a man in some sort of Raj costume from India's past, and a woman in a short Greek tunic with a bow and quiver on her back and a bronze helm on her head. Jason's suit was a dull black, typical of the style of dress in the 1880s, and he held a worn leather satchel at his side. His heart raced in his excitement, but his face never showed it.

Zap! Zap! Zap!

The glowing neon sign said TIMESHARES™ Incorporated above the desk. The badge on the man's chest read TIME TECH GLEN JOHNSON LEVEL 3 TECH.

"Your forms and birth certificate please," the Time Tech asked, his hand out.

Jason handed over the prepared materials.

The tech read over the information.

"Mr. Nips, I'm a huge fan of your company. My parents won one of your public lotteries and got treatments free. Would you mind giving me your autograph?"

"Sure, my boy, and thank you for asking."

"Wow, a real paper birth certificate from 1910," the tech marveled. "We don't get many of these. Your papers say you want to go back to your grandfather's time in 1887."

Jason looked down at his birth certificate. The perfect forgery had cost him a cool million dollars. In his mind, it was worth every penny. "Yes. I want to refresh my memories of the place. I didn't get the chance to say good-bye to my grandfather before he died."

"I suggest you don't talk too much to your grandfather. We don't want to risk Temporal Divarication, do we? As you know from your three previous briefings, Temporal Divarication happens when you deal with the immediate relatives of your past. We've found that in some instances just touching your parents or yourself can force a readjustment in the timeline. I think it was Mike Gray and his time studies that . . ."

"I've studied time travel with the designers of your unit. They've given me some good advice. I think I'll be all right. Thank you for your concern."

"I'm just doing my job," the tech said, obviously not liking being cut off from his normal lecture. "Show me your remote and you can go right through."

Jason took the device out of his pocket.

"Excellent. Just press that when you are ready to come back. If you don't press it, in thirty days you will come back automatically. Enjoy your stay."

"Thank you."

The one-hundred-and-twenty-five-year-old posing as a ninety-five-year-old walked into the temporal field and into his own history, breaking the number one rule of the Timeshares Company.

He appeared on the edge of Red Gulch, South Dakota. His mouth tasted of vile vinegar and the place stank to high heaven. He popped an illegal breath mint in his mouth, but he could do nothing about the smell. Cow dung mingled on the street with horse and pig dung as the animals walked about, ignored by the townsfolk. Nips hadn't remembered the stink of his hometown. He took out a piece of paper and read over his notes.

"One, I have to meet myself and talk about our grandfather. Two, I have to attend the ice cream social and get myself to buy Annetta Falkensturm's lunch box. Three, we have to use our inheritance to buy the oil land. Four, we have to save the life of our brother from the Yancy Gang."

Jason looked up from his notes and his eyes beheld a vision. Annetta Falkensturm and her mother just walked out of Tuttle's Grocery. She was a goddess in black and white. Her dress perfectly outlined her amazing hourglass figure. She had full breasts, a wasp waist, and wide hips. She swayed slowly down the boardwalk with her eyes modestly downcast. Jason thought she was prettier than any movie star. Her skin was white under her parasol, and there wasn't a blemish anywhere. She had to be the loveliest woman in the whole world. He had been a fool to not buy her lunch box at the social those many years ago. His heart ached at the sight of her, and he chastised himself for never pursuing her. He wouldn't be making the mistake of not buying her lunch box this time.

Struggling to tear his eyes off the girl, he moved to Hal's blacksmith shop. He had worked there far too many hours, and that would never happen this time around. As he entered the shop, the old fool Hal walked up to him, wiping his soot-covered hands with an even more soot-covered rag. "What can I do ya fer, old timer?"

Hal stood five foot and was as wide as he was tall. His hair was sticking out in all directions and he had a soot-dusted beard. His overalls hadn't seen a washing in a long, long time.

"I'm after a new horse with all its tack," Jason said. "I'm told you give fair prices. I want to buy the best you have."

"Well, we can take care of that right away. Jason! You come on a running with Thunder."

Jason saw his younger self pop out of a stall with a pitchfork of dirty straw. He dropped the fork and ran for the back of the barn. In minutes, he brought out a large stallion.

"This horse is the best I've got," Hal said. "It's a stallion, but calm as you please."

"What are you asking for it, new tack, and a rented stall for seven days?"

"I like the way you deal, mister," Hal said. "I'm asking one hundred and ten for the lot."

"I'll give you six twenty-dollar gold pieces if young Jason here can get some free time to show me around the town in the next couple of days."

The younger version of Jason looked up, surprised.

The greedy Hal jumped at the chance. "It's a deal!"

The older Jason reached into his bag and took out the very authentic gold pieces.

"Jason, my lad," he told the boy, "I'm your cousin, Jason Walch, of the Virginia Walches. So you and me share the same name. I was a good friend to your grandfather, Big Mark Nips. I'm sorry I wasn't here for his burial last month. Saddle up my new horse and take me to the best hotel Red Gulch has to offer."

"You knew Grandpa Mark?" young Jason asked,

wide-eyed with surprise. "That's great. Sure I'll get right to the saddling. The good hotel is a mile down the road, next to Getchil's Dry Goods Store."

They talked as they slowly rode to the hotel. The younger Jason was unusually ignorant, and that didn't please the older version. They talked about Grandpa Mark.

The younger Jason was all smiles.

When they got to the hotel, people were sniffing at the younger Jason's clothes.

"What's there to do in this little town?" the older version asked.

"There is the ice cream social this evening at sunset. I didn't plan on going this year, but I sure do like the taste of ice cream."

"Of course you do, and of course you and I are going. Get into Getchil's Store and get yourself some new clothes for the social. I'm going to get a room in this here hotel. When you walk out of that place, I want to see you looking like a New York dandy." He passed two twenty-dollar gold pieces to his younger self and was careful not to touch the boy's flesh.

"I don't rightly feel good about taking your money, Cousin," young Jason said.

"Not a bit of it, my boy," the older version said. "Part of the reason I'm here is to give you an inheritance your grandpa had me hold for you. Get some new clothes and join me for a long meal in the hotel. We'll talk over old times and go to the social together. Now get along."

Jason didn't even look back as he entered the hotel, feeling very pleased with himself.

Getting a room, he unpacked his few things and took out a pouch of three hundred dollars in twenty-dollar gold pieces. It was a small fortune in gold coins in his time, and it would be a great start for the young Jason in this time.

The old version couldn't help laughing at the younger version as he walked into the dining hall a short time later. The boy had on a white shirt with a string tie. The new brown vest matched the brown pants. He had on new boots, and to top it all off he was wearing a bowler hat. A fashion plate he was not.

They ate a great steak with beans and talked the afternoon away. The old version gave the young version the three hundred in gold, and the young version was lost for words.

"You should invest that money, son. But we'll talk about that tomorrow. Right now, we've a social to go to."

Young Jason put the money in the hotel safe and they took their time walking to the town's band shell.

The older version carried two blankets as they strolled into the park. A small band was playing a light tune, and many couples bounced to the music. There was a huge batch of wrapped boxes on several tables.

The older Jason couldn't wait for the bidding.

A man got up from the crowd and walked in front of the band. "You all know me. I'm Mayor Parker. We are going to start the bidding on these here packed lunches. The money we get goes to the widows and orphans fund, so be generous. Mary, start bringing up those boxes. Let's begin with that nice big basket with the red bow."

"That's Annetta's basket," the older Jason said. "You bid on that basket, you know you want to."

"Twenty-five cents," the younger Jason shouted. "Cousin, how do you know it's hers?"

The bidding was brisk, and soon it was up to two dollars.

"Go on now, outbid everyone."

"Cousin, that's a lot of money for dinner."

There was nothing that was going to stand in the way of the two young'uns getting together.

"I've got a twenty-dollar gold piece that says my young cousin here, is going to eat from that basket tonight," the older Jason shouted.

The crowd gasped at the thought of that.

"Well heck-fire, I don't imagine any gent here is going to beat that price. The red box is sold. Will the lady who made this one please come up."

Annetta Falkensturm, turning several shades of red, walked up to the stage. The older Jason tossed the younger one a blanket and a twenty-dollar gold piece to pay for the box.

"You take that girl up on the hill, under the old oak tree and have yourself a time, ya hear me boy?"

"Thanks, Cousin. I will try and do that."

The two went up the hill, arm in arm.

Jason leaned back on the bench and smiled as the beginnings of his plan began to unfold just the way he wanted. Halfway through the auction, a yellow-ribboned basket came up for sale. He remembered it to be the Widow Jenkins'. The girl was just twenty, blond and blue-eyed. She made the best meat pies in the county. In that long-ago time he had strolled out with her a few times, but found her way to bold to suit him. That wouldn't be a problem now. He waited until the basket was bid up to three dollars, before buying it with another twenty-dollar gold piece.

"Dear lady, I hope you don't mind that an old man bought your wonderful basket."

The girl in front of him was a vision in her light blue dress. "Why no, good sir. I saw what you did for your cousin and I'm proud to sup with such a gentleman."

He walked her up the hill and spread his blanket by

another oak tree. He heard the strangest snorting from time to time, but soon that was lost in the eyes and gentle smiles of the Widow Jenkins. It seems she liked older men and wasn't shy about it.

The next day young Jason was to meet his cousin in the hotel. As he rushed up the stairs, he saw the Widow Jenkins leave his cousin's room. Her hair was all messed up and there was a huge grin on her face. She didn't look him in the eyes as they passed by in the hall.

The door was open.

"Cousin, that was the Widow Jenkins leaving your room, wasn't it? She's the best cook in town."

"She has some other skills as well. I will be seeing her tonight when you and I have finished with our business. How did your picnic with Annetta Falkensturm go?"

"It was amazing. We watched the moonrise, held hands, and she even kissed me good night. She's the prettiest little thing I've ever seen. Her laugh's hard to take though. She sounds a lot like a rooting pig when she laughs."

So that explained the odd noise.

"I'm sure you can get over that little flaw. Now I want you and me to ride out to Devil's Canyon to look over that land."

"Why would we do that? It's nothing but bare earth and rocks. Lots of people have owned it, but no one has been able to do anything with it."

"Humor me, son."

They rode out, and the canyon was just as promised. A couple miles wide and seven miles long, it didn't support any growth.

The cracked earth was depressing. Outside the valley, there were a number of clumps of forest.

"Cousin Jason, I told you this land is dead. Why would anyone want to have a chunk of this?"

"There's oil there, my boy, and lots of it. That's why there isn't a lot of plant growth. We get into that oil, and you will be a very rich man. I know it doesn't look like much now, but I can see wells and processing plants filling this canyon in the years to come. Trust me."

"All right, if you think so." The young Jason didn't sound convinced.

"Mark my words. This is just what you want to own. You'll be rich in no time and giving your Annetta Falkensturm all the things a lovely young lady wants to have."

"Well, Cousin, that's more than enough reason to do a little, investing, I guess. Let's get back to the bank."

They rode their horses hard back into the city.

Grim-faced bank managers became all smiles when the two Jasons said they wanted to buy the Devil's Canyon. They asked for five hundred dollars and were talked down to two hundred and fifty. The ink was fresh on the land contract when the bankers started laughing at the deal. They admitted that they never thought they would sell the property.

The older Jason had to make a comment. "We're going to take millions of barrels of oil out of that canyon. What do you think of that?"

The bank manager was blunt. "I know there is oil down there but it is all shale oil. The oil is embedded in the rock. Good day, Mr. Nips. Thank you for your business."

Both Jasons had sour looks on their faces as they left the bank.

"Well, that didn't work out like we planned, did it, Cousin?"

"I didn't know about the shale oil, son. But I'll give you a hundred dollars in gold. You can bring in oil-drilling experts and see what they say. It's getting late, and I bet you have a meeting with Annetta Falkensturm."

"You are correct, Cousin," young Jason said. "I bet you are going to have a meat pie for dinner tonight."

"You could be right. Meet me tomorrow at Tuttle's at noon. Be dressed in your good clothes. I'll need some help carrying some things I'm going to buy. That won't be a problem, will it?"

"Not at all, Cousin. I'm a landowner now, even if it's dead property. I am squiring the best-looking gal in the state, and it's all because of you. I'll be there. Enjoy your night."

"Oh, I will."

The young Jason tried to pat the older one on the back, but the adult avoided the touch.

The older Jason's thoughts turned toward the Widow Jenkins. Minutes later, he knocked on her door and was warmly welcomed inside.

Morning came too fast, and the ever ready widow was as fast at cooking as she was with other things. Jason left her with a smile, a tickle, and a promise to return after lunch.

He rode Thunder to Tuttles. He remembered just what he wanted to buy. The younger version of himself got there a few minutes later.

"Look at that, Cousin."

The older Jason has set a large wooden box with six shotguns and a box and a half of shells on the counter.

"What do you want all of those shotguns for, Cousin? You gonna fight a war?"

"Never you mind, just take the other side of this box. We're going to the stagecoach stop. Your brother Ben is going to be on that stage coming in at twelve thirty."

"Really, how do you know that? I wasn't expecting to see him for another month."

"I know things."

They carried the heavy box to the stage office on the

other side of the street from the bank. Jason noted the six horses tied to the rail in front of the bank. He hoped the sheriff and deputy were coming this way, as he had asked them to do so over a late lunch the day before.

"Son, help me move some of these dry goods barrels to the edge of the sidewalk."

"I can do that, Cousin, but I don't think Getchil's is going to like that."

"Trust me."

They moved the barrels, and the older Jason set up the six shotguns against them. The younger Jason looked on in wonder.

"The stage is coming! The stage is coming!" boys shouted from somewhere down the street.

The next several minutes were a blur.

Brother Ben got off the stage and was surprised to see a cleaned-up younger brother. He gave him a big hug.

The stage driver started unloading suitcases from the top of the stage.

Shots rang out from the other side of the street as the bank robbers came out onto the street, firing. The first bullet took the stagecoach driver in the head. He dropped the heavy suitcase on young Jason, and the boy went down like a sack of potatoes.

It was just as the older Jason had remembered things. But it would turn out different this time around.

The older Jason started cutting lose with double-barreled blasts. He was only a passable shot, but he didn't have to be an expert. The buckshot ripped the bank robbers' arms and legs from their bodies.

"Stay down, Ben," shouted the older Jason. "Protect the boy. I've got them covered and the sheriff's coming."

He continued to quickly pepper the other side of the

street, going from gun to gun. Three bank robbers bled out on the street as the sheriff and his man ran up to add their gunfire to his. Jason quickly reloaded all the shotguns and began firing again.

There was only one robber left now, and he shot back at the sheriff. The older Jason rushed into the street to get a better angle, and his shotgun stitched the side of the robber. The robber turned and fired as he went down. One of the bullets took Jason in the knee.

In terrible pain, Jason fell on the Timeshares device in his back pocket, hitting the panic button and vanishing from the street and back into time where he belonged.

He woke up in a hospital bed. Drugs dripped into his arm, and he didn't feel any pain. There was a loud beeping noise near his head.

A pretty red-haired nurse rushed into his room and pressed a button to stop the beeping. "I've sent for the doctor. Don't you worry about a thing. You're going to be fine now that you are back where you belong. Your brother has paid for the very best care for you."

Jason was unable to say a thing. He felt so fuzzy.

A tall man in surgery scrubs walked into the room with a datapad in his hand. He scanned Jason's body and was all smiles.

"I was a bit worried about the bio-replacement of the knee. I'm certain now that you will have one hundred percent freedom of movement. It's a good thing we could get you in the regeneration lab so quickly. Your brother saw to that. You are going to be fine and up and moving in a few days. I'm going to let your wife and brother in to see you."

Jason smiled at the thought of his newfound wife and brother. He had succeeded in the past. Everything would be great now.

A much older looking brother Ben and a fat woman came into the room.

"Jason, brother, you promised me when I paid for that vacation ticket that you wouldn't get into trouble. What happened back there?"

Jason struggled to remember.

No!

The fat woman seemed to find something funny and laughed like a pig.

Annetta. His younger self had married her, and he suddenly recalled a lifetime of that horrid laugh.

He also remembered a life with Annetta. It hadn't been a good life.

Jason gasped as the replaced memories surged forward. His brother Ben had bought the land contract for a thousand dollars ten years after its first purchase as a kindness to Jason and Annetta.

Ben got richer and richer, and Jason failed time after time in money making schemes. He had eventually invested a great deal in the Refresh Company, but once again Ben's money bailed him out, and Ben was three-quarters owner of the corporation.

Jason turned his head away from the pair. He knew he'd made the mistake of his life, and there wouldn't be a second chance to set things back in order.

Time Sharing

Jody Lynn Nye

Jody Lynn Nye lists her main career activity as "spoiling cats." She lives northwest of Chicago with two of the above and her husband, author and packager, Bill Fawcett. She has published more than thirty-five books, including six contemporary fantasies; four science fiction novels; four novels in collaboration with Anne McCaffrey, including *The Ship Who Won*; edited a humorous anthology about mothers, *Don't Forget Your Spacesuit, Dear!*; and written more than a hundred short stories. Her latest books are *A Forthcoming Wizard*, and *Myth-Fortunes*, cowritten with Robert Asprin.

Milan, 1494

Lorraine couldn't decide which was worse, the terrible vinegar taste or the stew of odors that assailed her nose as she struggled to get into the heavy robelike dress and velvet cloak. They had been too hot to wear in the departure lounge of the Timeshares Travel Agency, between the giant crackling spheres that owed their heritage to Tesla coils, whatever the name the corporation called them to make them more palatable to the un-schooled yet moneyed class they wanted to attract. Well, she was no ordinary customer!

Mother was here, in Milan. It had taken some very specific information, threats, and bribes to get the correct information from Rolf Jacobsen, the president of Timeshares. She had based her hunch upon notes her mother had left on a pad of paper in the study of her empty apartment in San Francisco. It was not until she had insisted she would go to the police that Jacobsen allowed that perhaps, yes, he did know Genevieve Corvana and her whenabouts, as well as her whereabouts. Lorraine was proud to know that she was right. She could not, however, place the odd look on Jacobsen's face when she told him the rest of what she wanted. But she was here now, Marguerite wasn't, and nothing was more important!

She straightened her ornate lace and jeweled veil. Her thick brown hair was scraped back into a silk net beneath. Somehow, the exposure of her face and neck made her feel vulnerable, all the more since preparation for the trip had involved removal of her eyebrows and eyelashes. Randa Cuddy, Jacobsen's head of Esthetics, had assured her that the depilation was temporary but necessary in light of the fashions of the day. She straightened her back and marched toward the door. Suddenly a hand grabbed her by the hair and pulled backward.

"Oh, no, you don't! I got here first!"

Horrified, Lorraine wrenched herself free. The light that streaked through the gaps in the boards of the lean-to was enough to see the glaring eyes in a face that was so much like hers, with its firm, square chin, decided mouth, and wide hazel eyes, but broader across the cheekbones, the image of stubbornness. How? "Marguerite!"

"How did you get through?" her sister demanded. "I gave Jacobsen a huge bribe not to let you."

"You miserable waste of skin!" Lorraine snarled, feeling her blood pressure rise. She felt behind her and straightened out the net, which was hanging askew. "I am here to see Mother, and you can't stop me."

She shouldered Marguerite aside and headed toward the vertical sliver of daylight that must indicate a door.

"I was here first! You're not getting ahead of me!"

Marguerite pushed back, raking her clawlike nails over the back of Lorraine's hand. When they burst out into the bright Milanese sunshine, Lorraine could see that it was bleeding.

"Oh, how I hate you!" Lorraine shrieked, wrapping the ornamental frill of lace around her hand.

Suddenly, she became aware that many pairs of eyes were upon them. Men in simple linen shirts over hose and filthy shoes pushing wheelbarrows. Men in gorgeous padded doublets with exaggerated codpieces sticking out just below the hem. Women whose undergowns were tied at the throat as hers, but with the drawstring so loose that their breasts were almost completely on display over pieced bodices that were for support much more than for show. Women in carts and carriages wearing veils or holding up fans on sticks or seated under sunshades to protect themselves from the blazing light, possibly with a tiny live monkey curled around their necks or with a bird on a perch attached to the frame of their conveyance. She and Marguerite were providing free midday entertainment to their fellow passersby.

Lorraine drew herself up. "I am going to see Mother. Whether you do or not is of no concern to me."

Jacobsen had promised a guide. She looked around the crowded street. She didn't expect someone to be standing there holding up a sign, but who was it? Jacobsen assured her he would be easy to spot.

Suddenly, a very dark-skinned African boy in a glorious cloth-of-gold turban, an embroidered tunic, and bare feet skipped out of a storefront and came to bow to them.

"Signorina Corvana?" His diction was crisp but flavored with an exotic accent.

"Yes?" she and Marguerite chorused.

"My name is Iskander. I am here to take you to Signora Genevieve." He grinned at them, showing perfectly even, white teeth. "This way." He turned and began to thread his way along the crowded stone street.

"He looks as if he had orthodontia," Marguerite murmured.

"Three years' worth," the boy agreed amiably. When they blinked in surprise, he grinned again. "I am a graduate student at Stanford. My real name is Arthur Struthers. This is my summer job, tour guide in Renaissance Milan, in the service of my lord the duke Ludovico il Moro. Beautiful, isn't it?"

It was. Lorraine's first glimpse of another time and space should have been thrilling beyond words. How wrong it seemed that she had her entire mind upon the woman striding at her side, who had beaten her into the world by a mere thirteen months, and who had stolen all the attention from their mother ever since. She tried to pull her soul out of the quagmire of resentment and enjoy her surroundings. The stench was impossible to ignore, but so were the colors, made even more brilliant by the sun. Flowers bloomed in impossible hues. The people around them were as vivid, arrayed like so many exotic butterflies in silks, brocades, and linen. She, who had lived most of her life among the muted palette of northern California and spent much of her time bent over a microscope, found it exotic and wonderful. The clothing Jacobsen's employees had furnished her repelled dirt and insects, so minor discomforts were kept at bay. Thousands of humans, many more than she was comfortable rubbing elbows with, crowded the street, shouting to friends, hawking their goods, pushing barrows toward some distant market, all adding to the rainbow palette. The bowl of the sky, an expanse of purest turquoise, was decorated with a few fluffy white clouds. The city was like a master's painting crossed with a Where's Waldo poster. Why was Genevieve here? Why didn't she want to go somewhere more comfortable, where the streets didn't stink?

"Graduate student?" Marguerite asked. "One of Mother's graduate students?"

The young man nodded. "Yes. I am on independent study now that she has retired. Officially. But she is still my faculty adviser." The blinding grin took them off guard again. "Here we are."

The door of the wide, white stucco-covered house had no portico to protect one from the elements, but opened into a small but gracious hall with polished wood floors and frescoed walls. The cherubim that beckoned to visitors weren't as simpering and overornamented as many putti that Lorraine had seen in contemporary paintings. She tried to identify the style, but the name escaped her.

Iskander bowed and strode into the burgeoning crowd, leaving them on the stoop. A plump female servant in white apron and tightly-wound headcloth led them down the narrow hallway toward the rear of the house. She opened a door and stood aside. A wave of noise from within all but knocked the two women backward. The sounds of a woodwind and a stringed instrument warred with voices.

The room was filled with people. Men and a few women in smocks sat at easels, trays of color at their elbows. A few men, ranging in age from late twenties to perhaps fifty, linen coifs covering their sweating heads, painted faces of near-photographic quality onto wooden panels on which only a few dark lines suggested the landscaping and buildings that would soon surround them. Those details were being added to other panels by younger artists in their early teens to early twenties. Others, mostly youngsters, some very small, ground the colors in mortars held between their outspread legs as they sat on the floor. The delicacy of their task did not cut down at all on holding conversations with their fellows. A large sheet of paper had been tacked to one wall so that Lorraine could see that all the pieces in the room were intended to be part of a single installation, possibly an altar-piece. In the corner, a pair of musicians in rolled hats and hose strummed and tootled, unperturbed by the seeming chaos around them. More noise filtered in from outside, through enormous windows flanked by wide-flung wooden shutters. Around the walls stood sturdy machinery of iron and bronze. Lorraine could identify the small forge and anvils, but she could not have guessed at the purpose of the standing metal plate with holes of ever decreasing size drilled in it or the odd frame that resembled a loom without a shuttle.

One of the older women, wearing a linen veil on her graying brown hair and an enveloping ecru pinafore over a gown made of good ochre-colored brocade, brush raised, glanced up at the opening of the door. Her cheeks widened in a grin. She put down her brush and rushed to embrace them.

"You found me!" she cried. "So the clues weren't too difficult?"

"Mother!" Lorraine exclaimed. "Wait, you left those notes on purpose?"

Genevieve Corana smiled. "Of course I did. I wanted to see you."

"You did?" She pointed at Marguerite. "Then she needs to go back home. Right now. I have no intention of letting her ruin ..."

"*Me* ruin? What makes you think I want to be here with you, you wet blanket! I left home on the twenty-fifth of July."

"Well, I left on the twentieth!"

"How did we get here at the same time?" Marguerite demanded. "When I get my hands on that Jacobsen ..."

"Silence!" Genevieve roared. There was no mistaking a genuine teacher voice, or the cold glare that went with it. Lorraine and Marguerite quieted like guilty pupils. The rest of the room fell silent as well. "We will speak in my private study. There will be no more uproar. Have respect! Do you understand?"

Subdued, the sisters followed their mother through a wooden doorway. A playful frieze around the frame depicted demons dancing as though the portal led to hell.

Genevieve shut the door and leaned over to fling open the shuttered window in the dim room.

"You will not upset the atelier again," she hissed. "There are too many ears listening. You can cause untold trouble. Didn't Rolf's assistants give you the entire safety briefing?"

Reduced to children again, the sisters surveyed the hems of their elegant dresses.

"Yes."

"And you signed the waiver saying that you understood? And what the legal penalties are for disobeying them?"

"Yes."

"But Mother!" Marguerite wailed. "You disappeared without telling us where you were going."

Genevieve waved away the protest. "I messaged you both. I told you I was retiring. I said I was going somewhere I enjoyed, and I wanted you to be happy for me. I planned to let you know more in time. I had to establish myself first. It's taken a few years, but things are going well. You arrived here at the same time because I wanted to see *both* of you. I am glad you are here, darlings. We're going to have such a nice time."

"A few years?" Lorraine asked. "But you've only been gone since June."

"Linear time does not apply in this process, darling. You know that. I told Rolf that when you came looking for me, 1494 was the earliest that he could let you through."

"But an artist studio?" Marguerite asked. "You're a scientist."

Genevieve smiled. "They're not such different disciplines. Especially not here, not now. I'm happy here. The others think I am a noblewoman's daughter who became an abbess and decided to retire from the church. They're a little scandalized by that, but it made them accept me as a scholar, if not a good Catholic. I have formed warm friendships with wonderful women, and a few men, too. This is a marvelous place. I hope you'll come to love it as much as I do. I bought an annual timeshare of two weeks from Rolf for you to use. *If* you two can behave yourselves in my home."

Lorraine surveyed the room. A layer of dust stood on the windowsills and anywhere there were not piles of parchments heaped upon trestle tables, stools, and rolled up in cylinders on shelves. Mother had always been so neat. The furnishings, too, were rough and broad in design.

"This is a man's room," she said.

"Yes," Genevieve said, with a broad smirk. "I found the man of my dreams. This is his studio."

"A man?" Lorraine felt her heart constrict with fury. "Time's not linear, but you couldn't spend a single day to tell us your plans before you disappeared?"

Genevieve tucked her arms into her sleeves, an unconscious gesture, but a new one to Lorraine. It must have been something she had adopted in her pose as a former religieuse. "Sweetheart, I'm sorry. My duties were done. You two were well on your way. You are both grown up, with your own careers and families. I couldn't wait to get back here. To him. To the life we had together. It was all I could think about."

Marguerite's face had gone red, too. "Mother, that's ridiculous. You're in your sixties!"

"Hardly doddering old age. Nothing's stopped working yet except for my childbearing equipment, and frankly, I'm glad to be done with that. What is it you want of me?" Genevieve asked, with a frown. "Did you expect to find me warehoused somewhere, slowly moldering away, pining for you as you seem to be pining for me?"

"No!" Lorraine protested immediately, but she was too much of a scientist herself not to analyze her mother's words for the germ of truth. "I suppose I thought you would always be there. For us. For me. I thought that once you retired you might be able to spend more time with us."

Genevieve raised an eyebrow. "Did I say you were grown up?"

Lorraine felt her cheeks burn. "I am! But it feels as if all the time we ever had from you was stolen from your other projects."

Her hurt words won a contrite look from Genevieve.

"For that I am sorry. I do love you both with all my heart. I knew I didn't hack it well as a wife. I must not have been much of a mother, either. When the five-year contract with your father was up, we just let it lapse. You know we never held any rancor for one another. I was just not good at being married. Well, to your father," she added with a shrug. "I tried to give you happy childhoods. You had all my love and attention."

"Bull. That went to your classified programs," Marguerite snapped. "Those got all your attention."

"They were profitable enough to put you through college and graduate school," Genevieve said, defensively. "You didn't reject the benefits. My technological research enriched the lives of thousands of students and will continue to benefit humanity for a long time." She fought visibly for control and smiled at them. "I haven't stopped working. Come and see what we have been doing."

She took a heap of the parchments from the table and set them on the floor. From the collection on the shelves, she took one that was bound with a ring of bronze and spread it out. A pair of spindles topped with spheres shot lightning at one another around a filigree cage in which rotated a cosmos of stars. Fine, delicate handwriting surrounded the images. Formulae that Lorraine, a biologist, did not recognize, were written in neat blocks. To her surprise, she realized the letters and numbers were all backward.

"This is the original design for the Timeshares generator," Genevieve said. "I believe it is elegant in its simplicity, to clone a phrase. It uses far less power than the first time-travel engines, and is far more accurate, thanks to quantum entanglement." She paused to regard the perfection of the fine lines. "It looks so primitive now, but it has passed through over three hundred modifications to

get to the final design. This one." She took another huge
sheet from the pile and placed it next to the first on the
sanded board. "I had thirty-nine physicists working on
the project over twelve years, but the final design came
from here. How delighted we were when the beta tests
came back perfect eighty-three out of a hundred tries.
You cannot ask for better results. Oh, here's something
new we've been working on. It's a geothermal storage
facility for residential complexes."

"How beautiful," Lorraine said, examining the plans.
"The rendering is perfect. They look almost like drawings by Leonardo da Vinci."

"Of course they look like Leonardo drawings, my
dear," Genevieve said. "He drew them."

Before either of them could sputter out a two-syllable
expletive of disbelief, the door opened.

"Belladonna," said the tall man. He removed a dark
blue rolled velvet hat and cast it aside. He rumpled up
the linen cap underneath, tousling locks of lank red hair.
His beard was sandier in hue than his hair, shot full of
silver threads, especially at the corners of his mouth.
Genevieve held out her hands to him, and he embraced
her warmly. "His grace sends to you his compliments, for
what they are worth. Somehow he has heard of the new
cannon I designed, and wants it for himself. His wish,
of course, is my command, though I must warn my lord
de Medici such a thing may be done." He bowed to the
sisters. "My ladies, I am remiss in not greeting such dis-
tinguished visitors. I am Leonardo. I welcome you to my
home and workshop."

"My love, these are my daughters," Genevieve said.
"Marguerite and Lorraine."

Lorraine wondered if she should curtsey. All her
briefings on the culture of the time fled from her mind
like the vestiges of grade school Latin. His eyes, deep

blue, fixed upon hers. She was caught in their infinite depths, and she nearly gasped. The power of his intelligence and personality were in that gaze.

"I should have seen by the echo of her beauty in your visages," he said, his eyes twinkling at them. Lorraine knew that she would never forget that moment.

Genevieve helped settle him in the broad chair at the table and rearranged the big parchment sheets, rolling up the old plans and putting them away. Her business-like movements snapped Lorraine out of her entrancement. "I'll leave you to your work, my love. I will have Casperina bring you wine and food. The girls have traveled far and need to rest." She took their hands firmly. Lorraine snapped out of her trance. "I will show you to your rooms. They're on the third floor. I hope you won't mind, but the house is full at the moment."

The girls followed her up a flight of stairs. Even the beauty of the carving of the newel posts and stair risers couldn't conceal how narrow they were. At the top of the last flight, a slim corridor led to paneled doors of golden wood.

"Mother, how could you involve someone from the past in your classified work?" Marguerite hissed. "He knows about the Timeshares project! What about the noninterference pact that we had to sign?"

"That *you* had to sign," Genevieve corrected her. "Leonardo helped me design the system. I had run into walls again and again, where I just could not make the process work. I needed someone who was not confined to modern thinking about the technology. I read the letter he wrote to the Duke of Milan, and realized that Leonardo was the one I needed. I came here to watch him, and discovered he was watching me. His powers of observation surpass those of anyone else I have ever met, anywhere." She blushed. Lorraine was shocked.

"As your great-grandmother used to say so colorfully, 'chicks dig smart guys.' We fell in love. He has other women here and there, but he comes back to me. We bond over science, and that I share with no other woman. I am satisfied."

"But, he's an old man," Marguerite said.

"And I'm an old woman. But he's only forty-two. That's the way people age here in the Renaissance. He looks much older, and I come from a time in which nutrition and better care make me fortunate enough to look younger. But we weren't always old. And," she added with a wicked twinkle in her eyes, "for some things it really doesn't matter."

"Mother!" Lorraine exclaimed, aghast.

Genevieve laughed. She opened two doors. The sun fell on a bed, washstand, and chair in each room. "I'll have to lend you clean clothes, since you didn't bring luggage, but we're all close to the same size. Thank heavens for strong genetics. The timeshare is only for two weeks, but I have so much to show you. His grace has asked to meet you. It's a great honor. Dinner is in two hours. Iskander will take you on a tour of the city."

Once Marguerite had closed the door, Lorraine tried to draw Genevieve into her guest room. "Mother, please, can't we talk?"

Genevieve gently took her fingers from her sleeve and patted them with her other hand. "Later, darling. We'll talk more at dinner."

But dinner provided no time for private conversation. The son of the duke of Padua was present in the place of honor at the head of the long table, along with his wife and young sons, who waited on their parents. The other seats were filled by several prosperous merchants of the town. Most of the conversation was about trade, but in the middle of a fish course, a pike served with leeks and tarragon, it turned to Leonardo's work.

"So, I hear you are building a machine that flies?" the nobleman asked.

"Alas, it does not fly, except in my dreams," Leonardo said, with a smile.

"What is the problem?"

"Mainly that no means of driving its wings exists, at least at present. It is a problem I cannot yet solve, but rest assured I continue to try."

"You have created nothing that can press the air into it, as a bird's wing?" the man asked. "I have seen your drawings of anatomy. Something that would cause it to flap and rise from the ground? A gigantic bellows, perhaps?"

Marguerite, an aeronautical engineer, hastily swallowed a bite. "This is not a machine that flaps, your grace, but that spins, like a child's top, and can lift that way. Or should."

"Ah." The young lord's shining dark eyes lit on her in amusement. "So, are you a *woman* of science? Where did you learn the terms? They come easily to you, I see."

Lorraine, beside her, was horrified. They were supposed to be noblewomen, visiting their mother for the first time. They were not to speak out in this very masculine society. The unique niche that their mother had carved with care over these last few years was not theirs to occupy.

"Forgive my sister," Lorraine said, hastily. "My mother writes to us of these things. I feel we know them as well as we know scripture. Ser Leonardo is so well regarded, even in our faraway homes." She punctuated the sentence with a stomp on her sister's foot. Marguerite gasped.

"Oh, and where do you live?" the lordling asked.

"Spain," Lorraine said, falling back upon the cover story prepared for them by Timeshares. "My husband is a merchant in Barcelona."

"You have not fallen prey to their ghastly accent," he said. "I compliment you. And you, madonna?"

After one angry glare at Lorraine, Marguerite collected herself. "England, sir. My husband has estates in the Midlands."

"And have you children?" asked the wife.

"Two sons. One is in college. Oxford."

"Only two children, but one to the priesthood?" the lady at his left asked.

Damn! Both of them had forgotten that the universities were founded mainly to train priests.

"He has a calling," Marguerite said simply.

Such things evidently did not interest the son of the duke of Padua. "When you make your whirlybird fly, Ser Leonardo, I wish to be present."

"You shall be notified, my lord," the inventor promised.

Leonardo and Genevieve exchanged amused glances. Lorraine noticed it, and felt herself flush. So now she understood why there had always been books about Leonardo all over Mother's apartment. The oil portrait in profile of her on the wall Mother said had been done for her by a friend was in his style. Now Lorraine was sure it was an original painted by Leonardo.

The party retired to a room hung with rich, incense-scented tapestries where Leonardo played tunes for them upon a lyre of his own design. Mother hung on his every word like a lovestruck teenager. Lorraine resented not being able to talk with her privately or even make eye contact. All her attention was on that man.

Lorraine was horrified to realize she was jealous of Leonardo da Vinci. She was appalled at her overwhelming gall. It was ridiculous but it was true. She glanced at Marguerite. Her sister was just as jealous. She obtained some small satisfaction from that.

She felt eyes upon her. She looked up to see the deep-set blue gaze meeting hers frankly. She blushed. Thank goodness he could not read her thoughts.

Genevieve permitted the sisters to stay with her in the atelier, as she called it in the French style, but only if they sat quietly in a corner or if they helped with the day's work. If not, they could go out and see the city of Milan with Iskander. They tried, but since even the smallest apprentice knew more than they did, and the heavy skirts of their mother's formal court dresses got underneath everyone's feet, Lorraine and Marguerite had no choice but to sit silently side by side.

"You can go out on a tour if you wish," Marguerite said, peering out of the corner of her eye at Lorraine. "You're interested in fashion. Except Fashion Week won't be invented for five hundred more years."

"Ha ha," Lorraine said. "Why don't *you* go out for a walk? Those men in the market certainly found you attractive enough to follow around."

"Shut up," Marguerite snapped.

The easels had been pushed aside for the sake of the gun commissioned by Duke Ludovico, and the metal-working equipment brought into the center of the workshop. Leonardo consulted with his workers over the plans. Prototype barrels made of soft brass were cast then cut in half to measure thickness and tolerance. From what glimpses Lorraine could catch, the internal workings of the weapon were complex. It was meant to shoot several balls in succession, like the Gatling gun, still centuries in the future. Big, swarthy blacksmiths huddled shoulder to shoulder with goldsmiths and clockmakers, who

would create the fine mechanism that would operate the
gun. Mother took rejected design documents to the office and returned with "updated" plans that Leonardo
claimed he had waiting. The ink stains on her fingers
told the sisters that she was making the changes on the
plans herself, something the master guildsmen must not
know, or pretended they did not. The look of concentration on Genevieve's face was so familiar to Lorraine
that she almost felt as though she was a little girl again,
watching her mother work at home.

"Mother," Lorraine whispered as she went by with
rolls of paper in her arms. "Can we talk alone? Please?"

"Not now, darlings," Genevieve said, impatiently.

"Stop it," Marguerite hissed. "She said we had to sit
and be quiet. Can't you even do that? You're trying to
take up her time right in front of me!"

Lorraine fumed. She was growing bored, and the
wooden stool was uncomfortable under her less than
well padded bottom. Why had she traveled back over six
hundred years and across an ocean to sit and watch her
mother work? If she wanted that, she would have stayed
home and looked at all the videos she had of her mother
in the classroom and the lab. She was wasting the opportunity of a lifetime. She ought to feel appreciative of
her situation, to take advantage of it, but she could not
bring herself to go out to explore Milan and leave her
sister triumphantly alone on the field. And now there
was *that man*.

Time crawled by until the one-handed clock touched
twelve. They dined with the masters at a trestle table
set up in the workshop. The workmen were polite, but
their minds were focused on the project at hand. Their
attempts at small talk dropped away as they recalled details they needed to draw to their employer's attention.
Lorraine, who had made an effort not to sit next to her

sister, ended up among a group of men who talked across her as if she was not there. Beseeching glances she sent to her mother went unmet, let alone unacknowledged.

The afternoon seemed to stretch out endlessly. Lorraine was not a physicist, but she came to understand the dilation of time at the point of perception. No hours could have passed more slowly. Marguerite snapped every time she moved a foot or shifted on the stool.

"Stop fidgeting!"

"I'm not a statue!" Lorraine said, raising her voice so it was audible over the grinding and pounding of the machines. "Don't pick on me! I don't like this anymore than you do!"

Suddenly, all the noise stopped. Lorraine looked up guiltily to see that everyone in the room was looking at them, especially Leonardo himself. His brows were drawn down like a ruddy thundercloud over his prominent nose. Mother's face had paled. From their childhood, the sisters knew that she was really angry. She glided over to them and stood, her back rigid, her hands hidden inside her sleeves, giving nothing away.

"Go up and change into your own clothes. You leave tonight. I will call Iskander to escort you back."

"Mother, I'm so sorry," Lorraine said.

"Not another word," Genevieve snapped. "Go. I refuse to act as if I am dead so you two can learn to get along. Go away."

She turned her back on them. Lorraine was too stricken to protest. She had gone back six centuries to Milan to see her mother, and she was being sent home. Marguerite shot her a look of mixed anger and smugness.

It took only a moment for the workers to go back to their tasks and forget about the sisters as if they were not there. Lorraine rose and gathered her skirts with what dignity she could muster, and swept out of the room. Marguerite came behind her like the Roman slave with the laurel wreath to remind her she was mortal.

Undoing all the laces and ties took more time than it should have, but her fingers fumbled on them. Frustrated, Lorraine sank down on the small bed and had a good cry, but not for sorrow. She only cried that hard when she was furious. She hated Marguerite, but she almost felt as if she hated her mother, too.

A soft tap came at the door. Lorraine wiped her face with her linen undersleeve before she answered it.

The maidservant stood there. "Signora, will you come with me now? You are summoned to the dining room."

Probably Mother wanted to give her one more solid drubbing down before she left. Marguerite was already waiting in the hall.

"What is this about?" Lorraine asked.

"I don't know."

The girl stood by the door to usher them into the painted chamber.

Mother was not there. Leonardo sat at the head of the long table. They began automatically to back out of the room, but he beckoned them forward.

"Come, we must talk," he said, gesturing to the chairs on either side of him. "Please, sit. Would you like wine?"

"No." Lorraine stood at the foot of the table, keeping as great a distance between her and Leonardo as possible. Marguerite slid into one of the straight-backed chairs and yanked Lorraine's arm.

"Sit down," she hissed. "Do you want Mother angrier than she is?"

With ill grace, Lorraine seated herself. The inventor placed his long hands on the table and leaned forward over them.

"Now, what is all this about? I see how unhappy you are. You dislike each other, you dislike even me, and I am a stranger."

"Not really," Marguerite said. "I feel almost as though I know you. Mother always had books about you, copies of your work, around our house."

His face lit up. Lorraine felt her heart twist. She did not want to be attracted to him. "Did she? Then she knows how dearly I missed her as well. As you do. Tell me. Signora Lorraine?"

Lorraine pressed her lips together. She didn't want to talk to him, but he and her sister were looking at her. She shook her head.

"Then let me interpret. I am an artist. I see tableaux. You feel that I am what keeps your mother from you. It is not a logical thought. You act as if she is not free to behave as she chooses."

"How could she be?" Lorraine burst out. "Anyone would fall all over herself to be your lover!" She stopped, feeling her cheeks burn.

He tilted his head, the blue eyes twinkling. "You don't find it an honor that I have chosen her? Ah, no. You are truly women of a different age. Then tell me the names of some of the men of science who have superseded me, from whom you would find his attention an honor. I would be glad to know."

"None, really," Lorraine admitted. "I don't know what we can tell you, without skewing history."

"Your mother fears temporal paradox as well. Your faces tell me enough. I am honored by history's regard, then. It is most humbling. But I am not the one who is unhappy, signoras. Tell me your troubles. I will not judge, only listen."

"She always went away . . ."

"She never spent time with just *me* . . ."

She and Marguerite burst out with all of the anger and disappointment that was inside them. Expressing herself in Renaissance Italian only rendered the litany of her woes into a poetic cadence, but it didn't lessen the hurt of feeling abandoned by Genevieve, again and again, until this last utter disappointment. By the time her voice died away, she was feeling absolutely ashamed of herself, but Leonardo's kindly expression did not change.

"Your feelings are most understandable," he said. "You find her an attractive personality. So many others do, too. She is a song in a world of cacophony. She is trying to show you her new world. You do not accept her as she is or what choices she has made. You are possessive of her. Can you accept perhaps that she was only lent to you by history for a time?"

"Of course not," Lorraine said. "She is *our* mother. But she won't let us have what we want from her."

"But what is it you want? She is here. She has made you welcome."

"Under certain circumstances," Marguerite said, bitterly.

"But why are those so hard to accept? She wishes that you would love each other. You do, when she is not there, I think."

They glanced at one another. Lorraine saw an expression in Marguerite's eyes that made her take a mental step back. Her sister was actually afraid she would say she didn't love her. It forced her to be honest.

"We do," she said, and made the assertion more firm. "We really do love each other." Marguerite reached out to squeeze her hand in both of hers. Lorraine squeezed back.

Leonardo nodded. "I believe that is all she wants, for you two to cooperate, and to share what there is to enjoy together. Life is not long; even when you can jump back and forth between events, it does not increase the days you have to spend. Otherwise, I would want to live forever, leaping from year to year, seeing what marvels that men have dreamed. Do not waste the days."

"But she is sending us away, Ser Leonardo," Lorraine said, sadly. "If all we had was two weeks . . . she's making us go before it's up."

He touched his chest with two fingers. "I will advocate for you. I am good at presenting my case before courts nearly as difficult and tough-minded as your mother." He gave them a playful smile. Lorraine understood even more how her mother had fallen in love with him. She found herself halfway there, too. "You have a rare and marvelous opportunity that I can only dream of. I implore you to cooperate, if not for your own sake . . ."

"For hers?" Lorraine asked. She was surprised at how eager she felt. Leonardo smiled.

"No, for mine. Genevieve wants you to return to us once a year. I would hear of the marvels of your time. Will you do that for me, share with me the wonders that will come after this?" He looked from one woman to the other. "You are troubled that she has involved me in her work. But I keep many secrets. Yes, you think that writing mirror-fashion is a poor form of security. Most of that which I do not want known by anyone else I keep up here." He tapped his broad forehead. "I know of the great inventions of the future. I wish I could see them, but it is forbidden to me. I must not be influenced. I understand secrets. This will be a gift to me that I think she was hoping to make. But only with your cooperation. She is so disappointed that you may not return." He looked hopeful, and Lorraine realized that *she* could make a gift to *Leonardo da Vinci*. The thought made her feel humble.

She smiled at him. "How can we say no? I know I'd be honored."

"Me too," Marguerite said.

He sprang to his feet and came to take each of them by the arm.

"Genevieve will be so happy," he said, as he led them back through the corridor toward the squawk of voices and twang of music. "Now, come back to the workshop with me. How brave your mother is to sacrifice all her future life for our ideal. I consider our studio is a place where we transform thought into reality, answerable only to our patrons. Genevieve has explained the modern system to me, and though my way requires bowing and scraping to rich men who do not understand, it is better than shouting at the wall of what she calls faceless corporations. Here, the loss of dignity is temporary, but the science and art we reveal lasts forever. I believe it is better."

Lorraine peered around him to meet Marguerite's eyes. Her sister beamed at her, and she beamed back. It *was* better here.

The rest of the time they spent in Milan was wonderful, in every way. Lorraine had the breathless feeling that they were watching history being made. Leonardo tasked his apprentices to create marvels of contemporary science, tweaking his inventions forward a bit at a time until they worked. When the workmen got the barrel of Leonardo's model gun to spin freely on its axis, they all embraced one another for joy, Lorraine and Marguerite in the midst of a group hug.

With their mother, they visited the court of the duke of Moro. Though they weren't important enough to gain more than a moment of his attention, they were thrilled to see the pageantry of a ducal court in session. And in the evening, when the guests left and they were in private around a fire, Lorraine and Marguerite kept their word, and told stories of the future. Leonardo was as good a listener as a small child, hanging on every word. Beside him, her lap full of needlework, her mother smiled at them all. For the first time since they were small, the girls felt as if they were a whole family. It made Lorraine feel warm and loved. She was satisfied.

Before she knew it, the appointed time was over. Leonardo and his workers heaped them with gifts to take home. Side by side, the sisters packed the fans and hats and scale models into new cases bought for them in the market.

Lorraine was silent through the process, though not out of spite. She had had to come to terms with having a mother who was a part of history, all of it. She must share her, not just with one sister but with the entire world and future generations. The hope for an ideal mother-daughter relationship was gone, but she never really had it. She would have to settle for the one that she had, with which she had grown up, like it or not.

"We can't rewrite history," Marguerite lamented. Lorraine laughed, realizing she had been thinking exactly what her sister had been thinking.

"No," Lorraine said. "We'll write our portion of it." She held out a hand. "At least we have each other."

Marguerite looked at the hand suspiciously, and then her expression softened. "I suppose we do." She took the hand, and, to Lorraine's surprise, squeezed it.

The apprentices carried the cases out to the street where Iskander was waiting in an open carriage. Grinning, they helped the sisters up into the bouncy seats.

Mother came rushing out, her work veil tied tightly around her forehead. She did belong here, Lorraine realized. She never looked so at home in California. "I'm glad I caught you, darlings. I have something I need you to take back with you."

She handed Lorraine a heavy, square bundle. "I don't dare leave it here, darling," she said. "In any case, I know it was never found. If you don't think you can find it a safe place, give it to Rolf. He will take care of it."

Lorraine undid the knotted linen cloth and found a huge book. The binding of the enormous volume had knobbly rungs in it, as if a ladder had been plastered against the spine underneath the leather. The cover itself was made of wood. Inside, a frontispiece showed the two sisters, in their visiting finery. The girls gasped in delight.

"That's by Leonardo," their mother said. "He worked on it from a sketch he made of you one evening. A wonderful gift. An original, darlings, all yours."

Lorraine turned over the heavy parchment leaf and saw page after page of designs, drawings, and Leonardo's inimitable backward writing. The images were familiar: the round-winged helicopter, the mechanical carriage, the boat-hulled submarine, all of Leonardo's most famous inventions. With a shock she realized what she held.

"It's a codex. I've seen a couple in museums. Is this one special for you?" she asked her mother.

"More than that, darling," Mother said with a twinkle. "These are the ones that work. All Leo ever lacked was a power source. I showed him the formulae for internal combustion engines and nuclear engines, and he was so pleased. We bring so many things to each other." She smiled with almost catlike pleasure.

Lorraine felt a slight twinge of the old jealousy. She still didn't like sharing her mother, but if she had to, the most famous inventor and artist of the Renaissance was almost worthy. She hugged the codex to her. "Thank you. We'll treasure it."

"It's a one of a kind book," her mother reminded them with a knowing smile. "You'll have to share."

"I get it first," Marguerite said, immediately.

Had nothing really changed? Lorraine opened her mouth to say that she did. Then she closed it.

"All right," she said, handing her the codex. "Share and share alike."

Marguerite's mouth opened in surprise, and then she grinned, too.

Genevieve stepped back and waved to Iskander to whip up the horse. "See you next year, darlings. Together."

Two Tickets to Paradise

Vicki Steger

Vicki Johnson-Steger lives in Mount Pleasant, Wisconsin, with her husband of twenty-five years and Dave, an ancient cat. She and Dale have three children and four grandchildren. Vicki retired after nearly thirty years as an orthodontic lab technician so she could spend her days writing. Her first story was published in DAW's *Spells of the City*. In her spare time she haunts the magnificent Dinosaur Museum in Kenosha, Wisconsin, and volunteers at a local high school for the production of their yearly musical. A collection of fossils, rocks, and dinosaur bones litters her bookshelves.

Evelyn watched water swirl around the bathroom basin through puffy red eyes as she thought, *there goes my marriage down the drain after all these years.* A quick cell phone call late the previous evening from what sounded like a noisy restaurant let her know he'd be working late and sleeping on the sofa at his downtown law office—again.

Evelyn knew better. This wasn't the first time her husband had strayed. She'd seen the signs develop for

169

months. When she bundled his clothes for the laundry she noticed an unfamiliar scent. The woodsy aroma that clung to his shirt collars was not a fragrance she wore. The late nights, distant demeanor, restlessness and irritability, all signs her husband Peter McAdams was not acting like the man she'd known for most of her adult life. Peter had been working out at a gym on his lunch hours, recently updated his wardrobe, and had his temples darkened by a new hair stylist.

One evening while Evelyn sat alone gripping an empty wine bottle, she wondered how her husband could dismiss her so readily after all their years together. Just yesterday she discovered a shiny Jaguar convertible had taken the place of his silver Mercedes sedan and feared she too was about to be replaced by a younger model. Her hand shook as she opened its door and inhaled the distinctive smell of leather upholstery. Sinking into the sumptuous passenger seat she discovered an exquisite diamond bracelet cradled in a plush velvet box hidden deep inside the glove compartment. Evelyn's face drained of color and she suddenly felt faint. Her heart beat a rapid tattoo when she realized her husband of forty years had chosen this expensive piece of jewelry for someone else.

Evelyn's rage was palpable as she proceeded to her husband's closet. With scissors in hand she angrily snipped the crotch out of every pair of his trousers.

The following morning after her daily morning run along the lakeshore that bordered their exclusive property, she padded to the shower. Feeling refreshed, she emerged, swaddled in a luxurious bath towel, and ran her fingers through tangles of gray hair. From the bedroom windows she glimpsed the landscaper as he carefully tended the sunken rose garden that surrounded her newly constructed glass gazebo.

There on their king-size bed lay Peter's clothes, keys, and belongings. She heard the whooshing sound of water issue from his bathroom. After a quick check to assure her husband was still in the shower she pried his briefcase open. Her hands twitched as she fumbled with the clasp. *I shouldn't do this. There's probably confidential client stuff in here.* Still, Evelyn searched for evidence of the new woman.

She discovered a brochure from Timeshares Travel Agency stowed in the pocket of his briefcase. The strange stiff flyer appeared to be papyrus printed with thick black ink. Under the business name was a tag line: TAKE THE VACATION OF A LIFETIME.

That cheating bastard was taking his new woman on vacation. Her calmness evaporated quicker than the steam from her bathroom mirror. She dug through folders, sending correspondence to swirl around her in a paper storm as she searched for his vacation itinerary. There, under a yellow legal pad, she glimpsed a black state-of-the-art device.

He must've bought one of the new iPhones. She gritted her teeth as she rolled the sleek gadget over in her hand and hastily prodded it to find any concealed photos or text messages that may be secreted inside.

The metallic slam of the shower door startled her as Peter entered their room clad in a towel; his new physique proved the hours at the gym had been well spent. Evelyn glared at her husband, contraption in hand.

"So you bought a new phone. To converse with the new girlfriend, I suppose?"

"Evie, give that to me. It's not what you think." Peter grabbed in her direction.

"So is there a picture of the woman who's been sleeping with my husband in here?"

She held the phone behind her back as Pete lunged

to take it. While battling to keep him from retrieving the phone, she fought an intense urge to punch him square in the mouth.

They wrestled, thrashing about for several minutes on the bed before Peter overwhelmed her and reached the device, unaware it had developed a slight hum and an eerie pale glow.

In a whirl of color and wind they were transported.

The couple rolled onto hard ground as each struggled to catch their breath. Waves of nausea washed over them. An intense pain throbbed at Peter's temples while Evelyn reeled from double vision that made it impossible for her to focus for several minutes.

They lay at the base of a mountain, definitely no longer in Lake Forest. Unable to speak, they stared in bewilderment at their surroundings, then at each other's naked bodies. Somehow in the fury their towels had been swept away and now clung to a prickly bush cactus.

"What the hell happened?" Evelyn wheezed, her green eyes wide with fear.

"Well, um, I," mumbled Peter, "I–I, think we've been transported. But to where and when I, um, I'm not exactly sure. Give me that remote control thing and I'll get us back."

"Back? Back from where? And what does this phone have to do with anything?" Evelyn's voice broke.

"I'll explain everything when we get home, just hand over the transporting device. It's new. The travel agency just started offering them. It has a preprogrammed battery, good for only so many days."

She stood shivering, holding out her empty palms. "I don't have it."

Peter grabbed his wife's wrists, turning her hands over in disbelief before he dropped to his knees and furiously searched the underbrush. Evelyn stomped her bare feet and demanded an explanation.

"Now stay calm, okay? I'll get us back, promise. You need to calm down," Peter implored.

"Don't you tell me what to do, you cheating son-of-a-bitch," she bellowed as her open palm swiftly met his astonished face.

"We just need to find that device so we can return." Peter rubbed his stinging cheek before he returned to feverishly pat the surrounding ground.

Several feet away large bubbles burst to the surface of oozing muck as the travelers' eyes met, reflecting their mutual horror.

"Oh no," they said practically in unison.

Their only means of escape had been gobbled into a bottomless pit of quicksand.

Peter scanned the countryside. "We have to find a higher elevation and weigh our options. And we have to find help."

Miles of tall grass bent under the bitter wind as it howled and swept across the inhospitable plain. Peter grabbed Evelyn's hand to set out for help, but she quickly pulled away. Their pampered unshod feet were soon worn raw from tramping over the rough terrain toward a distant mountain.

The exhausted pair struggled for many hours to reach the summit. Treacherous cliffs surrounded them which were in turn encompassed by a vast, angry ocean. Three raging rivers of white water surged below, cutting off any means of escape. A great distance away a verdant patch appeared like a tiny emerald floating in a sea of rugged brush and sage grass.

Peter and his disgruntled mate, both now bruised and bloody, descended the ragged cliff. They discovered a small cave where they wearily collapsed, grateful to be protected from the unsparing wind that had taken its toll on their delicate skin. Evelyn had never been so hungry or thirsty, and her head threatened to split from a full-blown migraine. Her once manicured hands trembled from fear and caffeine withdrawal as she tugged the towel tighter around her body. She'd never been this miserable in her life, and that included a lengthy session at Bible camp the summer she turned ten—the year her parents divorced.

"You, you need to t–t–tell me what's happened and where the hell we are." Evelyn's teeth chattered from the cold. She crossed her arms as she tried her best to remain calm. Her husband hung his head and felt her penetrating stare as he drew a deep breath.

"I signed up to find the fountain of youth. Going back in time I thought I could return to a younger me, you know, revitalized. On my way to work last week I discovered this unique travel agency that could send me back in time to anywhere and anytime. So I figured why not give it a try. There was supposed to be another session with the travel technician to fine-tune things. The guy left early, had the flu or something, and I took the control that you lost in the muck off his desk. Anyway, I had to reschedule the appointment so I never got all the information. I guess I, um, don't know exactly where we are or what year was chosen."

"You dragged me back maybe hundreds, possibly thousands of years to find a way to grow younger before you left me for another woman? ARE YOU INSANE? Never mind, just get me home!" Evelyn snapped, her red, angry face shook violently, now more from anger than from the cold.

During the next few hours Peter McAdams unburdened himself as his confessions poured over his stunned silent wife. He admitted his discontent and struggles with middle age, his best years gone, life holding more past than future. The affair began innocently enough, borne of boredom. He simply wanted to start over. This time he desired fulfillment, something more than a huge home on the lakeshore, foreign cars, and club memberships to show for his years of hard work to make senior partner at the firm.

"I–I've been thinking a lot lately about, you know, what I missed by not being a father, not leaving a legacy—not having someone remember I was here. I'd really like a son or two before it's too late, or else what have I done this all for?" Peter cast his eyes down to look anywhere but at his shell-shocked wife.

Evelyn sat with her back against the hard stone of the cave, feeling suffocated as her husband's words crashed over her like an endless wave. The damp wall was less chilling than her husband's cold and hurtful confessions. This could not be happening. She felt as if she were viewing someone else's life. For a long time she simply lost the ability to form words.

"Why did you wait all this time to tell me that you had a burning desire to reproduce? You decide when we are in the middle of who-knows-where to bring this up? Couldn't you have mentioned this, oh I don't know, say maybe thirty years ago?" Evelyn spat, feeling like she'd just been smacked with a shovel.

"Well, since you brought it up—I tried to have this discussion with you many times, but you always blew me off. It was never the right time. Your beloved tennis or some charity event came first, or you were too busy remodeling something."

"All right, you cheating bastard, you can have a divorce. In fact, as soon as you get me home I'm calling Jake Perlman. You remember Jake from Princeton, the one I *should* have married. He'll be happy to represent me, and I hear he's single again. You'll be able to tote what's left of your belongings in that little red sports car you're so proud of."

Begrudgingly they huddled together for needed warmth as they shivered under their dingy towels. Evelyn sobbed until rays of morning light pierced the deep blue horizon. Stiffness in their joints caused such discomfort they could barely sit up. Peter sneezed; his sinuses were swollen by the pollen-filled air.

From the stony shelter they searched for anything to stave off the hunger pangs that gripped their stomachs. They sucked the bitter juice from a spiny succulent plant Peter stumbled on while they gathered dry grass for bedding. Terrified, they watched a strange looking pride of lions in the distance and realized that they would serve as a perfect carry-out meal for hungry cats.

"No hard shell to crack and a soft creamy center. We'd make a tasty appetizer for that bunch—even without ketchup," Peter snorted, his stab at brevity lost on his angry wife.

A small herd of woolly mammoths grazed several miles below the cave entrance, unaware their progress along the open savanna was being observed by two horror-stricken humans. What looked like a prehistoric lean tiger stalked a juvenile mammoth that lagged behind the protection of its herd. Its frantic bellow was stifled before the animal's flesh was torn greedily from its bones by long teeth that resembled curved blades and glistened in the sunlight.

Mouths dry, lips cracking, Evelyn and Peter knew if they were to survive they must find sustenance soon. At daybreak, while thick ribbons of fog cloaked the valley, they grudgingly left the security of their cave. Picking their way with care, they descended the rocky cliffs to head toward the spot of green, their only chance for survival.

By some miracle they managed to slip unnoticed by a pack of scruffy, unusual looking wolves. All trace of the previous day's chilly temperature was gone. The warmth of the rising sun drew a flock of giant black vultures. These harbingers of doom circled overhead while the pair pressed on to find shelter.

Peter and Evelyn stopped only when necessary to extract embedded thorns from their painful torn flesh. They steadily trudged toward a magnificent copse of lush trees. They knew they would not last much longer without water and relief from the blazing sun that scorched their burned, peeling skin.

Delirious and exhausted, they crawled under the canopy of an acacia tree and fell into a dreamless sleep. Lacy bits of sunlight dappled their raw skin. Unnoticed, an enormous green serpent unwound itself from a low branch. Its cold, piercing eyes regarded the dozing couple while its red tongue flicked the fragrant moist air.

They woke not knowing how long they'd slept, startled to find a young man and woman standing over them. Delighted at the sight of humans, they were surprised to see that the couple was naked, and unabashedly so. The beautiful woman's knee length hair cascaded around her in thick black swirls. The man's muscular tanned body could have been the model for Michelangelo's *David,* complete with dazzling blue eyes. The pair reached to draw the weary travelers to their feet. The woman applied thick liquid from the pulp of a nearby plant to their festering wounds. Almost instantly their deep cuts and bruises healed, and they gratefully followed their rescuers.

They reached a hut sturdily constructed of bamboo,

surrounded by huge leaves and palm fronds the size of tennis rackets. The warm breeze carried a spicy scent as they entered. The walls were resplendent, vines bursting with vibrant blooms that trailed inside, completely camouflaging the structure.

The young hostess held out a basket of luscious fruit that Peter and his wife greedily consumed, not concerned by the sticky juice that streamed down their chins. Their host split a large smooth coconut and offered their guests a drink. Later he arranged thick mats of woven palms for the approaching nightfall.

The four woke to the soft rhythmic thumps of generous raindrops and raucous screeches of birds mingled with the chatters of monkey conversation. A chorus of frogs joined in.

Peter noticed their hut mates communicated through a series of nods and smiles, as though connected in a way that made speech unnecessary.

"I'm Peter and this is Evelyn." Peter spoke slowly and deliberately, taking turns pointing to himself and his wife. He tried to coax names from the other couple, who gave him curious looks before he realized if they were the only two humans in this place, names were not needed. However, they appeared interested when Peter spoke and were eager to learn this form of communication.

Under Peter's tutelage, they mastered words and phrases at such a rapid rate that scarcely a week had passed when they were nearly as fluent as Peter and Evelyn.

The pair reciprocated and introduced the new arrivals to the benefits of warm mineral pools, showers under cascading waterfalls, and taught them where to find food and springs of pure, delicious water.

It was paradise, Evelyn thought. *Almost.*

Several days later Peter and Evelyn followed their

hosts to the entrance of a beautiful sanctuary in the middle of the garden. A stream of scintillating pale blue light surrounded a magnificent ancient tree.

"Forbidden," the man said. "This place is ..." He searched for one of the words Peter had taught him. "Hallowed." He explained that the fruit was off limits, too, even though it dangled seductively from every branch of a particularly beguiling tree. "The knowledge of the universe is in the branches. Forbidden."

Evelyn got the gist that to enter this sacred space and pluck from the tree would surely unleash dreadful retribution.

Time played out differently here as it seemed to flow in circles instead of the measured march toward a plotted destination. Every new day brought incredible things to discover within the overwhelming beauty of this enchanted region. There was an abundance of serene wildlife, and the creatures showed no fear of humans.

The absence of mosquitoes, biting flies, and other airborne annoyances that plagued them back home convinced Peter to cast his towel aside and embrace the nudist lifestyle. Peter noticed a renewed surge of vigor and stamina he'd not known since his carefree days of childhood, and his hair had grown thick and dark.

While he was having the time of his life, Evelyn sank into despair. She wondered if Peter would choose to stay behind should rescue come. Surely someone from the travel agency would come looking for them.

Paradise? Almost, but not quite. She craved her pomegranate martini lunches with friends, neighborhood gossip, morning beach runs, tennis, and clothes. She'd give anything to trade in her tattered towel for a sporty tennis outfit, and she longed for the companionship of her well-connected friends. Marnie, her friend and doubles partner, must be wondering why she'd been absent from their tennis tournament. Surely Marnie would launch an investigation to find her.

The police will be alerted, Evelyn thought.

Her mood lightened as she realized the authorities would certainly question neighbors, Peter's coworkers, club members, and anyone who knew them. They were bound to discover a large sum of money Peter had paid to Timeshares Travel Agency, the last people to have contact with Peter before he disappeared. The travel agency must have a way to retrieve those trapped in another time without a transporting device.

After all, they were liable for this epic screwup, and their business was bound to suffer if they "lost" customers.

While Evelyn contemplated her plight, she heard the soft throaty call of an exquisite heron that was wading in the reeds in search of a mate. Iridescent dragonflies skimmed the surface of the clear water where Evelyn knelt for a drink. Absorbed in self pity, she splashed water on her tear-stained face and was astonished by her young reflection.

The crow's feet and creases had vanished, and her short spiky gray hair was the color of glowing copper. She felt her lithe, thin body burst with the energy of a teenager. The road map of blue spider veins on her thighs had vanished. She peered once more into the water, not believing her eyes.

Maybe it wasn't too late to save their marriage! Surely Peter had noticed her transformation.

What Peter had noticed was the other female.

Pain seared Evelyn's heart as she observed him stealing glances at the beautiful young woman who was unaware of being watched.

Peter no longer seemed interested in returning home. In fact, he had grown accustomed to the quiet splendor of this sequestered place.

Early one morning while sitting under a coconut palm, Evelyn decided that when rescuers came, she would leave him here. This would save her the cost and humiliation of a sensational divorce. She'd simply tell friends that Peter was working overseas for an extended period, which could buy her time to plan a plausible story for his disappearance.

As the tension mounted between her and Peter, Evelyn noticed that the other woman was growing quite irritable toward her man. Busy brooding about the state of her life, Evelyn failed to notice the kind, handsome, seemingly flawless man who stole glimpses of her whenever possible.

While Evelyn gathered figs and mushrooms one day in a shady glen, she discovered Peter and the other woman; a crystal pond reflected them hand-in-hand and deep in whispered conversation. Evelyn crept closer to hear her husband regaling his enthusiastic subject with tales of Chicago and all its wonders.

You'd think he was the most powerful man in the world the way he's going on, thought his furious wife. It sickened Evelyn to see the simpering female hang on every word uttered by that philandering old goat.

Her stomach churned as she listened to Peter. He promised his new trophy it would be no time at all before he had them back in Lake Forest. His new woman sat spellbound by the incredible places he described—theaters, restaurants, yachts, as well as maids and room service. Their new life together would be completed by a couple of children to fill the immense lakeshore home.

Evelyn's fingers closed around a rock. *One swift blow to the temple ought to do it,* she thought. *One blow, and . . . wait. If Peter is talking about Chicago, he must have found a way to get back home.* And it was evident he planned to take his new conquest back with him while he left his wife behind.

Evelyn had planned to leave Peter here when the Timeshares folks finally showed up. Now it seemed Peter had a similar idea.

Evelyn's mind spun. If she wanted to be rescued she would have to stalk the two from the shadows to stay close. If the other woman returned with them, so be it. *Out with the old and in with the new, huh? Let her spend a Chicago winter in that outfit*, Evelyn mused.

She quietly pursued them, creeping along at a generous distance until night fell. It seemed like hours before the two stopped to curl into each other's arms under the protection of a sprawling tree.

Bone tired, Evelyn crouched behind a nearby thicket, worried that Peter suspected he was being trailed. He had periodically stopped suddenly to look behind him. She clapped her hand over her mouth to stifle a scream as the smooth scales of something long slithered across her bare ankle. A snake? She looked, but couldn't see it. Eventually, the distant rhythm of her husband's measured snores lulled her to sleep.

Evelyn woke, encapsulated in the gray mist that hung heavy as damp gauze. To her horror, Peter had vanished—along with his prize. She frantically retraced her steps to the crystal pool, terrified they would leave without her.

The earth quaked beneath her feet and thunder boomed, nearly felling her. Was the nearby mountain about to explode? The morning sky darkened and a deathly silence closed around her. Birdsong, animal chatter, croaks—all the natural sounds she'd grown used to hearing were replaced by an ominous, eerie stillness. She shuddered as a chill wove its way up her spine.

Suddenly Evelyn knew where her husband had gone.

She raced toward the middle of the garden, practically running into the abandoned man who pounded up beside her. They halted before a barrier of thick blue flames that surrounded the forbidden tree. Evelyn could barely see Peter and his new woman through the blue light.

Shards of white-hot lightening burst from the sky while Peter and his woman shook behind two leaves the size of elephant ears. A golden piece of fruit lay at their feet, bearing two sets of bite marks. A heartbeat later, the couple vanished.

The flames disappeared, and in their place stood a radiant angel brandishing a flaming sword.

"The violators have been banished from paradise!" the angel announced. Then he, too, was gone.

Evelyn felt a soft touch on her bare shoulder.

She turned to meet the kind sapphire eyes of the man left behind. Held by his magnificent gaze, she felt their unexpected connection and instantly realized everything that had been missing from her life.

Evelyn no longer yearned for status that came from club presidencies and committee memberships, vacations to Monaco or cruises on expensive yachts.

In that moment she glimpsed her future with him and quickly bid farewell to her former life—along with her towel.

Tenderly, hand-in-hand, they made their way back to his hut.

After a delicious breakfast of fresh papaya and fish grilled over coconut shells, Evelyn studied the place and pondered how best to remodel it while her new mate sought a way to permanently rid paradise of that damn snake.

The World of Null-T

Gene DeWeese

Author of forty science fiction, mystery, and fantasy novels, Gene DeWeese was, once upon a time, a technical writer who wrote manuals for B-52 navigation systems and "intuitive" programmed instruction texts on orbital mechanics for NASA's Apollo program. He's lived in Milwaukee the past forty-seven years with his multitasking wife Beverly and assorted single-minded cats. His most recent books are a *Star Trek* novel, *Engines of Destiny*, and a small-town-sheriff mystery, *Murder in the Blood*.

The memory is not the event—not even close!

Function without appropriate form is inefficient, but form without appropriate function is not only useless but an insult to the customer.

—Anonymous know-it-all

In the Timeshares Era, there's no such thing as a middle ground position when it comes to being a Chrono-Cop. It's either the most important or the most useless job on Earth. Any ChronoCop will tell you we're unsung heroes whose battered fingers are figuratively plugging endless holes in the leaky dykes of Time. The ChronoCorps, they say, is all that stands between Earth and a ChronoTsunami. Just don't press us too hard for precise definitions of terms, which are slippery at best even when Time is a constant, let alone the variable to end all variables.

On the other hand, if you ask one of the Timeshares people (we're *assuming* they're people) you'll be told with a wink or a sneer that the ChronoCorps is nothing but a collection of feather-bedding Chicken Littles no better than those despicable but imaginative twentieth-century scammers who managed to sell "gravity insurance" to some gullible flat-earthers (is there any other kind?) when the early artificial satellite photos began suggesting, even to them, that the world just might really be round after all.

As for what we ChronoCops thought of the Timeshares people, suffice it to say that the recruiting requirements include a firm belief in Murphy's Law, which means whenever anyone tells us "nothing can possibly go wrong," we assume they're either lying or are so arrogantly overconfident they shouldn't be trusted with sharp objects, let alone the ability to time-hop pretty much at will.

And then there's the Matiolin Society.

Maybe.

No one knows *what* to think of *them*. For all the hard evidence we have (zero), we can't even prove they exist, and the "name" is nothing more than what our computers tell us are the most-often-produced set of sounds in the one and only static-filled "message" they sent. No one's ever even seen a society member, only their building, which "appeared" not long after—or maybe just before—the Timeshares people's flickering convoy parked in a twenty-four-hour orbit and began beaming down everything we'd need to get started in the time-travel business. A sort of time-travel kit, some assembly required.

Anyway, somewhere in there, the Matiolin Society building appeared, not in orbit but hovering a few feet off the ground right next to the ChronoCorps HQ.

And that was it. They/It didn't offer an opinion either way on ChronoCops. Or the Timeshares people. It just hovered, looking sort of like a gigantic misplaced crystalline Christmas tree ornament, and waited.

Or watched. Or reviewed their notes from their last stop.

Or took long naps. Like I said, nobody had a clue.

Those of us in the ChronoCorps hoped there was some significance to the fact that the Matiolins had parked next to our HQ, not the other guys'. We could only hope it was for the right reason—they'd be close enough to help or save us if/when the Murphy's Law poster boys did something both stupid and dangerous. And believe me, under the Timeshares "rules" that were included in every kit they shipped down, there was room for way more than enough trouble to go around.

See, the official and happy-making line touted by the Timeshares people goes like this: Time is the ultimate elastic, and nothing a traveler can do will keep the timeline—the *real, core* timeline—from being dragged, perhaps with a little figurative kicking and screaming, back to where it belongs before any "real" damage can be done. Therefore, say the experts in charge of soothing analogies, you don't have to worry about the infamous butterfly that flaps its dusty wings in China and causes a hurricane somewhere around Cuba, half a world and a couple centuries away. What you have instead is more like an elephant jumping on an industrial strength trampoline in your backyard. He bounces a few times, maybe rattles a couple teacups in the upper reaches of your china cabinet before getting bored and wandering off, leaving Time to heal itself, which it does by repositioning the rattled teacups a millimeter or so from their original place, which takes it a couple microseconds and is never even noticed.

But, say the few remaining scientists not on the Timeshares payroll, if the changes are large enough and complicated enough, then all bets are off.

Anything can happen.

Like Time Knots.

"Anecdotal and unproven," say the Timeshares people. "They're the Timeshares Era equivalent of UFOs, and you know how real *they* turned out to be."

"Anecdotal but inevitable," say the ChronoCorps theorists. With the Timeshares people's No-Fault-No-Limits approach to time travel, you don't need Murphy's Law to know there are going to be tangles in the timelines, and some will get so bad they can't be untangled.

Which is usually when one side or the other will cite the so-called Hitler episode, when everybody and his third cousin twice removed suddenly decided it would be a great idea to go back and kill Hitler, only to discover that a similar number of skinheads were already back there providing him with a lifetime supply of disposable bodyguards. In the resulting tornado of successful, unsuccessful, and semi-successful assassinations, every assassin and every bodyguard was killed at least once, Hitler hundreds of times, along with a bunch of innocent bystanders. Each incident, no matter the outcome, generated its own little time thread that added to the tangle.

All of which turned out to be a remarkable piece of good luck according to the pseudomemories that soon

began surfacing in the minds of the not-quite assassins—
the ones who had changed their minds at the last minute
and decided to stay home. Each time Hitler was success-
fully disposed of, these pseudomemories said, he was invariably replaced by a more pragmatic, less wacked out
version who got rid of Von Braun and redirected the scientist's rocket money to the Luftwaffe, which prolonged
the war by several years and left the postwar U.S. Von
Braunless and without a space program. The pseudomemories themselves continued to surface, albeit with rapidly
decreasing intensity, until it seemed that everyone who
had so much as dreamed about participating in the assassination had their own little packet of pseudomemories that quickly and seamlessly merged with their "real"
memories until the two were virtually indistinguishable.

The Timeshares people and ChronoCops of course
put their own separate spins on the incident. We kill-
joy ChronoCops insisted that the important lesson
to be learned was that Time Knots were not only real
but would, if limits weren't imposed, become both frequent and inevitable. Some of our theorists even went
so far as to say that if a knot grew big enough, it could
reach some sort of critical mass, at which point it would
start expanding on its own, like a nuclear chain reaction. It could, they warned, become unstoppable and, for
want of a better term, freeze time itself into one huge,
universe-size Time Knot.

The Timeshares people, on the other hand, only
scoffed at this "unfounded Chicken Little thinking" and
reminded everyone that while the United States had
been developing the first atomic bomb, one of the program's Nervous Nelly scientists had gone completely off
the rails and ran around warning that the bomb might
trigger a chain reaction in the atmosphere and wipe out
life on Earth. Luckily no one had paid him any atten-

tion, and the Timeshares people, never inclined to pass up an opportunity, soon began claiming loudly that the whole Hitler episode was, in fact, incontrovertible proof of what they'd been saying all along: *Time could and did repair itself spontaneously no matter how much travelers changed things.*

The pseudomemories, they cheerfully explained/improvised, were in fact real memories of what had happened in the depths of the time knot, and they were now being released as the so-called Time Knot itself unraveled (decayed?) and vanished, leaving the timeline unchanged except for the presence of a bunch of memories of things that hadn't really happened and therefore weren't even relevant to the real world.

You shouldn't have any trouble guessing which side won the propaganda war. Suffice it to say that within a few weeks, historical event markers everywhere began being papered over with suggestions as to how your average ChronoTourist could change the outcomes of those events. Ever wonder what kind of president Custer would've made? Head for Little Big Horn and give him a little extra firepower and find out. Or if you wondered how many terms FDR might've had if he'd been Time-napped from, say, January 1945 and taken to a twenty-second-century surgical center for umpteen bypasses and as many other repairs as they might find were possible?

Then, when all the changes were made, you could hire a camera crew and record the results of your changes. FDR, for instance, got two more terms and turned down a slam dunk for a third, and Custer became the first and only president to not only be impeached but also convicted. The video of his trial, especially the Crazy Horse testimony, easily beat OJ's long-ago adjusted-for-media-inflation ratings numbers, and the rest was history, of a sort. You think reality shows were popular back in the olden/golden days? Try alternate reality shows.

At one time there were fifteen networks devoted to cranking out nothing else. Even the sporadic wink-and-a-nod oversight the Timeshares people had once provided vanished, as did larger and larger chunks of the ChronoCorps budget. If it weren't for private donations of all sorts from all sources, legal and illegal, we would've gone entirely out of existence.

And no one would've noticed.

I even began hoping that the Timeshares people were right after all when they claimed that Time was virtually indestructible. If it wasn't, something was bound to seriously bite us on the ass sooner or later. A runaway Time Knot that ate the universe, maybe—or at least a galaxy or two.

Or something no theorist had thought of, like the ChronoEquivalent of metal fatigue. After the millionth or billionth Stretch and Snap Back excursion, the super-elastic fabric of Time itself would get fed up and rebel. "Screw it!" it would shout. "I wasn't designed for the sort of aggravation you morons are putting me through!"

And Time would let go and turn to powder. Or molasses.

How'd you like *that*? Or maybe it would reset into another, slightly less grandiloquent Big Bang and tweak a few of the emerging natural laws in hopes of getting some less goofy life-forms next time around.

All of which was interesting, at least to me, but utterly useless.

As was everything else I'd thought about since the whole world had gone time-travel nuts. I mean, what could I possibly do that could have an effect, either good or bad? True, I could travel through time and space and do anything I wanted, but so could everyone else, and if you tried the one thing that might help—getting rid of time machines altogether—there'd be a thousand other travelers determined to stop me. Like the Hitler episode only way bigger.

But then, one day, my phone jangled loudly even though I was certain I'd turned it off long ago.

When I fumbled it out of my pocket and put it to my ear, an early-model Hawking Voice said, "Check your other pocket."

Frowning, I looked around.

"Your other pocket," the Hawking voice repeated, "not your surroundings. You don't have a lot of time."

I let myself shiver for a moment. "To do what?" I asked.

"To check your pocket and look at what you find there."

I almost said, "But there's nothing there," but realized I would be lying. There was something there.

Now.

I could feel it moving.

"See?" the Hawking voice said.

Pointlessly, I braced myself and reached into the indicated pocket. And came out with a foldable sheet of digital paper. It must have been down to its standard one-inch square storage mode when I'd first realized it was there. The motion I'd felt had been its efforts to unfold itself.

Now, freed from its pocket prison, it snapped open like a spring-loaded umbrella. There were no words on the paper, no instructions on what to do next, only a single, constantly morphing image made up of several shades of red so similar to each other that the entire sheet seemed to be in deep shadow.

A shadow I instinctively knew I did not want to penetrate.

Except, I realized, I *had* penetrated it, not once but many times.

I could remember it vividly, positively. Just as I could also remember with absolute certainty that I had *not* ever seen it. None of which should have been surprising since Time had been converted into multilevel Swiss cheese.

"Now, now, Eldred," said the Hawking Voice. "You're resisting."

I froze, realizing where I must be: In a massive Time Knot, trying to referee the countless pseudomemories that were assaulting my mind more harshly than ever before.

"Just relax," the Hawking Voice said, "Let the Knot sort itself out. This is what it was made for."

A Time Knot? Made on purpose? I shook my head, or at least I tried. Truth be told, I had no idea if my head was moving or not.

Or if it even existed outside my own imagination anymore.

"Don't concern yourself with trivia, Eldred," the Hawking voice said, beginning to sound more natural. "I won't let anything happen to you. Just relax and go with the flow."

Easy for him to say. His head didn't feel like someone had drilled a hole in his skull and was tamping the pseudomemories into it at a fearsome rate.

Then I began to remember things—which is very different from being on the receiving end of a painful torrent of images and sounds and thoughts—none of which had anything whatsoever to do with me. Except for this one little snippet: The current scenario was ending, it said, and the results were being compiled.

In my head.

Except I didn't remember having one.

I closed and opened my unseen eyes a few times and was relieved to discover that they really did exist.

And not just two. There were billions of them, each reading and storing a separate stream of data. In the head that, milliseconds ago, hadn't even existed.

The head that *was* the Matiolin building.

"Good going, Eldred. You feel better now?"

I nodded, ignoring the sparks that were still stabbing randomly at what passed for my synapses these days.

And I did feel better. The roar of the data stream was still there, but all it gave me was a mild headache.

And even that would soon be over.

As soon as the data transfer was complete, I could begin the analysis. This time the process should be far quicker than last time. For one thing, the Scenario's complexity index had been lowered by a factor of two, but it still encompassed thousands of years and countless more timelines of all lengths.

Abruptly I switched to the search functions which, as usual, I hadn't known I had until I realized I needed them. The detailed analysis could wait. The cursory analysis the search function could provide would give me all the information I really wanted right now: Had this scenario, like all those that had come before, succumbed to the Styrofoam Syndrome?

"I take it you're ready to go, Eldred?" The Hawking Voice sounded almost human now.

As expected, it didn't take long to skim the timelines and snag the pertinent data. The only surprise was the disappearance of New Coke. Instead of digging in their heels, this last scenario's decision makers had given in to plummeting sales and consumer complaints and decided it was pointless to continue to resist. After all, they made the same profits no matter which label they used.

Unfortunately, the same good sense was not applied

to the one problem that had helped to shoot down every scenario so far: the Styrofoam Syndrome.

In all other respects, the scenarios were typical. Similar amounts of violence and altruism, of cruelty and kindness. Similar streaks of insanity and brilliance, often in the same individual or group.

But sooner or later, the Styrofoam Syndrome always strikes. People in those scenarios begin defying common sense in any activity having to do with tomatoes, and we daren't release them into the general, forward-moving population for fear that this remarkable behavior would spread to other areas.

And it's always the same. At some point, one or more of the growers invariably seem to forget that the primary function of a tomato is to taste good, and they start making them prettier to attract customers' attention and begin making them firmer so they're easier to ship. They are of course violating one of their primary rules: that any successful operation must be one in which form follows function, not the other way around. I mean, what good is a tomato that can be shipped across the country without a single unsightly blemish but tastes like Styrofoam?

Once that point is reached, it's all over. The Syndrome is self-sustaining. As sales drop, fewer and fewer tomatoes are grown in the ground, and even fewer are grown in the kind of ground that produces good flavor, largely because by then no one believes the type of ground makes a difference. With growers interested only in shipability and experts blathering about appearance, real tomatoes are gone. Within another century, no one would recognize the taste of a real tomato, and they've gone from being the most delicious of vegetables to being a fading part of folklore.

Sadly, I made a few last minute changes to the waiting scenario and activated the Reset.

As the new scenario enveloped me, I could hear the Hawking Voice sigh.

"Good luck, Eldred," it said. "Try to get it right this time."

Bruck in Time

Patrick McGilligan

Patrick McGilligan has been a senior editor of the *Dragonlance* series of novels for nearly twenty-five years. He has written numerous books about motion pictures including, most recently, *Oscar Micheaux: The Great and Only*, a biography of the pioneering African American novelist and filmmaker.

The sound of gunfire zinged all around Bruck as he splashed across the knee-deep shallows, pretending to be heavily burdened by the pack he was carrying on his back. It wasn't heavy at all. He toted some kind of weapon that was jammed or broken or something. Again and again he pointed it at the enemy on the opposite bank, and every once in a while one of the blue suits fell over—but it wasn't because of his weapon, which only made bang noises and fired puffs of smoke.

Everyone shouted and screamed—nothing distinct or intelligible—it was all one loud roar punctuated by gunfire and cannon explosions. Bruck waved his useless weapon in the air excitedly, yelling "Double knuckles!" for some reason he couldn't explain, when he accidentally swung his rifle into the face of the gray suit galloping through the water next to him, knocking him into a daze. The soldier sank to his knees before pitching forward with his eyes rolling up.

Bruck plunged ahead in seeming slow motion, blood spattering him from all around and running dark red in the water. He slipped on some rocks that were bloodslick. But none of it was his blood. He was unhurt and in fact barely winded as he reached the opposite shore, and, joined by a mass of others close around him, slammed into a wall of blue suits, cursing and punching and grappling.

Many gray suits stumbled back into the water with long gleaming blades stuck through their bodies. The soldier running closest to him suddenly clutched his head, dropping his bugle. He was very young, like most of the soldiers. Bruck caught a glimpse of the soldier's face clamped under a gray cap—startled blue eyes, lanky blond hair. The soldier careened away, head spurting blood. Bruck had a curious flash; he recognized the blond soldier as one who had died yesterday too.

Now the bullet zinging and cannonfire faded into the distance, replaced by loud clanging swords and the close clash of grunting and wheezing bodies. The yelling had almost died out. Epithets and groans were more common. Across a brown field the gray and blue armies met and mingled and fought against each other in a furious commotion. The air was filled with smoke and dust.

A veteran mercenary, Bruck felt his bloodlust stir as he swung his empty rifle like a sword, effectively clearing a path before him as a wide-eyed enemy lurched aside rather than face a seeming berserker. Bruck sniffed the air joyously, frowning to realize that although surrounded by dead and dying he missed a familiar scent.

The smell of death.

That was about a minute before the battle and everything else stopped.

If only he could remember. He was a fighter, he remembered that much, a damn good fighter who had fought in hundreds of battles. The details escaped him. The memories seeped away. Well, memories didn't mean much to soldiers anyway. If a soldier lives long enough for memories, the saying went, he's lived too long.

In his time, which was long ago and somewhere else, he would sign on for any campaign, any war, any fight, if paid in good coin. He had even fought, on occasion, without payment of any kind, because fighting is what he did and sometimes the fight was more interesting than the pay. Sometimes he just didn't care about the pay.

He was best at fighting with his knife and his sword. That certainly felt like the truth of what he remembered. But he was also growing accustomed to new and unusual weapons.

The last thing he remembered plainly was he had been drinking in his favorite tavern, the Bull's Bollocks. The place was crowded with rowdy patrons, shouting and laughing and singing. Bruck had been drinking at a table alone for some time, watching the chaos and merriment swirling around him with increasingly glazed eyes. People tended to give him a wide berth, noting his bare muscled arms, the weapons slung at his waist, and the apparent glowering expression on his face.

In fact, Bruck was in a buoyant mood. He had been paid well for a raiding party across the border just last week. Someone had to be taught a lesson. Bruck and other mercenaries had torched a barn and house. A foolish man had come running out of the burning barn, waving a knife. He ran straight into Bruck's sword.

The sour mead came in huge bubbling pitchers at the

Bull's Bollocks, and the serving girl knew to keep them coming. Bruck was on his sixth or seventh pitcher when the tall barrel-chested stranger came over and asked if he would care to join him as his partner at the gaming table. Bruck didn't mind at all—indeed he liked the fact that the tall barrel-chested stranger had picked him out of the crowd in such a friendly fashion. He took to the stranger right away for some reason, as though they were kindred warriors. Something about the way the fellow winked at him every time he said something, but also just spoke with his eyes when he wasn't saying anything at all, like they were old friends in on a conspiracy.

The stranger, who was dressed in peculiar clothes that were soft and formfitting, brought Bruck to a gaming table in the back where a pair of men waited.

They looked to be brothers. The one Bruck took to be the younger had narrow eyes and a pockmarked face. He nodded suspiciously at the newcomer. The older brother had curly red hair and a bristly beard the same hue; he glared at Bruck, making an impatient gesture. Bruck took his weapons off and sat down.

The three had been drinking and playing games for hours. The tall barrel-chested stranger said he had been winning steadily. But his previous partner had quit and gone home to his wife. Bruck ordered a round of pitchers, and they opened up a new game.

Bruck remembered all of that, and the tall barrel-chested stranger winking at him as they started up the game, and the brother with red curly hair and bristly beard still glaring at him.

That was how many days . . . weeks . . . months ago?

Funny how often the battles were between blue and gray suits. The first time Bruck had fought on the side of the blue suits, and then a month or so later he had

Patrick McGilligan

worn a gray suit. Only about a week ago he found himself outfitted for action in a blue suit, and just yesterday there he was, yet again, charging across the river in his gray suit.

Gray suits, blue suits. It didn't matter to him what uniform he wore.

Different types of fighting each time, of course. Climbing hills. Slogging through swampy forests. Little hand-to-hand skirmishes. Big sprawling noisy battles.

Gray, blue. Didn't matter.

Bruck was brooding over a beer as he sat, people watching with the Marquis in the Bar None. The place was loud with electrified music and crowded with folk jumping up and down and wiggling rhythmically. It maybe was Bruck's tenth beer. Piss weak beer, and it came in so many types and colors he couldn't keep track of the choices. He sure did miss The Bull's Bollocks, as much as he could recall of it anyway.

This was the Marquis' favorite place. The Marquis was not a real marquis, but that was the name he used when introducing himself to women at the Bar None. Bruck stared at the Marquis, who was staring at some of the dancing women, his eyes riveted. The Marquis liked to boast about all the wars and battles he had fought in, and women liked to listen. He had the look of a fighter, strong and tough like the tall barrel-chested stranger, but it was mainly a look.

Bruck recognized the fact that the Marquis was a pretend fighter, not a real one like himself. That was okay; the Marquis was his friend, his only friend.

In a fight or a battle the Marquis needed Bruck to watch his back, though he pretended he didn't. Bruck always tried to fight on the same side as the Marquis and as near to him as possible, though it didn't always work out that way.

The Marquis needed Bruck, and Bruck needed the Marquis too. The Marquis explained things to Bruck he wouldn't have understood otherwise. And the Marquis was the only other person who knew about Nestor— the tall barrel-chested stranger. Bruck always forgot the tall, barrel-chested stranger's name unless the Marquis was around, saying stuff like, "Just you be patient, little buddy. Pretty soon Nestor will be back ..."

Funny, the Marquis calling him "little buddy" when the Marquis was a short, solid guy and Bruck was maybe an inch or two taller than him. Always winking, though, just like his friend Nestor, the tall barrel-chested stranger.

The Marquis got up from the table, swaggering away toward a dancing girl with braids, throwing a wink over his shoulder at Bruck. One night the Marquis got into a heated shoving match with a brawny lout, and Bruck had to step in and shoulder the Marquis aside. The brawny lout took a swing at Bruck, and Bruck ducked under the fist and slammed his head into the lout's stomach so hard the guy crumpled on the spot. The other people in the bar applauded. The Marquis winked and grinned.

"Thanks, little buddy."

A waitress came by with another beer. Bruck disconsolately handed her his empty. Looking across the room, he saw the braided-haired girl feeling the Marquis' muscles, giggling.

He didn't have the heart to tell the Marquis. Bruck wasn't sure exactly what he knew or remembered anymore, but one thing he was pretty sure of was Nestor would not be coming back soon.

Bruck took a long, slow drink of his beer, nearly draining the tall glass, still straining to remember. He patted his pocket—something valuable in there, he dimly recalled. His thoughts were cloudier and cloudier.

He signaled for another beer. He drank too much these days, always drinking when he wasn't fighting.

Staring across the room he thought he caught a glimpse of a man with curly red hair and a bristly beard, but then people shifted around and the man melted into the crowd. Or was he imagining things?

The waitress brought him another foaming beer. He looked around for the Marquis, but his friend too had melted into the loud, smelly, shouting, dancing crowd.

At night he dreamed of playing double knuckles with the tall barrel-chested stranger against the two brothers, one younger with narrow eyes and a pockmarked face, the older one with curly red hair and a bristly red beard.

The game had been going on for hours. It was long after midnight, and the tavern had all but emptied. The only people left were the four players, the proprietor who sat on a stool behind them watching stoically, a groggy serving girl with her arm stretched around the proprietor, and two or three die-hard regulars who stared with goggle eyes as the pile of coins rose higher than ever before at the Bull's Bullocks.

There were hundreds and hundreds of coins in the pot. Bruck had wagered more of his earnings than was wise, and several times he had been tempted to fold his cards and walk away. But he was still enjoying himself, and each time he had been tempted to quit, the tall barrel-chested stranger had winked at him and he had stayed.

He was a fighter, not a gamesman, but the tall, barrel-chested stranger proved very, very good at double knuckles, and the brothers were losing and falling farther and farther behind. The young brother grew even more silent and peevish, while the red-haired and -bearded one glowered nastily as, finally, he emptied his pockets and pushed his last few coins into the center of the table.

The tall barrel-chested stranger seemed to savor the drama of it all. He hesitated before he reached into his purse and found the right number of coins, flipping them carelessly onto the pile before reaching for his final card.

Bruck and the younger brother played their hands. The unremarkable result made the serving girl yawn. The two looked to their partners for the climax.

The red-haired bristly-bearded brother defiantly slapped his cards down, a smirk on his face. For a moment the tall barrel-chested stranger looked surprised, then winking at Bruck, he gracefully spread his cards to show a hand that vanquished his opponent's.

Even before the grin on Bruck's face had started to widen, the place exploded. The younger brother shouted an epithet and stretched a long arm across the table toward the coins. Bruck reacted in a blur, reaching down and grabbing a long knife from his cache of weapons on the floor and bringing the blade up and down in one fluid whirl, plunging it hard into the table and cleanly slicing off the man's outstretch hand.

The hand appeared to scuttle away and slide off the table as the younger brother screamed and fell back from the table. But then, with a sick feeling, Bruck realized the brother's screams were mixing with the loud groans of the tall barrel-chested stranger, who had been knocked back in his chair by a thick dirk hurled by the older brother. The blade was stuck in the broad target of his barrel chest. Bruck quickly found his sword and stood, waving his weapon in the air, anxious to avenge his partner.

There was no more opportunity for violence, however. The red-haired bristly-bearded brother had draped his arms around his shrieking brother and, with a baleful look over his shoulders, dragged him and his bloody stump away. The proprietor and handful of observers shrank into the shadows. From somewhere in the room, Bruck could hear the servant girl sobbing. Perhaps, he thought, she'd been sweet on the pockmarked loser, who was now bleeding grievously.

The tall barrel-chested stranger was still alive and strong enough to reach down and yank the dirk out of his chest and toss it on the floor contemptuously. The effort took a lot out of him, though. He gestured weakly to Bruck, who swept the mountain of coins into a sack and then scurried around the table to catch his partner just as he began to slump to the ground. The tall, barrel-chested stranger whose name was Nestor—yes, Nestor, Bruck recalled—pointed to a narrow stairway at the rear of the room, and Bruck half walked, half carried Nestor upstairs, blood wetting both their clothes.

Inside a small sparse room was a pallet, a wooden chair, and a dressing table with a mirror. Bruck helped Nestor to the pallet. Nestor refused to lie down, instead sitting with his legs outstretched, his head propped against the wall, still winking and chuckling despite his wound and shallow breathing.

"I've seen worse," grunted Bruck, after examining the wound, and it was true—he had. But this wound was bad enough that it might kill Nestor if not treated. Bruck would make sure Nestor was settled and comfortable, he wanted to check the winnings, and then he would go and bring a doctor.

Spotting a small flask on the dressing table, Bruck took a sip of foul liquor and handed it over to Nestor, who drank from it several times until it was emptied and he tossed it on the floor, laughing. First things first: As Nestor watched him with glittering eyes, Bruck dumped out the coins and counted them, dividing the haul into two piles.

Whether because of how much he had drank or the shock of his wound, Nestor was beginning to babble. Bruck, almost done, wasn't listening closely, and Nestor, still laughing, raised his voice insistently. Clutching his bleeding wound with one hand Nestor dug through his pockets with the other and, after arduous effort, produced a rolled parchment and a polished triangle of stone that he thrust at Bruck, urging him to pay attention.

Rising from the floor, Bruck deposited his share of the coins in his sack and put Nestor's in his purse, which he tossed onto the pallet next to the wounded man. He then sat down at the dressing table, staring at the two items he held in his hand and listening to Nestor's babble.

The stone triangle had a row of numbers along one edge that changed as Bruck rotated them with his thumb. As Nestor called out numbers in a precise order, Bruck rotated the numbers one by one into the sequence being urgently dictated by his wounded partner.

Slumped against the wall, his bleeding still copious, Nestor talked nonsense about fighting good fights and traveling through time. Yes, fighting and traveling through time—that was the strange thing that he kept saying.

This was the best trip ever, Nestor said.

Bruck listened more carefully now, fingering the numbers on the stone triangle, following the sequence dictated by Nestor, even as he wondered if Nestor was dazed and hysterical or crazy or dying.

"The best trip ever ..."

Bruck had not closed the door to the room, and he had been listening very intently to what Nestor was saying. Otherwise, he would have noticed the pairs of feral eyes lurking in the dark shadows outside the door. Too late, he realized that the red-haired bristly-bearded older brother had crept up the stairs and was standing there, listening, with a handful of savage looking men behind him, waiting.

Bruck felt a pang of regret as the red-haired red-bearded brother dashed into the room with a terrible cry and plunged a long sword into the heart of the helpless wounded Nestor.

Nestor slumped over lifeless, the grin on his face permanent now.

Bruck had just rotated the last number into place. But he dropped the rolled parchment on the floor and it skittered away as he ran out of time.

Even as the killer pulled his sword out of Nestor's dead body and gleefully turned to Bruck, the killer's blade dripping with blood and his confederates surging behind him, Bruck had begun to shimmer and vanish.

The red-haired bristly-bearded brother was too slow, reaching for Bruck but grabbing nothing, reaching, stretching, grasping futilely with hate-filled eyes.

That was always the last thing Bruck remembered before waking up, the reaching, stretching, grasping hands and the hate-filled eyes of the red-haired bristly-bearded brother.

The line shuffled forward. It was a long line, and there were many other lines inside the building. After each man received his orders he moved outside where there were vast treeless spaces, and grouped areas of machines and equipment, and hundreds if not thousands of men, all attired for imminent battle.

Today Bruck's weapons included a bow and arrow and several long curved swords tucked into his sash. He carried a shield and wore a winged helmet. Pads of armor were fitted over black pants, a black shirt, and a burgundy vest, everything edged in gilt.

Everywhere around him similarly dressed samurai awaited the signal.

Bruck felt a little foolish.

If only he could remember.

The worst thing was not the fighting all the time. He loved fighting, though he sometimes had to remind himself of that fact. The worst thing was not not knowing what he was fighting for—most of the time. Sometimes he knew the cause, though usually they didn't tell him and it didn't really matter.

The worst thing was how false and foolish and pretend it all felt.

The Marquis came by and pointed at Bruck, laughing. Bruck laughed back, pointing at the Marquis, and in a way that cheered him up a little, even though the Marquis quickly moved on to another part of the field, where today he had been picked to ride on horseback.

Bruck was an expert rider. He could have ridden circles around the Marquis and most of the others, but he didn't care if he was running and carrying a spear or riding a horse. He didn't care if he was dressed in blue or gray or samurai armor or the uniform he wore several times, with variations, when fighting in something the people in charge insisted on calling World War II. They numbered everything in this place, even wars.

If only he could remember.

Holding the triangle of stone in his hand, he rotated the numbers around into sequence again and again. And although he had been doing the same thing for days and weeks, each time the numbers locked into a new configuration, he waited expectantly for the shimmer and the rocketing, dizzying, nauseating sensation that might send him home again, though that never happened.

Seven numbers.

Bruck had about ten thousand probable sequences to work through, provided he could keep track of all the numbers he had tried before, the Marquis had told him with a laugh.

"Just wait till Nestor gets back . . ."

Bruck looked up, shading his eyes against the hot sun, and there—he spotted him again. A man with curly red hair and a gnarly reddish beard, huddled with another group of samurai, dressed slightly differently, over there on a small rise. Was the man staring at Bruck?

Was he the same man Bruck had glimpsed at Bar None?

The man in the dream?

Bruck felt a sudden excitement, a renewal, hope and expectation. The bile rose in his throat as he pocketed the stone and tightly gripped his sword. Around him others were stirring, standing.

A man came by with a bullhorn shouting instructions.

Bruck felt real again, for the first time in weeks, ready for a real fight.

"Action!"

Memories of Light and Sound

Steven Saus

Steven Saus injects people with radioactivity as his day job, but only to serve the forces of good. His work has appeared in *Seed* magazine and *Andromeda Spaceways* inflight magazine. He also has several flash fiction works in the online magazines *365 Tomorrows*, *Everyday Weirdness*, and *Quantum Muse*. You can keep up with him at www.stevensaus.com.

"At least I get to wear a nice hat," Monica laughed. She held its floofy rim down as a gust of fall wind threatened to pull it off her bobbed hair. "You know, baby, when I said I wanted to visit Manhattan someday, this isn't quite what I meant."

Anthony adjusted his bowler, shielding his dark eyes from a stray beam of late afternoon sunlight. "It's an important time period," he said. "The Roaring Twenties. Flappers, speakeasies, all that jazz. Besides, the Statue of Liberty isn't wading in seawater like it would be if we came here in our time."

Anthony grabbed the leather handle of the suitcase the Timeshares agent had provided for them. They had managed to buy one of the first unaccompanied tours.

They wore period clothes for the trip and had an automatic recall trigger. Timeshares had arranged for a native to provide a packed suitcase, an itinerary, and lodgings. The reduced traveling mass and short length of their vacation reduced the price enough to let regular people like them afford the trip.

"The hotel is right across the street. Good for one night only." The traffic only justified checking the street once, but the back part of Anthony's brain twitched so he checked for cars again.

The hotel's foyer spread out before them as Monica handed her fur coat to a doorman. Anthony pointed to the marble pillars along the walls. "See? I got you Roman columns."

She giggled, and Anthony wrapped his arms around her, the soft cotton of her dress thin under his arms.

"It's our honeymoon," she whispered in his ear, her pale fingers playing with the trace of gray at his temple. "I'm more interested in another kind of column."

Anthony's face grew hot. He only had a few years on her, but her forwardness still took him by surprise. "We'll do something about that after I check in," he said with a smile.

He walked to the counter and rang the bell while Monica examined the oil paintings on the wall. The other men in the lobby looked at her. Anthony's smile got bigger as he leaned on the counter, watching the men watch her. It didn't matter how much they looked. She had chosen him, the loser boy who had finally been successful. Now, on his honeymoon, he could finally make things right with—

The clerk's rough voice stopped his daydreaming. "You a wop?"

The blunt question punched through Timeshare's historical briefing. Their warnings echoed his grandfather's stories of a time when his family was not considered white. Anthony's heart beat faster as he turned to face the desk clerk, fingers pressed into the polished wood of the counter.

"What the hell did you say?"

Monica was at his side, her words cutting into the clerk's reply. "We're from Cleveland. Ohio. It's our honeymoon!"

The clerk nodded to Anthony. "Sorry. Didn't figure, but the owner doesn't want no dagos staying here. Drives off real business, you know how it is. Gotta be careful with all the boats coming in."

Monica tapped the counter. "We don't have much of that in Cleveland, thank goodness. Husband, dear, why don't you sign us in and pay the man?"

"Of course," Anthony forced out, fumbling with the strange paper money.

He signed his name as Michael.

Anthony relaxed on the bed, pleasantly surprised at the comforting sensation of the thick quilt against his bare skin. He fluffed the pillow, pressing his head into the soft, real feathers. After years with bland foam, he found the prick of an occasional quill fascinating. The sweat from their lovemaking slowly dried on his skin while Monica rinsed off in the extravagant claw foot bathtub. Both of them had paid more attention to each other than the room, which was now littered with their clothes. He let his attention wander as she splashed, taking in the ornate gilded wallpaper, the swirled plaster ceiling, the gas lights and radiator. Eventually it rested on his trousers. On the small bulge of folded papers in the pocket.

The muscles in his stomach clenched. Anthony closed his eyes. "Monica, there's something I need to tell you."

"What, that racism is annoying? Or that you've

rested enough?" She had gotten out of the tub and leaned against the doorway, dripping and naked. Monica grabbed her hat and plopped it on her head. "You like?"

"I wouldn't have married you if I didn't."

Her gaze slid down his body, one corner of her mouth rising higher in a wicked grin. "Doesn't look like you like it quite enough," she said.

Anthony rolled his eyes. "I am older than you."

Monica snorted. "It must be the hat." She tossed it onto the bedpost, then jumped onto the bed in a slick wet heap.

"Even medical marvels have their limits, you know."

"*Modern* medical marvels," she said after kissing him. She rose up on one elbow. "You can't worry about this stuff, baby. You've got to be practical about the past. You know how this all turns out, history. You can't change it now, so let it go." She ran a finger across the short hairs on his chest. "Maybe you should concentrate on right now."

He sighed, feeling the topic get away from him. "But I need to—"

"Husband of mine," she said, inching her way down the bed, "we can only afford one honeymoon. Get your mind off the past and on the present."

And for a little while, he did.

The next morning, Monica snored softly as Anthony picked his trousers up from the floor and pulled the papers from his pocket. Golden light from the early sunrise shone through the window. The soft clank of the radiator echoed in the cool autumn morning. The folded sheets were bound with a scrap of string. One ragged edge showed where Anthony had removed them from the binding. He untied the string and unfolded the yellowed paper, smoothing the wrinkles against the floor. He put aside the copied record from Ellis Island and began to read.

Anthony skimmed over the handwritten Italian of his grandfather's diary. He remembered the translation, merely using the sheets as sentimental cues. The earliest entries began a few weeks from now, in the coalfields. His grandfather had stopped keeping the diary the day Anthony's parents had died. The day Anthony began to live with the old man.

Anthony was glad of that. He replayed that part of his childhood again and again. So many fights with his grandfather. So many times his grandfather had tried to keep Anthony from screwing up his life. All the times when he caught Anthony smoking, stealing, or sneaking out at night. The times when he insisted Anthony stay in school.

Monica turned in her sleep. The bedsprings' creak echoed the springs of his old bed in Grandfather's house. That night he'd thrown himself on the bed in teenage melodrama, arguing over the sound of protesting springs. The last night.

"You cannot go out with them, Anthony. You are grounded. They are bad boys, and you cannot go with them."

The ancient jazz from his grandfather's record player was yet another way the old man was behind the times.

"You don't understand! You can't understand. You're not even from this country. You don't get it!"

He could not remember what any of it looked like. All he remembered were the sounds and silences of that night. The sudden silence of his grandfather—confused and unable to speak. The echoing wail of the ambulance siren. The beep-punctuated quiet of the hospital room as Anthony waited for the doctors to tell him it was a massive stroke. The total silence of the funeral home when his smart-ass teenage mouth could not say a thing.

"What's that, baby?" Monica said.

Anthony mashed the pages back together. His hands twisted the string around them on autopilot. The radiator clanked again, louder, giving him a moment to stall. He held a fragment of the past, a relic of a memory older than himself. He could not take anyone else judging him about this.

"Nothing," he said. She flinched at the flatness in his voice. "Just some notes about things to see in the city." Anthony pushed the papers back into his pants pocket.

"Okay, baby."

He watched her breasts rise and fall with a deep breath.

"Are you coming back to bed?"

Anthony put on his trousers. "No. Let's get dressed. I want to get started on our tour."

The lion did not roar.

Monica's eyes were large. "How does it move around?"

Anthony closed the pocket watch in his hand and looked up at the lion. It stopped circling the cage—it had just enough room for that—then sank down and began chewing at the bald patches on its haunches. It ignored the stinking bowl of kibble and scraps in the far corner.

"I don't think it can. These small cages in zoos were normal even when I was a kid." He could smell the musk of the big cat over the metal of the cage; they were far closer to the lion than they would ever be in the naturalistic enclosures of a modern zoo.

"Is that why it's chewing on itself? Because it has no room? Because it feels trapped?"

Anthony started to reply when a swarm of schoolchildren flowed around a corner and past them, a pushing, shoving, river of shouting youth. Behind them, a schoolteacher in a muted floral dress prompted stragglers to keep up.

Monica pointed at the kids. "They're so cute, Anthony."

"No."

"I wasn't—"

"I can't afford kids. We've talked about this before." Anthony looked at his watch again. "We've got to get going, anyway."

"Fine."

Anthony looked up; the hardness of her voice was also in her eyes.

"We won't talk about it, Anthony. I'll meet you at the front gate."

He watched her walk away, her stride keeping pace with the students. A chuff from the lion got his attention. It had stopped gnawing at itself, its face instead turned straight toward him. Anthony understood how antelope felt.

"I can't afford it," he whispered. "I can't afford to make another mistake."

It was afternoon when they got to the docks, and even if the conversation was not forgotten, Anthony was not going to mention it. The early afternoon sunlight angled across the water as the ferry lowered its ramp. When it did, humanity poured out, swirling among the few people waiting nearby. The passengers' brown clothing offset the sea of olive skin and dark hair. Pale manifest tags from the passenger ships were still pinned to their clothes. The sound of immigrant voices reached Anthony, a linguist's stew of Europe, the words too fast in too many languages to understand. The smell of disinfectant came next, carried on their clothes from Ellis Island, pushing away the smell of the sea.

Monica leaned into his shoulder, a whispered breath in his ear. "Why are we here, baby? Isn't the Statue of Liberty next on the itinerary?"

Anthony turned his head slowly from side to side, both negating and trying to take in each of the faces as they went past. He tried to imagine each one forty years older, to match them to the face he had argued with years ago. His heart twisted more with each small wave of people that passed. He was only able to see a few of them. There were too many—the ferry was emptying too fast.

They both swiveled at a joyful cry. A man, still in dirty work clothes gathered up a woman and child into his arms. The woman was speaking fast, high, excited, and then was stopped by the man's passionate kiss. A small wordless sound escaped Anthony's lips, his mind filled with memories of his father returning from business trips.

Monica looked at Anthony, then at the family, and then at Anthony again. He felt the wetness in his eyes, a tear running down his left cheek. He watched her piece together the snippets of his story, shared over coffee and pillows during their engagement. Her eyes widened, mouth shaping into a small O.

"Your grandfather," she said.

Anthony nodded, wiping away the tears from both cheeks. There were still a few people getting off the boat.

"The records say he was here. I haven't seen him yet," he said, gaze roving back across the faces. She punched his shoulder.

"Why didn't you tell me?" Monica stepped in front of

him, pressing closer. The lavender of her perfume mixed with the lingering antiseptic scent. She grabbed his chin, forcing him to look at her. "Talk to me, husband."

Anthony closed his eyes, listening to the waves, the seagulls. The crowd was thinning; he could pick out individual voices, words in different languages. He took a deep breath, willing the dark despair back down his throat before opening his eyes.

"Talk to me, baby," she said. "Let me in your head."

"It doesn't matter." Anthony looked past her face, past the sunlight in her hair to the ferry beyond.

"Bullshit." Anthony's attention snapped back to her. Her cheeks burned red, the light flashed in her eyes. "It does matter. You brought me here, you chose this for our honeymoon, and you didn't tell me the real reason why."

It sounded stupid as he said it. "I thought you would be mad."

"Jesus," she whispered, pulling away and turning to look back at the boat. "I want to hold you and slap you at the same time."

The few immigrants who remained clutched multilingual handbills promising work while following better dressed men into the city. Anthony slowly reached out to her. When his hand brushed the soft hair on the side of her neck, she tensed, and then leaned back into him.

Her voice was soft. "This is your grandfather who had the stroke, right?"

"Yeah," Anthony said. "I was an idiot, arguing with him over stupid things. Probably sent his blood pressure through the roof. Caused it."

Monica slid under his arm until she was facing him again. "Good to know some things don't change," she said smiling, and kissed his cheek.

Anthony pulled her close and spoke into her hair.

"They're raising the ramp now. I missed him. I only know he was on this ferry, then in the mines two weeks later." He sighed. "We only have a few hours left before we have to go."

Monica kissed him again. "We can finish the tour. We can just go to that speakeasy, baby, and try to enjoy ourselves."

Anthony tried to smile as they turned away from the dock. "This is the past, and I have to concentrate on the present, right?"

The alley outside the club stank of piss and nausea. Inside, it was clean and glittering. The jazz quartet's jackets shone silky blue, and waiters brought gin in teacups to the tables. Cigarette smoke hung in a low cloud over the dancing crowd.

"Are you sure it's safe?" Monica asked when the music paused.

"Relax," Anthony said. "There's no raid here tonight. They checked that when they made up the itinerary."

With a musical slide of notes, the trumpet player led the band into another song. A young woman, hair bobbed and hose turned down, danced past their table. Her arms and legs flew in a frantic Charleston.

Monica drank the rest of her gin in a quick motion. "C'mon baby," she said, grabbing his hand. "Let's dance."

Despite the month of lessons at home, Anthony's limbs did not want to cooperate at first. A live band and a busy dance floor just seemed different from the living room floor and old recordings. But after a few missteps and one slightly mashed foot, he started to feel his body relax into the music. Monica's mouth had broken into a huge grin as their hands flitted from knee to knee.

Then Anthony saw him.

The busboy was clearing a table, as awkward as Anthony had originally felt on the dance floor. Anthony stumbled, his limbs suddenly numb and unresponsive. The earliest pictures of his grandfather had not prepared him for how much the young immigrant would resemble the man he had grown up with. The wood floor banged into Anthony's knee, a sharp spike of pain sweeping aside the rest of his confusion.

"Are you okay?" Monica asked as the band finished the song.

"He's here," he said, gesturing to the busboy. Monica glanced over while Anthony picked himself up. "I'm going to talk to the owner."

A ten dollar bribe and ten minutes later, Anthony watched confusion ripple across his grandfather's face. The stern man he expected was not there. The lines, the weariness from the mines, had not yet appeared. He was just a boy, alone in a new land, summoned away from his new job by a tip for more money than he would make in a week.

"How can I help you?" his grandfather said in his thick accent.

Anthony opened his mouth to speak, but his chest and throat tightened around the words. Monica spoke into his silence. "Are you Antonio Marinelli?"

His grandfather's eyes widened. "I am he. Who are you?"

Anthony felt the vibration in his pocket. Monica looked at him a second later; her recall device had vibrated its five-minute warning to her, too. Their vacation was nearly over. Anthony took a large drink from the teacup.

"What are your plans, Mr. Marinelli?" he asked.

His grandfather took a long look at Anthony, and

then laughed. "Plans? I have a room I share with five men, and they say we are lucky! The padroni get me a room, this job, but they want me to work more. They tell to get me to go work in the mines, but . . ." His grandfather sank back in the chair. "Is it worth it? Perhaps I return to Italy soon instead. America could be a mistake."

The recall vibrated again. Three minutes. Anthony covered his grandfather's left hand with his own. "It will be worth it, I swear. All of it."

His grandfather's eyes narrowed. "Do you know me?"

Anthony kept his eyes locked with his grandfather. He spoke fast, hoping the man's English could keep up. "It will be hard. After you leave the mine, when you think you are done with work and children, an ungrateful child will be in your home."

His grandfather tried to pull back, crossing himself with his free hand. "Una maledizione!" he whispered.

Anthony held tight. "No curse. You will think this child is a failure. He will be too stupid to appreciate you. One day, though, he will be successful. He would have made you proud. He will realize how much you meant to him." His grandfather stopped pulling his arm away, instead leaning toward Anthony. "But by then, it will be too late to tell you."

His grandfather lapsed into muttered Italian again for a moment, and then said, "Are you an angel? A demon?"

"I am no demon, Nonno." Anthony said. The room began to fade as his recall device pulled him back through the centuries. The music of the band faded, too, sounding less like a live band and more like a record played long ago.

Anthony threw himself on the bed, and then glared

back at his grandfather through his bangs. The old man looked small next to the oversized black light posters, his starched white shirt and teeth glowing.

"You cannot go out with them, Anthony. You are grounded. They are bad boys, and you cannot go with them."

The ancient jazz from his grandfather's record player in the living room was yet another way the old man was behind the times.

"You don't understand! You can't understand. You're not even from this country. You don't get it!"

Anthony stared at his headboard, not wanting to even give his grandfather the satisfaction of eye contact. But out of the corner of his eye, Anthony saw the old man smile a little, his lips curving into the words, "You're welcome."

Anthony shook his grandfather's hand one last time. "Thank you," Anthony said.

And they were gone.

A Night to Forget

C. A. Verstraete

Christine Verstraete is a Wisconsin journalist who did see the *Titanic* display in Chicago, but doesn't remember anything out of the ordinary happening. She's had short fiction published in the *Dragons Composed* and *The Heat of the Moment* anthologies, in *Mouth Full of Bullets*, and coming in *The Bitter End*. She is also the author of a middle grade novel, *Searching for a Starry Night: A Miniature Art Mystery*, a 2009 Eppie finalist for the e-book version. Contact her at her Web site: http://cverstraete.com or stop by her blog, http://candidcanine.blogspot.com.

The building's faded brick and dirty windows made Jessica Adams question whether she'd found the right place.

She eyed the ad once more before exiting the car. Matt should've come and checked the place like he promised. Would've saved her a trip, and a ton of aggravation, she muttered.

Her mood sour, Jess inched closer and tried to peer beyond the layer of dirt in the front window. The inside of the store was dim, its secrets well hidden. She rubbed the dirt from a section of a pane of glass, her effort providing a slightly improved view of the items piled haphazardly on the window ledge. The collection included a faded cruise program, a black-and-white image of a woman in an elegant, ankle-length dress, and a pair of lady's gloves, the tiny pearl buttons dull with age, the cloth's once pristine white a memory.

The quaint scene seemed better suited to an antique shop than a place offering the kind of vacation she had in mind. She'd envisioned a private beach in the Caymans or a secluded cabin in the woods, just the two of them. Instead, Matt had begged off, telling her he was too busy for vacations. So, a little peeved, she went alone to investigate the new agency he'd seen advertised in the paper. She had half the mind to book a vacation for herself.

Her bravado faded now that she was here. She read the small, hand-lettered sign tucked into the bottom window pane and scoffed: TIMESHARES—ADVENTURE FOR THE AGES. The place was as likely to book her dream vacation as she was to win a million dollars. It sounded, well, kind of odd and a bit too good to be true.

"Good old Matt," she groused. "He did it again."

Disappointed, Jess refolded the newspaper page and shoved it in her bag. She needed a good strong cup of coffee. Maybe someone at the coffee shop could recommend another travel agency so the trip wouldn't be a total waste.

She was about to leave when a flicker behind the glass caught her eye. Had the owner arrived? Guess she could at least see what the place offered and hope that the pickings weren't as slim as she expected.

Finding the door open, she stepped inside. "Hello? Anyone here?"

She blinked several times, waiting for her eyes to

adjust to the dimness. The view was staggering—row upon row of shelves stuffed with old books; faded manuscripts covering the walls and stuffed in baskets. Then there was the art: paintings, the varnish brown and cracked, hung in every available open space.

What a mess.

Still, the more she looked around, the more her curiosity grew. Each painting had a note tucked into the frame with the title, name, date: The Battle of the Bulge, Napoleon, Cleopatra.

Annoyance gave way to fascination as she wandered around. Was the owner branching out? Probably a good idea from the look of the place, she thought, as her finger rubbed a layer of dust off a painting.

Her questions about the missing travel agent faded at sight of the next painting. She studied the majestic ocean liner streaking through the mist: *Maiden Voyage, The* Titanic, the paper said. Not that she needed a note. She'd know the image anywhere.

The tragedy of the *Titanic* had captured her imagination since she was a child, thanks to her mother. Besides classic children's stories like Jack and the Beanstalk or Mother Goose, her mother's favorite, often-told tale had been about how her great-aunt had boarded the *Titanic* as a child. She had perished with many of the other immigrants traveling in the bare-bones quarters in the ship's bowels.

Jess had repeatedly studied the faded photo of a young, unsmiling Polish girl dressed in a matronly long dress, babushka on her head, and clunky, old lady shoes on her feet. The patched, battered carpetbag she held accented the girl's poverty.

She'd always suspected that the story of how the poor girl made it to England and onto the *Titanic* was just that—a fable. Family legend said the girl's uncle won the third-class ticket playing dice (her mother said others insisted he stole it) and gave it to her in hopes of giving her a better life. So the story went.

Jess had begun her search for answers when her sixth grade teacher made everyone research and write an essay on a historical topic. To her surprise, she not only discovered that her mother's story was true, but a helpful librarian led her to a list of *Titanic* passengers— which included her great-aunt.

Despite her continued research, she never learned more about the girl. Not that it mattered. That someone she "knew"—at least through stories—had been involved in such a tragedy made the event more personal. Ever since, she'd felt a strong emotional bond to the vessel.

An unexpected voice broke Jess's musing, making her jump. "What're you doing sneaking up on people!" she cried. Her outburst trailed off as she eyed the stooped little man behind her. He barely reached five feet and stood wringing his hands, his face sheepish.

"I'm sorry, miss, I didn't mean to frighten you." He gave her a timid smile and pointed at the painting. "That's always been my favorite," he said, his voice soft.

She returned his smile and turned back to the painting. "Mine, too. Someone in my family died on the *Titanic*."

"You don't say?" The man stroked the silvery mustache that draped the outer edges of his lips like antique lace. "I'm assumin' you've seen the documentaries on the raisin' of the ship. Been to the exhibit?"

"Yes, I watched it on TV, but I haven't been to the exhibit yet."

"No? Well, it's somethin' you should see, especially with your connection. Hmm, I've just the thing if you're interested, something no *Titanic* fan would want to miss, I'm sure."

His smile and oily tone made Jess pause, but the bad feeling passed just as quickly as it appeared. She pondered the idea. Maybe she could take a trip and see the exhibit at the same time, something Matt would hate. That made it even more attractive.

"Well ... maybe it's a possibility. I'd like to go someplace different, and if I can see the exhibit, that'd be great."

He clapped his hands in delight. "Excellent, excellent! Any particular place you would like to visit?" He leaned toward her, his face anxious. The tip of his tongue licked his lips.

The image of a snake unfolded in her mind. Jess recoiled slightly, surprised at the thought. She'd better finish and take a break. Maybe she wouldn't be so jumpy once she ate. Blood sugar must be low.

"I've thought of going overseas or renting a cottage on Martha's Vineyard. I've never been there."

He scurried around the table, grabbed a giant black book from the shelf, and blew off the dust. She sneezed and tried to see the book's title but failed as he flipped it open. He began to scan the pages of small writing.

"Hmm, no, there's nothing *Titanic*-related going on out east right now. Wait, yes, here we are. A new exhibition is opening at Chicago's Museum of Science and Industry."

Jess swallowed her disappointment. Romantic visions of floating down Venice's canals in a gondola, staring at *Mona Lisa*'s smile, visiting the British Museum, or even celebrity watching at Martha's Vineyard faded.

Nothing against Chicago, of course. She'd visited her cousin there as a child, and never forgot the thrill of seeing the perfectly furnished miniature Thorne Rooms at the Art Institute on Michigan Avenue. She still treasured the book her cousin bought her. But her dreams of actually seeing parts of the *Titanic* had always been linked in her mind with a much more exotic setting.

"Here," the little man said, pushing an envelope into her hand. "Take a peek at the tickets and itinerary. You won't be disappointed."

Her questions about how he'd gathered everything so fast disappeared like fog on a sunny day as she opened the envelope. She slid out the ticket dated April 14, then glanced at the schedule and felt a surge of excitement. A limo would pick her up at her home in Wisconsin and take her downtown. There were stops for lunch and snacks at first-class restaurants. Shopping sites and other attractions along the route were listed. If she preferred, a private plane was available for an extra fee.

"You can stop anytime. Turn it into a several-day or all-week excursion if you want. We have connections at the finest accommodations. You'll find the suites fully furnished, complete with a new wardrobe, our compliments."

Her eyes widened. "A wardrobe? B–but that isn't necessary. I have my own clothing. How much does that add to the price?"

"I know our surroundings here . . ." he waved a hand, ". . . are less than satisfactory, but this is one of our oldest branches. Still, we believe in pampering our guests to the utmost. The smallest detail isn't too small. Everything is taken care of for you at no extra charge."

He handed her a handwritten bill and nodded.

"Everything is included, hotel, travel, museum admission, drinks, and meals. The garments as well. Inclusive."

She glanced at the itinerary again. "Okay, I'll take it."

"Wonderful!" His face glowed. "Someone will pick you up this afternoon at four o'clock."

"Today? I still have to pack and—"

"You only need a few personal items. I'm sorry, but booking the ticket starts the time clock. Our trips operate a bit differently than most. We want to get you in before everyone else for your private showing. You can cancel if you feel this is inconvenient."

She hesitated but a moment. "No, I guess that's fine. I'll look for the driver."

Her mind was still a whirl as she quickly showered and threw some toiletries, a couple outfits, jewelry, and shoes in a suitcase. She arranged for her neighbor to water the plants and sat to wait, still wondering if she was doing the right thing. It was crazy, impulsive ... and she had to admit, more fun than she'd had in some time. She didn't bother to call Matt. Let him wonder where she'd gone.

The drive was uneventful, the driver pleasant, the accommodations wonderful. To her surprise, she walked into her hotel suite and there above the queen-size bed hung the painting she'd seen at the travel agency, *Maiden Voyage, The* Titanic.

A knock on the door made her forget the odd coincidence. She opened it, surprised to find a woman holding two of the most amazing dresses she'd ever seen. The black gown was trimmed with sparkling black jet and ruby glass beads. The gray and white striped linen day dress had a neckline ruched with gray silk and handmade lace.

"Good afternoon, miss. I've brought your clothing for tomorrow. The gray gown is for your morning excursion. The black gown is for the evening dinner. Your dinner will be brought in tonight. Is there anything else I can assist you with?"

"No, thank you," Jess answered. "I'm going to relax and turn in early I think."

"Very well. I will be here at seven to help you dress. Have a good evening then."

The next morning, Jess giggled as she slipped on the vintage undergarments she found in the drawer. They felt strange, but she was willing to play along. Her assistant arrived promptly at seven. She coiffed Jess's shoulder-length hair in tiny curls and pinned it up with glittery hairpins, helped her into the gray *Titanic*-era gown, and fastened the row of hooks in the back. Jess stared at herself in awe. The present faded as she slipped her feet into beaded vintage shoes that felt like they were custom made.

The driver dropped her at the exhibit entrance where she received a program from two young ladies wearing simpler Victorian gowns. It felt odd being ushered into the softly lit exhibit rooms alone and told to take her time. She could get used to such privilege, she thought.

Inside, time stood still. She passed glass cases containing gold buttons, broken pieces of comb, fancy mirrors, and other personal effects. A white shirt once worn by a ship steward hammered home the reality of what had happened and brought a tear to her eye. Had the man met her great-aunt? Had he wondered at the fate of those below deck or tried to help them?

She strolled from room to room in silence, her emotions in turmoil. The quiet unnerved her. She almost wished there were others around to lessen the impact. Gleaming silverware and a polished china cup and saucer with the *Titanic*'s signature cobalt-and-gold pattern sat in one case. A child's doll, one arm and leg gone, its dress in rags, was perched next to a logbook. She bit back a sob as she saw the entry with a child's name and age.

Two hours later, she looked up in surprise to see one of the costumed attendants. "Miss? Your driver is here. Your tour continues after dinner tonight."

Disappointed, but intrigued, Jess returned to her suite and changed to go shopping. She relaxed a couple hours before her assistant arrived to fix her hair and help her dress, this time in the stunning black gown. The dress rustled as she turned to admire her silhouette. Some light makeup, a beautiful cameo brooch, and a small beaded reticule completed her look. *Eat your heart out, Matt.*

She entered the museum dining area, the room aglow with gleaming cobalt-and-gold *Titanic* china, and shimmering crystal. Other diners dressed in their absolute best nodded in greeting as she strolled to her table. She smiled as the handsome man to her right introduced himself as Mr. Bernard Brady and pulled out her chair.

"Good evening, Miss Adams. They told me to expect you for dinner, but they didn't say how lovely my table mate would be."

She smiled, greeting him and her other dining companions. They did think of everything, she thought. The conversation flowed as Jess picked up her menu headed with the name of the ship. It read:

April 14, Titanic
First Course Hors D'Oeuvres; Oysters
Second Course Consommé Olga, Cream of Barley
Third Course Poached Salmon with Mousseline Sauce, Cucumbers

The list went on, a full ten courses, ending with eclairs, Waldorf pudding, and French ice cream. It was decadent. She sighed and wondered how much she'd be able to eat in this tight-fitting dress, but couldn't resist the crisp cucumber scent of her fish when it arrived. It melted in her mouth.

Music and dancing followed dinner. Jess couldn't remember when she'd so enjoyed herself. Her companion, a witty man in his forties, exuded an old-world charm she found refreshing. She looked forward to tomorrow's dinner.

Not ready to end the evening, Jess was thrilled when Bernard asked if she'd like to take a stroll with him later, "along the deck," as he called it. She smiled in agreement and went to do her own exploring.

As she turned a corner, her eyes widened at sight of the full-scale replica of the *Titanic*'s grand staircase. She stared, almost afraid to touch anything for fear it would fall down. It had to be a front, she figured, like those fake buildings the movies used that looked real, but had nothing except wood supports behind them.

The banister felt solid. A tingle shot up her arms, but she ignored it. She bent down to touch the step, the coolness of the marble giving her goosebumps. Heart pounding, she went up one step, then another. At the top, she shivered as the air turned cold.

She held back the panic and pushed through the icy curtain, surprised to see how the room shimmered around her. Her grip on the banister tightening, she struggled to keep the vertigo at bay as she watched the room grow brighter.

Finally, the strange feelings passed. Muffled sounds reached her ears. She recognized the strains of violins . . . soft laughter . . . voices. She searched in vain for the hidden stereo speakers, amazed at the care someone put into making everything seem so real.

Someone called her name. She looked to the right,

surprised to see her handsome dinner companion coming down the uppermost staircase.

"Miss Adams, it is a pleasure to see you again."

"Mr. Brady, it's good to see you, too." She smiled, feeling the warmth of the blush in her cheeks.

"Please, call me Bernard. We do not need to be so formal, do we?" He took her hand and kissed it. The light brush of his mustache sent a chill up her spine. "How about we take that stroll, shall we?"

She nodded and gasped aloud as the air glimmered with wisps of gray smoke that slowly coalesced into solid form. Her mind tried to make sense of what was happening as the staircase filled with other couples who nodded and smiled as they passed.

Funny how her companion's body appeared to have a slight translucence to it. Yet as he leaned over to kiss her cheek and take her hand, his touch felt as warm and real as hers. Her skin tingled as he pressed his palm intimately against her lower back. There was nothing imaginary about him, or about the feelings he stirred.

He leaned over and whispered in her ear. "Please, tell me if I am being too forward."

His breath tickled her neck. She loved that he was playing this Victorian manners thing to the hilt. It was incredibly sexy and more provocative than anything she'd ever experienced.

They turned down a richly decorated hall. For a fleeting moment, Jess wondered at the expense the agency had put into personalizing her trip. She smiled at the passing couples, noting how the walls sometimes seemed visible right through their clothing. The light must be playing tricks, she guessed.

Her escort stopped in front of cabin A-21 and pulled a key from his pocket. "I need to get something. You may wait here if you feel it is inappropriate to come inside."

She watched him turn the key, shocked to hear the lock click. As the door swung open, she noticed the familiar painting of the *Titanic* hanging above the fireplace mantle. After a moment's hesitation, she followed him in. It wasn't a surprise when Bernard closed the door and took her in his arms. That they shared the rest of the evening together didn't surprise her, either.

Hours later, Jess sprang from bed at the sound of thumps and yells outside. She looked at her still-sleeping companion in confusion. Then it hit her. The date ... today was the fourteenth of April, 1912.

"Bernard!" She shook him awake. "Hurry, we have to get dressed. What time is it?"

He gazed at her and smiled before reaching for the gold pocket watch on the nightstand. "Time?" He yawned. "It is only twenty three minutes past ten. There is plenty of time yet." He patted the bedcover.

Her panic growing, she slipped on her gown, urging him to fasten the back buttons. She tried not to sound rude as he began to kiss her back.

"Bernard, please, we have to hurry."

He responded by trying to slip the gown off her shoulders. She stepped away from him. "No, you don't understand. We have to go. Now! The ship is sinking!"

"Sinking?" He laughed. "Surely you jest and have a horrid sense of humor. The *Titanic* is unsinkable."

The noises in the corridor outside grew louder. A minute later, someone pounded on the door. "Mr. Brady, sir? This is the steward. Hurry, sir, to the deck and please get into your lifejacket. We need to get everyone up on the deck, quickly. Leave all your belongings, please, and come to the deck immediately."

Jess saw his face pale as he answered. "Yes, I will be there in a moment."

He looked at her. "Then it is true?"

She nodded.

He grabbed her shoulders. "How did you know that? Tell me. Are you a witch, some sort of soothsayer?"

She'd had enough. It was time to return to reality. "Bernard, I think this has gone on too long already. Please, tell whoever's in charge that I won't be angry. Let's end this. I got more than my money's worth."

His face reddened as he buttoned his shirt and slipped on his shoes. "Madam, whatever you are insinuating, I never received any kind of money. I am deeply sorry if you feel I compromised you in any way."

Ignoring him, she ran to the door and yanked it open. A gasp escaped at the sounds of yelling in the distance and the look of fear on the passing passengers' faces. He joined her at the door.

"Now do you believe me?" she asked. "Hurry. We have to go."

On deck, the first-class male passengers were stoic, bravely leading women to the lifeboats, almost pushing them in when they balked. She watched, dazed, not believing what she was seeing. It wasn't real. It couldn't be.

The crowds surged forward, propelling Jess along. She tried to hold onto Bernard, but felt his hand slip from hers. She kept moving, her heart aching, but she dared not look back. She didn't want to see him standing there, trying to be brave in the face of what lay ahead.

A crew member rushed by, yelling as lifeboats were released half full. The ship creaked and moaned. Stunned passengers staggered around, ignoring others near them.

Jess gazed at them, her panic rising. Suddenly, she knew what she had to do.

Her heart raced as she struggled to keep her balance against the growing tilt of the ship. She rushed to the lower level deck, studying the face of each passenger until she saw a girl huddled in a corner, her floral babushka awry. Jess held her breath as the girl turned her way revealing the same heart-shaped face as the one in the photo back home.

Jess pointed to the upper level and held out her hand. Tears spilled from the girl's eyes as Jess raced to the upper deck, pulling her along. She arrived in time to find the crew struggling to release the last lifeboat and fight off those who threatened to topple it. Jess kissed the girl's cheek and pushed her into the arms of one of the female passengers as the boat was lowered to the water.

Her face wet with tears, her teeth chattering, Jess sloshed through the rising water to Brady's cabin. She found it open, everything inside scattered and thrown about. She stared at the painting bobbing in the rising water. The image of the ship also dipped beneath the painted sea, the stern pointed at an odd angle.

Pulling the original ticket from her pocket, Jess hurried down the hall, her dress becoming wetter and heavier by the minute.

Her eyes straight ahead, she tried not to look into the faces of the other frightened passengers ambling around as she retraced her way to the grand staircase. She moved toward the exit, praying, hoping, that she could still turn in her ticket for a refund.

A Passion for Time Travel

Donald J. Bingle

Donald J. Bingle is a frequent contributor to anthologies in the science fiction, fantasy, horror, thriller, and comedy genres, including the DAW's *Zombie Raccoons and Killer Bunnies*, *Gamer Fantastic*, *Imaginary Friends*, *The Dimension Next Door*, *Future Americas*, *Front Lines*, *Fellowship Fantastic*, and *Slipstreams*. He is also the author of *Forced Conversion*, a science fiction novel set in the near future, when everyone can have heaven, any heaven they want, but some people don't want to go. His latest novel, *Greensword: A Tale of Extreme Global Warming*, is a darkly comedic eco-thriller about a group of misfit environmentalists who are about to save the world—they just don't want to get caught doing it. Don also co-owns the company that sells the TimeMaster roleplaying game. He can be reached at www.donaldjbingle.com.

Timeshares.

Evan Pogue rolled his eyes glumly as he headed for the company's reception area. He'd been informed that the prospective clients were clearing security in the main lobby of the building and would soon reach the fifty-sixth floor by express elevator.

He couldn't imagine why a timeshare huckster would need the services of Williams, Reavis & Buddenbrook, the agency *Ad Age* had named Chicago's premier advertising establishment for the discriminating and daring marketer. Didn't these vacation condo flimflam men usually just make do with a tacky bamboo stand on the street corner near middle class hotels in popular tropical tourist destinations? High pressure direct sales were their stale bread and rancid butter.

Still, as the chime announced the arrival of the elevator, Evan plastered on a smile and moved toward the opening doors, his arm outstretched to greet the next contributor to the agency's bottom line. Meeting a prospective client cold was always stressful, but advertising is a high-stress field. He could handle it, no matter what Buck Buddenbrook had intimated during Evan's last performance review, after Evan had been removed at the client's request from the Pee-Pee-Peekaboo-Baby doll account.

"Welcome to Williams, Reavis & Buddenbrook," Evan oozed with all the faux sincerity he could muster, and for an ad man, that's quite a bit. "I've been looking forward all morning to hearing about your company and what we here at WR&B can do to help you lure the weary traveler to the vacation location of a lifetime." Evan knew, of course, that it was more like trapping the unsuspecting traveler in the high interest monthly assessment of a lifetime, but principles were the first thing left on the cutting room floor when most commercials were made.

The taller of the two men strode forward and met Evan's hand with his own. "Warner Eckerton, vice president of marketing." The man nodded toward his companion. "This is Flynn Colby, our director of customer satisfaction."

Flynn Colby had a scientific look, like he spent more time with customer surveys and spreadsheets than he did out in the real world. Both men were also surprisingly pale for executives of a vacation destination vendor. Evan would have figured that all those guys got to stay in the company's unsold beachfront inventory on a regular basis as a perk.

Evan guided the group to a cherrywood-paneled conference room with a great view of Lake Michigan as everyone spouted the usual banalities about the view and the office and how good it was to meet each other. Evan could do a meet and greet in his sleep; it was all part of what he called the Big Schmooze.

His fetching assistant, Nancy, showed up magically with chilled glasses and sparkling bottled water. The stuff was shipped in from Tahiti, for God's sake, and was accordingly much more expensive than domestic water, but that was the magic of advertising, wasn't it? Evan always served it, just to send a subconscious message about the power advertising has over consumers. He opened his bottle and took a refreshing sip, giving an enthusiastic "Ahhh" as he finished and put the bottle back onto the veined granite tabletop, the label of the recycled plastic bottle facing outward toward his guests. The water importer was a client, too, after all.

Nancy exited the room after serving his guests, her hips sashaying. She shut the conference room door as she left.

Time for the pitch.

"Everyone here at WR&B is excited that you called us for a meeting today," Evan lied. No one at the agency had ever heard of Timeshares, but he was sure their money was as green as anyone else's. "We have a full range of services, from traditional television commercials to sport and concert events sponsorship, magazine slicks, free-standing newspaper inserts, radio spots and promos, sweepstakes, contests, Internet pop-ups, viral marketing, whisper campaigns, and, of course, direct mail."

He smiled broadly, but neither of the men from Timeshares spoke up, so he continued on after only a beat. No reason to make the client uncomfortable in his own meeting.

"As you I'm sure know, vacation marketing generally falls into two broad categories, volume drivers and competitive comparisons." Guys in the biz knew this kind of thing, but when neither client spoke or even nodded in understanding, Evan decided to explain.

"Volume drivers advertise the allure of the trip destination in order to increase the number of visitors to the destination. You know, pictures of palm trees, sunset beaches, laughing couples, bikini-clad models, that kind of thing. They drive more customers to the market, increasing the size of the customer pie. It helps your competitors, too, but if you operate only in limited markets, it helps drive volume to your markets rather than some other island or beach or country." Evan didn't want to blather on without knowing more, so he simply asked, "Do you operate only in a few locations or is your business worldwide?"

Eckerton spoke up. "We go everywhere."

Evan was pleased but surprised. Since no one in the office had heard of these guys and a quick Internet search of their surprisingly bland name had turned up nothing but a plethora of generic timeshare come-ons and some weird science fiction references on a time travel Webring, he had assumed they were small-timers, maybe new in the business. He probed further. "Tropical?

Or do you include all-weather terrains? Skiing, hiking, urban landmarks, that kind of thing?"

Eckerton spoke again. "We go everywhere."

"Excellent," Evan responded with enthusiasm. "Well, then, since you have your fingers in all the pies, competitive comparisons are the way to go. These can go in three basic directions. Price competition—you know, the old 'we get you there for less' kind of thing; ease of experience—all inclusive, no hassles, package deals; and quality—high end pampering, fancy lobbies, dolphins in the pool, thread count of the sheets—all that jazz."

Eckerton leaned forward. "I don't think you understand what our company does, Mr. Pogue. We don't run hotels or condos in tourist meccas, we offer time travel to historic destinations. You can go to any place and time you want."

Evan shook his head to clear his mind. That fantastic crap on the time travel Webring was real? He'd thought that the hubbub in the press a few years back about the invention of time travel had just been PR hype for the movie *ChronoScooters*. "So I can go to any historical event ever and see anything that ever happened?" This was a blockbuster concept. The only problem was it would freaking sell itself. What could they possibly need him for? "So, what's the catch?"

"Catch?" replied Eckerton, a bit of umbrage in his voice.

"Er, 'catching point,'" Evan extemporized. "Office lingo. What is the impediment to customers trampling each other in a frenzied desire to purchase your services? Price?"

"High," replied Eckerton, "but affordable, especially given the unique service we offer." He tilted his head to one side and pursed his lips. "Overall, I think we are satisfied with our total volume of interested customers."

Evan's brow furrowed involuntarily, but he quickly unfurrowed it. Not only was it bad form to show confusion or consternation to the customer, he didn't want to accelerate the time when he would need a Botox treatment. He looked at his clients with a calm, friendly smile. "If you have all the customers you want at a price you are happy with, then I don't understand what you are looking for from us here at WR&B," he said, then increased the wattage of his smile. "Not that we're not always happy to help. A few subsidized trips for movers and shakers will make your vacations in history the 'in' thing to do. We can have people standing in line at your offices as if they were at the latest nightclub, if that's what you want. Adds a cachet of exclusivity to a volume business."

"That's not it at all," replied Eckerton. "We have a product mix problem."

"Product mix?" queried Evan. "You only have the one product, right?"

"Yes and no." Eckerton relaxed back into his chair. "We only offer time travel vacations, but we have multiple destinations. That's where the product mix issue comes in."

Evan thought hard. The furrow on his brow returned, but he let it slide. "But you said you can go anywhere anytime. Right?"

Colby spoke up. "Subject to certain technical limitations."

Aha! "Such as?"

Colby shrugged. "The time portal is fixed in location and needs to be somewhere inconspicuous. So we can't, for example, take anyone to the doomed voyage of the *Titanic*. The ship moves, so when they wanted to return, the portal would be miles away, hovering over the water. Same with airplanes, space shuttles, and submarines."

Evan frowned. "But everything moves. The Earth rotates on its axis. It revolves around the sun."

Colby smiled. "Orbital mechanics are fixed and predictable. Everything else is a bit problematic, although we have had some success with trains. Of course, the timing is a bit tricky."

The furrow disappeared on its own. "That makes sense. And the portal needs to be inconspicuous because you don't want people just popping into existence where there are witnesses, right?"

"Quite right, Mr. Pogue," replied Eckerton. "This isn't like a movie or a virtual world. It's not remote viewing. This is reality. The vacationers are actually at that time and place they visit. They can be seen and heard and can interact, although there are stringent rules about the interactions. You know, the obvious things: no out of time objects, No anachronistic references or incongruent references to technology, Leave nothing behind. The rules are strict, but everyone understands the need.

"The inconspicuous imperative does limit destinational choices, however, even if the rules are followed. You can't just walk into the Oval Office during the Cuban Missile Crisis—the Secret Service would be all over you. Although I am pleased to report that we have filled in all of the empty seats in Ford's Theatre the night of Lincoln's assassination."

"Even with those limitations, there's still a lot of world and a lot of time available," Evan said with a nod. "What's the problem exactly? I can't help you until I understand it completely."

"Precisely why we are here," Eckerton responded. He motioned toward his companion. "Let me have Flynn here explain. He's on the front lines of customer satisfaction from the intake and destination selection phase to the post-return customer comment cards."

Flynn Colby opened a folder, scanned some notes, and then looked back up at Evan. "Despite the relatively few technical limitations on Timeshare's time travel encounter adventures, there are a number of practical impediments that limit the menu of desirable sites. In some cases, the inconspicuousness factor comes tangentially into play. Since the Timeshare visitors are actually there at that time, since in fact all Timeshare visitors that shall ever visit that time and place are actually there at that time, certain visits have inherent caps on the number of slots available. Warner's reference earlier to Ford's Theatre is a simple example. We can't put people in the Presidential box or in the aisles or on the stage, but we can put them in otherwise empty seats. Open areas with large crowds are the easiest for our kind of travel. The reason more and more aging baby-boomers claim to have been at Woodstock as time goes on isn't because they are all lying, it is because Timeshare injects vacationers into the mix on a regular basis."

Evan laughed. One of the great mysteries of the modern age explained. Could they possibly solve another? "You mean, if I wanted to be in Dallas . . ."

"Yes," sighed Colby, "we could put you into an available spot on the grassy knoll."

"And . . ." prompted Evan. "What would I see?"

Colby shook his head. "Sorry, our lips are sealed on that score. You'll just have to go see for yourself if you want to know."

"Don't put it off, though. Numbers are limited there," Eckerton interjected. "So we've jacked up the price on that one to what the market will bear."

"Like many of our customers," said Colby, "you've focused right in on near history in your home country. And there's good reason for that. Reality imposes its own limits, language chief among them. Going back to a place where people speak a foreign language you don't understand can be a big disappointment according to the customer comments I've reviewed. Even middle English is incomprehensible to most modern Americans. The discomfort of the required period costume, the smells, the air quality, and the lack of decent sanitation facilities are also often cited by customers as detracting from the quality of the vacation experience."

Eckerton leaned forward again. "That's why we want to run a campaign to get out of our battles and brothels rut."

"Battles and brothels?"

Colby winced. "We don't use that term in the customer satisfaction department. But what Warner is saying is that given the language barriers and the limits on how conspicuous we can be, a lot of our business has gravitated to two types of activities—both of which are somewhat distasteful to the powers that be in our company. The first is—to put it bluntly— sex tours. Certain customers wish to go to a time before AIDS, before current mores and laws, and simply cat about."

Evan grimaced. "There were diseases back then, too, weren't there?"

"Most can be handled with a simple prescription these days," explained Colby.

"But wouldn't those visitors be breaking the rules of Timeshares not to, er, leave anything behind?"

Eckerton gave a broad smile. "The time travel process has a radioactive component. By arranging the shielding appropriately, we are able to induce temporary sterility in our travelers with no long-term effects. Our waiver warns travelers that those attempting to start a family should not travel."

Yikes! Evan found himself crossing his legs without having consciously thought about it.

Eckerton gave a knowing laugh at the movement. "It's just like irradiating fruit at the supermarket to kill pathogens."

Colby laughed, too. "Except here we're irradiating nuts."

Uh-huh. "Let's move along," said Evan. "You said something about battles?"

"Sure," said Colby, his eyes flicking down to his notes. "Seven of our top ten destinations are violence-oriented. Civil War reenactors, history buffs, and fans of slasher films are among the hobbies of that market demographic."

No surprise there. "What's your top travel site? Gettysburg? Little Big Horn?"

Eckerton gave the answer. "Those are popular, but both relatively limited by conspicuousness and danger factors. Our top destination by far is the pass at Thermopylae in 480 B.C.

It took Evan a few seconds to figure it out.

"The Three Hundred."

Eckerton nodded. "Where three hundred Spartan soldiers held off an army of a million Persians."

"That sounds a bit conspicuous and dangerous itself."

"Not really," sniffed Colby. "Though some historical accounts put the count into the millions, there were actually only seventy-four thousand three hundred and twenty-eight Persians in the fight, so we can fill the hills behind the brutally violent skirmish lines with thousands and thousands of spectators, all while still fitting well within the parameters of the available historical record. We've actually set the site capacity limit at close to two hundred fifty thousand, not counting the actual Persians who get slaughtered or the Spartans who defend to the last man. Crowd-size estimation techniques sucked in ancient times."

Evan was appalled. "Wouldn't somebody notice the difference between the size of the crowd and the number of bodies eventually?"

Eckerton reddened. "We've contracted for body disposal activities with ... a number of organizations. We take the bodies in when we pull the vacationers out. All in period costume, with injuries appropriate to the situation. We weed out anyone with metal plates, pins, and prosthetics. We pull any crowns or teeth with fillings." He cast his eyes down at the table. "We don't talk about it much. Strictly confidential, you understand."

Evan understood the distaste the creators of Timeshare must have felt about how their device was being used. "History buffs. Let me guess. Watching snuff films is not among the categories of hobbies listed on the customer comment card."

Colby bristled at the reference to snuff films. "History is all about dead people. If you go far enough back, everyone you encounter is dead by now. We don't kill anyone."

"You just let people watch."

Eckerton jumped into the exchange. "This is precisely the product mix issue we have. Our current mix is ... embarrassing. Our founders didn't invent time travel so that we could pimp out history to man's baser instincts. Instead, we would like to emphasize other aspects of our travel opportunities. That's why we came up with our Sects and Violins tours."

Evan ground his teeth together at the sound of the punny product name. This guy was vice president of marketing? But Evan kept his mouth shut and let the client blather on.

"You see, given the language barriers, we thought that we might get increased travel to Europe and to premodern centuries by packaging a set of tours around great musical performances—a Woodstock thing for the more discriminating musical palate. You can hear Beethoven, Mozart, Bach, each performing or conducting his own works. You can listen to the first performance ever of the *1812 Overture* and marvel at the coordination required to make the sound of the cannons arrive at the precise moment needed, though they were situated miles away. You can listen to the glory of every church bell in Moscow joining in for the closing crescendo."

Evan could see the appeal to the symphony set, but that was a limited crowd. "Just classical?"

"Rock and roll is big, as we mentioned before. And blues has some hardcore fanatics, but is pretty severely volume limited. So, we've upped the price on those, although you do get a quality bootleg recording with every blues vacation."

Made sense. "What about the Sects part?"

"Great moments in religion," Eckerton gushed. "Hide in the shadows as Martin Luther tacks his theses onto the door at the Castle Church in Wittenberg. Join the masses at the Sermon on the Mount, lunch included!"

Evan understood the marketing play in being able to partake in an actual miracle of loaves and fishes as you listened to the Beatitudes, but he wondered if sitting in a crowd in the sun for hours while people spoke in incomprehensible languages about you was really that great of a vacation experience.

What the hell. People went to the beach all the time. At least no one would be playing a radio too loud next to you.

His mind began to piece together the components of a campaign to promote musical and religious destinations for Timeshares. It would take a lot of work. A lot. First thing, get rid of the awful Sects and Violins moniker for the package deals. But enough of those details for now. Time to compliment the client and close the deal.

"I think that we can help move more culturally rewarding religious and musical destinations into your top spots. What sort of budget did you have in mind?"

"I don't think you understand," said Eckerton with obvious concern.

"Several of our ten top sites are religious destinations or at least related to religion in some way," interjected Colby.

"But you said seven of the ten were violence oriented."

"There's some overlap. Let's see, there's the sacking of Jerusalem and the razing of Solomon's temple, burning Joan of Arc at the stake, the mass suicide at Masada, and, of course the Nazi death camps in operation. Religious persecution is popular in some quarters." Colby looked down at his notes. "I think there's one more religious destination in the top ten. Let me see ..."

Of course. "Jesus," blurted Evan. "The resurrection. The top religious destination's got to be the resurrection of Jesus, right?"

His would-be clients looked at him as if he were a crazed child.

"Not even in the top one hundred," intoned Eckerton.

"Not really dramatic," added Colby. "Just a guy you don't recognize walking around with his friends chatting in a language you don't understand. Nothing to see, really." He tapped his notebook with his finger. "Here it is. I should have remembered. It is one of the reasons we came." He looked up at Evan.

Evan couldn't stand the tension. "The Ten Commandments? The parting of the Red Sea? Mohammed moving a freaking mountain? What?"

"The Crucifixion. Big crowds, so not space limited, and plenty of cruelty, violence, and death. We've been packing them into the Hills of Galilee since we first opened for business. Popular stuff. Ask Mel Gibson. Second only to the Three Hundred in attracting the death and torture fetishists."

"Very distasteful," droned Eckerton.

Evan's mind was awhirl. Distasteful was too mild a word for peddling the Crucifixion like a no-holds-barred cage match. His lip twitched as his blood pressure rose, but he maintained a rigid hold on his outward demeanor. "What exactly do you want WR&B to do about it?"

"Isn't it obvious?" replied Eckerton, a look of surprise on his face. "We want a campaign that will make our customers seek enriching, ennobling, and educational cultural experiences filled with music and art instead of seeking violent, gory, and sadistic experiences filled with sex and death."

"Instead of?" Evan threw up his hands. "Instead of? That goes against everything in television, movies, literature, games, sports, and advertising since time began." Clients expected the impossible. With a hefty budget and a good campaign, he could increase customer demand for time trips featuring music and religiously uplifting themes, but decreasing the demand for lust and mayhem was impossible—crazy impossible. "You want an ad campaign that will make people stop wanting sex and violence?"

"We have money," Eckerton replied.

"And time," interjected Colby. "We have all the time in the world."

"Not enough," shouted Evan, his friendly facade shattering. "Not enough to change human nature, not for the better." He couldn't work miracles, and the public was apparently only interested in seeing someone who could if they were being brutally murdered.

The anger flooded over Evan, his heart rate increasing,

his fists clenching, adrenaline racing through his body. He hated clients who were unreasonable. He wanted to punch Eckerton with animalistic fury. His hands longed to strangle Colby until his eyes bulged out.

That was the problem, the problem no amount of mild-mannered marketing could ever fix.

Evan crushed his half-full bottle of overpriced, overmarketed Tahitian water and flung it across the room, storming out past his buxom assistant, sending advertising tear sheets for the latest torture porn flick and upcoming World Championship Cage Match fluttering in disarray in his wake.

Evan had a passion for advertising, sure, but mankind had a passion for the Passion. Neither was likely to find any peace.

Not anywhere.

Not anywhen.

No Man's Land
Allister Timms

Allister Timms is a Welshman who lives in Maine
with his wife and daughter and works as the copy
editor for *Down East*, the magazine of Maine. His
work has appeared in *Down East* and *Miami Living*, and he is currently working on his first cowritten YA fantasy novel *The Golden Grip*.

I crouch, hands clasped over my head. A whizbang explodes behind our stretch of trench fittingly named
by the soldiers the Bish o' Prick. The shell showers earth
and shrapnel high into the air. This one looks to me like
a dark etching Dürer might have engraved of an enormous tree uprooted by a twister.

But I'm blessed with such flights of fancy. Lieutenant
Pritchard says that if I daydream anymore I might pres-
age my own death. But he's an Oxford man and tends
to talk like that.

My feet are cold. There is about a foot of water and
mud covering the duckboards. Rain is falling in steady
streams. Even the elements, it seems, can't help but imi-
tate the war. If there is a sun, I don't know it. And when
I do catch a glimpse, it's murky. Like it's been doused in
coal tar.

I'm getting a little rest and time to think. Part of my company was out all night in No-Man's-Land, gathering information on the strength and number of machine guns Fritz has in place. The appearance of a sagging moon made our task harder and cost the life of Private Richards. I had joked with Corporal Jennings that the moon sagged on account of all the heat from the mortars both sides had flung at each another. He had laughed. And then he wept when Richards got it in the head. Richards was only eighteen. A buckshee private from Llandudno. Jennings closed his eyes. Another flare went up, burst, and cascaded down in a drizzle of dying lights. We scrambled out of the crater, leaving Richards behind in the waterlogged hole.

I try to sleep in my billet until the stand to order comes down the line. I listen to our artillery pound away at the fortified German positions and they in turn pound us. It's like a game of tennis that titans might play.

I look at my watch. It's July 30. Time's against me and I know it. Another day and the Battle of Passchendaele will be in full offensive and 300,000 men will die. It's recorded in all the history books. And now I could be one of them. The battalion has been given its orders. As an officer, I'm privy to what the other men only sense and fear. Who would have known that the uniform I purchased over the Internet would have turned out to be an officer's uniform. And a lieutenant's at that.

No wonder I can't sleep. Not after what's happened. Like the comforting words a madman repeats to himself to prove that he's sane, I remove the flat, iPhone-like Speed of Light device that Timeshares provided for this journey and type in the numbers. Over and over I punch them in. Turning numbers into a prayer.

Nothing. Like it's been for a month. Nothing but the

image of an hourglass and sifting sand. I want to toss the device over the trench and watch as a German sniper blasts to smithereens my only connection to my existence in the twenty-first century. But I can't bring myself to do it.

It was something the boy said. "Sir, Private Hawkes is dead."

Five little words. That's all it took.

They'd screwed up. Timeshares had blundered. I gave the tech the exact year of 1917 and the exact location of Passchendaele. And, most importantly, the precise date: July 28. That was the last diary entry of Toby Hawkes, my great-grandfather.

I should have guessed from the layers of white-gold bling-bling the young tech wore around his neck and the lazy chew of his slack jaw that I should have rescheduled.

"You've got that time figured precisely, right?" I'd asked. I know it sounds paranoid, but time traveling, even for recreational purposes, isn't anything to treat lightly. One wrong digit, and I could have ended up in 1717 in a field of grazing cows.

"I could do this with my eyes closed," the tech replied, stabbing the keypad of the slim electronic device with Passchendaele's degrees of longitude and latitude.

"It's just I scheduled my appointment with Dr. Arundel, that's all," I remarked.

"No worries. The doc is out with the flu. He just gives the briefing. It's me who flicks the switch."

Flicks the switch. This secular description of a complex and highly specialized field of molecular transference and time travel should have clued me in. But I shrugged and stepped inside the tubular contraption that looked like a frosted shower stall.

Thank God I'd been shrewd enough to ask about the briefing.

"Okay, the briefing," grinned the tech. "You'll need this." He shoved the small electronic device he'd been holding into my hand. "That gizmo is your ticket home, so don't lose it. What you do is . . ." and he perfunctorily explained about the numbers to dial that would connect me to Timeshares and scramble my atoms to bring me back to the current time. "Any questions?"

I looked at the Speed of Light device in my hand and watched the emblem of Timeshares, an ancient hourglass with sifting gold sand, blink across the screen. I secured the device in my trench coat.

The tech fastened the door on the Time Sequencing Modulator. I clutched my army haversack stuffed with gear: my great-grandfather's diary, gas mask, helmet, shovel, dried rations, candles, water canister, extra pair of puttees, eating tin, packs of Woodbines, laces, three pairs of extra socks (I wasn't taking any chances here), ammunition pouch, and an officer-issued revolver. It had taken me a good two weeks to locate all this paraphernalia, except for the diary, on eBay. I hadn't realized Timeshares would have provided a costume for me, included with the price of my "vacation."

I clenched my fists as the Time Sequencing Modulator screened my genetic makeup with a soothing blue pattern of lights. The small space began to heat up. Comfortable at first, like a hot tub, but then it got hotter. I pulled at my stiff collar. Fidgeted as the temperature rose.

I grabbed at my great-grandfather's diary to calm myself. I recited over and over his last entry: "Hobbs and I have come to blows over the money again. I knew he'd turn out to be a power-hungry bastard. I had me bleedin doubts about him right off. Should have followed me gut and never taken him under me wings. I swear to bloody god, he's going to kill me. So I'm writing this down in case I don't make it home to dear Old Blighty."

A blinding white light suddenly enveloped the inside of the modulator and I felt like a Rubik's Cube of flesh, twisting and turning, turning and twisting. And then I felt nothing but a lingering taste of cottonmouth, like I'd eaten rhubarb for an eternity.

It's unwise to travel the trenches by day. The enemy's snipers are always looking for new targets. And they are good. Better marksmen than our boys. Pritchard tells me it's on account of their grand Teutonic past that favored arms to art. I respond it was probably because they drank less rum and got better training.

I pass NCOs issuing the day's orders. Soldiers filling sandbags. Others dumping creosol and chloride of lime. Still more men pumping the brackish water out of the trench while singing hymns. The British Tommy loves to sing, even when he is about to die. Maybe he knows it could happen anytime. Perhaps it's his way of preparing his immortal soul even as he pumps putrid water.

I walk by a couple of big brown rats. Hefty buggers who, despite their bulk, are ever so nimble on the parapet. The one at the end of this little expeditionary force stops and inspects me. I try to remember a refrain or a bar from Tchaikovsky's *Nutcracker Suite*. I think even though he's a rat, he would have made a lovely king of mice commanding his soldiers. But he doesn't stay long enough for me to remember a note. So I schlep on, keeping my head down.

I find William Blake in his "coffin." It's his morose way of describing his pillbox crafted out of sandbags.

And, yes, it's that Blake. The eighteenth-century painter, engraver, visionary poet, and patriarch of English Romanticism. Turns out Timeshares isn't restricted to my own century. They've been busy capitalizing on Faulkner's famous dictum that "the past is not dead. It's not even past," and adding their own consumer slant with, "And now it can be anything you want it to be!"

Blake wears a frown as he says, "War on Earth is energy enslav'd."

I slump down on an overturned barrel and stare. Even after a month, I still find it hard to reason—which Blake keeps telling me is man's greatest folly—that I'm sharing the trenches of World War I with the eccentric poet who was considered mad during his lifetime and a genius in modern times.

I have the itch to ask him if it's true that he and Mrs. Blake recited Milton in the nude in their garden in South Molton. But I just can't bring myself to do it.

I tap the last Woodbine from the package, pack it on the butt of my revolver, and toss it into my mouth. I only cough a couple of times now when I take a long drag. It was a lot harder in the beginning. I felt like I was coughing my lungs up, and there is mustard gas for that.

A rowdy bout of mortars rain down.

"So, what shall we discuss today?" asks Blake.

He asks me this every time. And I answer it with the same reply: "Timeshares."

It's what binds us together and sets us apart from the other soldiers. But with this broken homing device, God knows I'm stuck here now just like the rest of the infantrymen. And I shouldn't be. It's a fucking mistake. The soldiers, they know they might die here in France. I was one hundred percent certain I *couldn't*. So my fate now seems more sealed than the men around me. They've got hope, whereas I don't even have that. Even if I do survive the coming battle, this time isn't mine. I don't have a family to go home to. Shit, I'm not even born for another ninety-five years!

Blake knew I was relieved when I found him. And I might have just passed him by like I did so many of the other men. I only stopped because he was vandalizing military equipment.

I stepped closer for a better look. I had to cough to get his attention.

Right away I sensed something different about him. He looked me square in the eyes with sad, innocent ones, like the eyes of a seer. They were so at odds with his fierce-jowled face.

If he hadn't met my gaze, I wouldn't have looked down.

That's when I noticed what he had been engraving into the butt of his rifle. It was an hourglass.

I splurted out, "What . . . what do you know about that?"

"Nothing sir," he replied surly.

"You tell me right now what you know about that hourglass, or I'll have you digging a latrine while the flares go up."

He shook his large head. "Infernal intellectuals. I wonder if that's why I'm such a good shot?"

"I'm warning you, soldier."

Enigmatically he said, "Time can as easily flow forward as it can back." (If I had known who he was then, I'd have thought it was simply one of his proverbs.)

"Timeshares," I whispered, as if to a lover.

"Yes," he replied. "The Eternals, it seems, have brought us together."

Machine gun fire rattles over No-Man's-Land. It sounds like rain falling on leaves.

Blake hunches down in his coffin. He's drawing a bead on some unfortunate. I always try to see him pull the trigger. But it happens like some prestige. The only evidence of his kill is the empty cartridge floating in the muck at his feet.

I ask him again to tell me about Timeshares in his world. "It's not an order," I say. "It's a favor, of one friend to another."

Blake slides the bolt back on his rifle. "Timeshares is a dowdy little hovel on Carnaby Street. I like to wander all over London, exploring, thinking—it's when I get my best visions. I was curious about the sign of the hourglass hanging outside the shop. Time has always intrigued me: each end of an hourglass seems to me like twin aspects of eternity. So I stepped into the unassuming shop and came out here."

"But why did you?"

Blake frowns and it produces a faint smile on his lips. He stuffs a hand into his mud-splattered trench coat and pulls out a handful of dark little seeds like minuscule shots. "Poppy seeds," he tells me, shaking them in his closed fist. "Wherever the angel tells me there will be a great war in the future, Timeshares sends me to that place, and it's where I sow the seeds of poetry. I came here to leave a gift; to remind man that war threatens creativity, destroys the breath of the Almighty. Man's wars are nothing but the fever of the human soul. I even went back to antiquity, to Homer's day, hoping to discourage him from writing his war epic. But the fool thought me an upstart poet trying to steal his muse."

A shower of flares explodes over our heads. They fall to earth like wounded angels.

Blake stares at me. In his eyes, I swear I see a sea of swaying poppies, exactly like the flowers that will one day cover these fields of Flanders. "And you?" he asks.

I lean closer, to be better heard. "I came here to save a man." Then I toss my head back and laugh like an ass. "And it turns out to be me."

I show Blake my broken homing device. "I can't return. And tomorrow's the most devastating battle of this war. Time is literally running out. I don't want to die." I can hear the tremor in my voice. "I came here to right a wrong, but now all I want to do is save my own skin. It's futile trying to change history. You can't. No matter if your intentions are good or bad. And I'm only now realizing this. I'm alone to suffer my fate like all the other men here."

Blake reaches into his trench coat again. He shoves a photo of a young woman into my hands. "She's a looker, isn't she? Nice legs, too. That Mrs. Blake knows how to ride a cock horse to Banbury Cross."

I smile, but it's a little forced.

Blake shoves me. "Ah, come on, where's your sense of humor? Jesus and Mary, you're making me weep with your drama."

He furrows his brow, which makes him look exactly like his painting of Nebuchadnezzar.

Rain. Mud. The coils of barbed wire slick. Each barb the cold bite of reality stretched out inside of me.

Dawn is approaching. The stand to order came hours ago in the fug of night. Not that day is any clearer. It's just less ambiguous. Stark reality glares all around us even without the sun. The dead bodies. The craters. The bloating mules. The endless barbed wire. The screaming and crying of wounded and dying men.

I can't believe I let Blake talk me into this. Maybe he is as mad as history makes him out to be. But what other choice did I have?

The Timeshares homing device is dead. And Blake says he doesn't have one.

My mouth goes dry. But it's not the cottonmouth I experienced time traveling to the trenches. This is produced by fear.

Blake chants at my side. "Tyger! Tyger! burning bright, in the forests of the night, what immortal hand or eye, could frame thy fearful symmetry?"

"Is that a passage from the Bible?" asks an ashen-faced young Tommy.

"Shut it," commands the sergeant.

The long line of soldiers becomes deathly silent.

My heart feels like it's an hourglass sifting my life away.

The major's whistle shrieks. "Charge," he screams, leading the way.

Over the top I go with the rest of the battalion.

The rattle of machine guns. Blood. Screams. A severed leg. A madman cackling in a crater.

And I'm running and flinging poppy seeds like Blake instructed, like he saw in his vision. I don't even remove my revolver. Just toss the seeds among all the carnage, expecting a bullet in the skull at any moment.

A blinding flash. A loud bang.

Someone's shaking me.

"Hey buddy, you okay?"

The smoke clears. I'm sitting on a highly polished sanitized floor. The clicks and zips and metallic beeps of computers bombard me.

"Did you have a blast or what?" asks the young tech, his bright, white-gold tooth shining like a piece of shrapnel in his mouth. "Shit, you did, didn't you?"

By Our Actions
Michael A. Stackpole

Michael A. Stackpole is an award-winning writer, screenwriter, podcaster, game and computer game designer, and graphic novelist. His most recent novel, *At the Queen's Command*, is the first in his Crown Colonies series. He lives in Arizona and, in his spare time, enjoys indoor soccer and dancing. The idea for this story came to him after too much research and too little sleep. His Web site is www.stormwolf.com.

The Timeshares helicopter thundered around the mountain. *This has to be bad.* The mantislike airship unsteadily lowered itself into the meadow. The pine trees downslope of the cabin hid it, but the fluttering roar of the copter's rotors echoed from the mountains. Men shouted below and he caught the flash of the first of Jacobsen's phalanx coming up the crooked path.

Logically he should have put the ax down and readied himself to greet his old employer's envoy, but he couldn't. Jacobsen had violated the promise to leave him in peace. *Doesn't matter. The answer's no.*

Perry gripped the ax tightly to stop his body's trembling.

Then Jacobsen himself appeared, still dressed for the heart of the city. Perry's mouth went dry. *It can't be.*

Jacobsen adjusted his tie—college striping, full Windsor knot—and played at brushing a spot of mud from his black suit's knee. He smiled, making it carry up into his eyes, and made eye contact. He extended his hand several muddy steps shy of level.

"It's good to see you again, Perry. The mountain air has done you well, old friend."

Perry stared at the proffered hand as if it was a snake. His own right hand bore the ax. He swung it up, then rested it on his shoulder. "You shouldn't be here. Please go."

"Give me five minutes, Perry." Jacobsen glanced back over his shoulder as his hand drifted down. "On the copter."

Perry shook his head. "Whatever you need, I can't do it. Won't."

"I need to convince you otherwise."

"You can't."

The white-haired man's eyes narrowed. "We've lost a leper."

The shakes hit Perry so hard he dropped the ax. "You lost . . . how could you? You promised!"

"Sometimes promises have to be broken."

"And this one broke time?" Perry closed his eyes, then muttered a prayer. He used the time afforded him in picking up the ax and burying it in the chopping block to get control of himself. He shifted fear into anger, his eyes opening into narrow slits. He spitted Jacobsen with a stare. "How could you have been so stupid?"

Jacobsen turned, starting back down toward the helicopter. "I will brief you en route. We really have no time to waste."

"Funny to hear that from you." Back in the early days

of Timeshares that had been a running joke. They had all the time in the world since they could go anywhere, do anything. Perry might have laughed out of habit, but Jacobsen's flat delivery underscored the urgency of the situation.

Perry swung into the copter easily enough—old habits never really die, just lay dormant. The chemical scent of aviation fuel filled his head, adding to his queasiness. The rolling clack of doors closing, the thrumming thunder filling the cabin, all things that reminded him of days he'd hoped to forget.

A bodyguard handed him a helmet and plugged him into the communications system. The helmet selected the executive frequency as Perry strapped in. As if the click of Perry's restraints had freed the craft from gravity's grip, the helicopter leaped into the air with a lurch. It left Perry's stomach on the ground.

Jacobsen, belted onto the bench beside him, passed him a tablet reader. "Everything you need to know is in there."

Perry shook his head. "Why did you do it?"

Jacobsen's gaze hardened as he reached over and turned the tablet on, then tapped open an app. A picture appeared. "That is Senator Harrison Smelton, religious conservative from north Texas. He chairs the Senate select committee on scientific research. He came to us and suggested that he was going to hold hearings into exactly what we do at Timeshares."

"He never should have known about Timeshares." Perry had been one of the company's first scouts. It had been made painfully clear to him that time travel wasn't going to be a Greyhound Bus kind of a vacation. The ultrarich, maybe some research trips, but not common knowledge in the early days. If folks even imagined time travel was possible, every economic boom and bust cycle would be blamed on profiteering by Timeshares customers. Timeshares had created the cover story of a virtual-reality touring package and even provided the same in some franchise operations. Those satellite facilities helped screen for potential high-end customers, but Jacobsen had been dead set against government regulation from the beginning.

"After you left, we had a couple clients dog-bone us." Jacobsen tugged at his shirt cuffs. "We dealt with most of them, but one of the early ones made a killing selling some artifacts he'd buried and dug up later. He hadn't gone for significant stuff, just did a time capsule with some rare baseball cards, comics, that sort of stuff. Smelton courted him for campaign contributions. They became chummy and, one night over cigars and a bottle of scotch that had also been in this guy's trove—stuff that went missing during Prohibition, nice planning on his part—he confessed. Then I got a call."

Perry flicked his finger across the tablet's screen. The picture went from one of the senator alone, to his standing with a young man, early twenties, in front of the Timetank. Flick. A third included their guide.

He looked up. "The Senator extorts a family trip to Jerusalem, 28 A.D.? April, around Passover?"

Jacobsen pointed at the third picture. "We followed your playbook. We sent a guide. They were all three done up as lepers so no one would get near them. This was strictly a holo-safari."

"*That* wasn't what I recommended. That wasn't what you agreed to." Perry shook his head. "Some events are just too hot. People feel compelled to interfere, to interact. What did the senator do?"

"*He* didn't do anything." Jacobsen sighed, a wall of static onto the com channel. "He got hurt, attacked. His guide, too. They hit their panic buttons, heading back. The son, Kevin, is gone."

Something isn't right. "What aren't you telling me?"

"It's delicate."

"You came for me. It's way past delicate." Perry searched the man's face for a flicker of humanity, but found none. "Oh, shit. You didn't do a psych vetting on the kid, did you?"

Jacobsen shook his head. "Kevin is a schizophrenic. The boy thinks, among other things, that he's possessed. His father was taking him back to get Jesus to heal him. To cast out a demon. Two days without meds, figured out where he was, he freaked out, attacked his father and the guide. "We think he hurt Jesus. Maybe even killed him."

"Not possible. I've been back. I saw . . ." Perry blinked. "So the Kaku Theory of Temporal Elasticity isn't holding up?"

"Doesn't look like it."

The Kaku Theory suggested that the arrow of time had a lot of momentum moving into the future. To disrupt its trajectory would take a vast amount of energy. Even if a change were made, Kaku had postulated that a divergent history could change enough that time travel wasn't discovered; thereby canceling out the change that spawned that timeline in the first place. It was the old science fiction trope of the grandfather paradox all dressed up with a bunch of string theory and arcane math into a suggestion that no one needed to worry about a bug being killed or anything else weird happening on timetrips.

"We're getting changes in the timetraps. They're slowly building up." Jacobsen sighed again. "We need you to fix things."

"You have other Stopwatches who speak Aramaic, Greek, and Latin."

"But nobody like you." Jacobsen punched the tablet's screen and an accounting sheet appeared. "I pay your bills, so I know what you buy, what you study. You've steeped yourself in this stuff, all this biblical history. You know what's going on then, and not just because you've been there. You're the only one who can fix it."

"You have the wrong man." Perry handed Jacobsen his tablet, his hands shaking. "I can't go back there."

"Perry, you're the *only* man. Truly."

"I can't be."

Jacobsen's face drained of color. "We've tried sending others back. They can't make it. Closest we've gotten is 67 A.D. Damascus. Because you were in Jerusalem, because you've seen what happens, the events are a reality for you. You have access to a little bubble of time that is fast collapsing, or so our advance research department thinks."

Perry shook his head. "It's against all the rules for me to go back. If I see my future self, I'll know I live, and that will change history. I'll make things worse."

Jacobsen snorted. "Do you honestly think that you *then* would recognize you *now*? The weight you've lost? The beard?"

The haunted look around my eyes?

Perry sat very still, the copter's vibrations the only cause of his movement. That trip to Jerusalem hadn't been his last scouting run, but almost. Prior to it, he'd been the guy who liked to go where the action was. Thermopylae, Tutenborg Forest, Gettysburg, Hue, Stalingrad, and the Horns of Hattin—if there was a war going on, he jumped to the head of the line. It wasn't that he'd taken great delight in war, but he just understood it as a living creature, watching armies crawl over landscapes, devouring each other. It was a whole different level of seeing things, with technology over the years just making the battlefields bigger and the wounds more hideous.

Perry's childhood hadn't involved a lot of church-going or religious instruction. His basic indifference to religion made him a natural for the Easter Run. He accepted the job, more interested in seeing how the Romans worked in the Middle East than anything else. It was just another run.

But after what he saw, it just wasn't something that could confine itself to a report.

Perry glanced down at his hands. "Father, take this cup away from me."

"Pardon?"

"The Gospel of Mark, chapter fourteen, verse thirty-six." Perry shook his head. "I can't do this."

"If you don't, none of us will exist."

"No more lepers."

Jacobsen nodded. "I swear to God."

"Playing the blasphemy card right now, not a good choice."

"You'll have everything you need." The gray pallor of Jacobsen's face began to warm. "Just ask."

"What I need is for you to be quiet." Perry brought his hands together. "And I need a chance to pray."

Perry timed-in outside Jerusalem and immediately went to his knees. Timeshares was pretty good of dropping people in on schedule, but actual physical locations were dodgy. He'd been aiming for olive groves outside of Jerusalem. They dropped him north of the Damascus gate, on Golgatha.

He knelt there, burying his face against his knees. His stomach twisted in on itself. The scents, the dust, animal dung, hints of smoke, and the stench of human habitation.

Even the stink of death because, in the Roman fashion, a couple of bandits had been crucified nearby and left to rot.

On the road to Damascus, so all can see Roman justice.

They had dropped him where it had ended. He squeezed his eyes shut against tears and against remembering. His fists tightened. Two days hence, a man would hang on a cross until he died and, by that act, he would shape the history of mankind.

And I have to make sure it happens.

He struggled to his feet, wrapping his linen sheet around himself more tightly. Timeshare's experts had suggested he travel back as a centurion. It would allow him to be armed. The implication that he might have to kill a senator's dangerously psychotic son was not lost upon him. Dicey prospect, but Jacobsen signed off on it.

Then he probably sold options to short his own stock in case I do.

Perry staggered his way down the hill, growing stronger with each step. He remembered clearly where he'd been on his previous journey, and there would be no crossing of paths. Jacobsen had been right, however. The old Perry wouldn't have recognized the new Perry. Moreover, had he seen him, the old Perry would have viewed him with contempt. The way he walked, the look in his eyes. It wasn't what Perry ever would have imagined for himself.

The previous Perry likely could have guessed there were four gospels. The new Perry had committed them to memory, and had learned to read them in the original and all translations. He'd started that study as a way to deny what he had seen. He wanted to find room to doubt. He'd grasped at the fact that there were no contemporaneous accounts of Jesus' life. Josephus was writing at least forty years after the Crucifixion. The Gospels were written yet later, and no eyewitness accounts of Jesus' ministry had been discovered. Some scholars went so far as to suggest that Jesus was a fiction picked up by Paul and transformed into something that took on a grand life of its own.

The Roman soldiers at the gate didn't give him a passing glance. He joined the stream of straggling pilgrims come to Jerusalem for Passover. They had no clue as to how close they were to history being made, their empire being swept away—and had he tried to warn them, they'd have considered him utterly mad.

They would ignore me as did Jacobsen.

The scent of unwashed human flesh, open sewers, and the occasional rotting dog would have overwhelmed most people from Perry's time. Tourists always had a clean, Hollywood impression—more sound lot than sandlot. On the couple of tours where he'd acted as a guide, his charges constantly made asides about the horrible scars left behind by diseases that had died out in their time, or the way that in-time people were so small and stiff and prematurely old looking.

As Perry moved through the narrow, twisting streets, he listened for any gossip. He heard nothing about the Nazarean, so he finally asked and was directed south. Everyone remembered the rabbi's triumphant entry into Jerusalem earlier in the week, so pointing out the home where he shared supper with his disciples was simple.

Perry arrived after the sun had set. Part of him wanted to go closer to the building, to listen to Jesus explain what the disciples were to do to celebrate his memory. He would have been interested to see how many of them were confused, and if any shivered with the ominous portent of his instructions. He longed to see Mary

Magdelene, to see if she was treated as friend or wife, and to watch her tenderness in caring for Jesus.

He could not, however, do that. It was unlikely that Kevin Smelton would interrupt the Last Supper, but he still had to keep a watch out for him. In fact, Perry was pretty certain where and when Kevin would strike. Biblical accounts of Jesus' death were fairly exact on details save where he spent the night after being hauled away from the Garden of Gethsemane and questioned. That was the only slip space in the accounts, and Perry had come prepared to stop the young man.

Perry caught no sign of movement save for the occasional silhouette that dimmed the limning light around the shutters. The night began to cool off, but Perry didn't notice. His mountain retreat had prepared him for worse, and he wondered if he had known this day would come. Had he really expected Jacobsen to black out special high-demand blocks of time when so many people would have paid fabulous sums of money to visit them?

I should have known better. I did.

Movement from the house caught his eye. A red-haired man emerged and scurried off. *Judas*. Perry had always figured that if someone was going to interfere with the passion of Christ, they'd come and stop Judas, but this was where the Kaku Theory about self-correction worked little micromiracles. The religious politics in Jerusalem demanded Jesus be broken and exiled or killed because he was challenging the power structure. It was like the death of John Fitzgerald Kennedy. Yes, Lee Harvey Oswald had been the one to kill him that day in Dallas, but if he hadn't, the Cubans or Russians, the Mafia, Ku Klux Klan, or an assortment of other psychotics would have done the job. It wasn't a matter of *if* but a matter of *when*.

At least for JFK it was fast.

More movement from the house and Perry readied himself. Jesus emerged along with the rest of the apostles. He wore his hair long and unbound, much as was seen in many portraits. His beard, however, had grown in quite full and had not been neatly trimmed. He wasn't a terribly tall man, but that should have been no surprise. None of them were. Had Perry not stooped his shoulders and lowered his head entering the city, he'd have towered over the Romans and they would have thought him a German barbarian.

As Jesus led the others through the city, Perry followed, initially keeping to the shadows. More people came out to follow Jesus as well. Some, children who just liked a parade, soon dropped off. Many young people like the disciples, men and women both, drifted in their wake. They held back, not sure if they were interfering or if they were welcome. While Jesus made no sign to encourage them, neither he nor the apostles made any attempt to chase them off.

So Perry joined the modest crowd. Their presence gave him reassurance. They allowed him access, to get close, which he wanted to do. It was critical to his plan, of course, and he told himself that was why it was so important.

And yet he couldn't deny there was another reason.

On his previous trip he had seen Jesus twice. Once from afar, as Jesus entered Jerusalem on a mule, being feted by adoring crowds. Perry had hung back with the lepers, but hadn't been terribly interested in Jesus per se. What had fascinated him was that the same crowd which welcomed Jesus as a savior would, in a week's time, call for the release of a thief and rebel instead of this man they claimed to love. It was just one more instance of the savagery he'd seen in countless battles and, in this case, ironic as the Prince of Peace would be led to the slaughter.

Then, later, he watched the procession to Golgatha. Jesus, his back bloodied, the crown of thorns causing rivulets of blood to course down his face, being forced to drag his cross along. The final humiliation that, like being forced to dig your own grave, being reduced from a human to the output of your muscles and bones. Being made into an animal, and less, because of the parts of you that were no longer required were the parts that defined you as human.

It was that idea that had gotten to Perry. It had taken time to sink in, but the truth of Jesus' sacrifice had eluded believers and scholars alike. They viewed his physical death as the grand sacrifice, but it wasn't. That was an afterthought. The man's identity, his essence, his *being,* had been stripped away. Jesus' teachings and philosophy, his kindness, forgiveness, and compassion had defined him. And yet with every step from the Garden of Gethsemane to the place of skulls, it had been stripped from him.

And yet his mission was so important he allowed it. His love for others was so great he gave up everything. What had been nailed to the cross was just a piece of meat that roused itself once, that wondered why it was all alone, and then it surrendered. No tears. No self-pity. No regrets. Just surrender.

That had gotten under Perry's skin as nothing else ever had. He'd seen enough on his other trips, he'd had his own military training before Timeshares, so he'd reassured himself time and again that he could do what he saw others do. Had the Spartan's needed man 301, he could have done it. He could have slaughtered Romans with the best of the Germans, or fought to the death in the arenas of Rome. The prospect of having to do that didn't confound or amaze him.

But to die to make a point?

To die in the hope that people would take his message seriously enough to change their culture, that made no sense. That was betting everything on the longest odds ever. Countless had been the cults that had made a similar bet and had vanished into history.

But Jesus had done it because he believed.

And Perry had never before believed in anything that much in his life.

But he found himself believing, so he did his best to destroy that belief. But all the studies couldn't kill it. He couldn't intellectualize and compartmentalize that which he had seen in dying Jesus' eyes. It changed him, destroyed him. The power of it drove him out of the life he knew and into one of peace.

Or one that should have been peaceful.

Hiking along toward the back of the pack, Perry wanted, badly, to get close to Jesus. Not to say anything, but just to look in his eyes again and let him know that he would succeed. Maybe, just maybe, that might ease the pain. It might give him just a bit more strength.

It might change history yet again.

Perry followed as they made their way to the Mount of Olives and into the Garden of Gethsemane. Jesus took his leave with Peter, James, and John. He wanted to go after them, in part to learn which of the gospels had the truth of the incident. Did an angel appear to strengthen him, as in Luke, or was he already resolute and needed no supernatural reinforcement? Did his disciples fall asleep, again as in Luke, or did they remain vigilant?

His hands closed into fists again as a cool breeze

rustled tree branches. Men like Senator Smelton would stand up and proclaim the Bible to be the literal word of God, yet little contradictions in the texts were things they swept away without a concern. Those contradictions were little "tests of faith," just like fossils and evolution. But would Jesus put those tests of faith in the Bible? That didn't seem to be in keeping with his nature or philosophy.

Perry smiled to himself. *It's a passage in Mark that has me here, but I didn't make it into Luke or Matthew.* That concerned him slightly, but since Mark had been a source for the other two accounts, not terribly much. That he wasn't in John either bothered him not at all. It had been written for a Roman audience, so his part would have been considered irrelevant.

A murmuring arose among the disciples and followers as they heard voices of men approaching. Jesus, looking haggard, his hair stringy and robe soaked with sweat, appeared with the other three. Judas, torch in hand, led the group who had come for Jesus. As the followers shrank back, Judas approached and gave Jesus a welcoming kiss.

Jesus pushed him aside, not roughly, but as if parting a curtain. He looked at the priests and temple attendants. "Who is it you seek?"

One slender hatchet-faced man with acne scars high on his cheeks, drew himself up. "Jesus of Nazareth."

"I am he." Jesus took a step forward. "You should not trouble these others."

A servant darted forward to grab Jesus by the wrist and tug him roughly toward them. Peter drew a sharp little fish-gutting knife and slashed at the man's face. He took off half his ear. The man retreated screaming and tension spiked.

Jesus gave Peter a reproving stare, then bent and

picked up the portion of ear. He reached out and pressed it to the man's head and held it there for several heartbeats. Jesus' hand came away bloody, but the ear remained whole.

Perry's jaw hung open. Perry couldn't see any swelling or redness or any other sign that it had ever been cut. He had agreed with scholars who dismissed the miracle stories as storytelling techniques needed to fix Jesus in the pantheon of heroes of that age. Virgin births were commonly ascribed to great men. Multiple accounts existed of magicians repeating Jesus' miracles, Simon Magus the best known among them. The miracles were the equivalent of Parson Weems' fantasy of George Washington chopping down the cherry tree. They were meant to illustrate a point, not to be taken literally.

And yet he'd just seen Jesus reattach a severed ear. It wasn't possible, and Perry wasn't alone in believing that. Those who had come to arrest Jesus nervously fingered their swords and staves. The disciples and followers dropped to their knees, not in submission to the captors, but in reverence for what the other side considered blasphemous sorcery.

Jesus opened his arms. "When I was in the temple, you did not come against me. Now you are here. This is your part to play. You are part of the darkness. Do what you must."

The priest nodded and two of his men started forward. Peter likewise headed for them, so Perry played the part ordained for him in the Gospel of Mark. He stood up and screamed as if terrified. He ran toward the priest and his men. Two of them grabbed him. Perry twisted from their grasp, shrieking as loudly as he could. The men tore away his linen cloth, and Perry dashed into the shadows.

His performance had the expected effect. Giving in to

their own panic, Jesus' followers scattered. The priest's men gave chase until called back, then they bound Jesus and led him off to the palace of the high priest.

Perry had run, but not far. He'd headed back toward Jerusalem, but crouched down beside the road, half hidden in the ditch beside it. He waited and watched, then as the priest and his entourage came down the road, he crawled from the ditch, crying and begging for mercy.

One of the men grabbed him by his hair and hauled him up, then slapped him. "You said the meek would be blessed. What of the craven?"

Jesus glanced back. "More courage lurks in quiet than ever lived in boastfulness. He is not your concern."

The priest held up a hand. "Are you one of his followers?"

Perry nodded.

"Bring him. A witness who is not paid would be useful."

Perry's captor spun him to the earth at the rear of the procession, and then kicked him so he'd march along. Perry scrambled to his feet and sidled along, ever watchful. He expected nothing on the way to the palace, but after Jesus' questioning, and before he was taken to Pilate, Kevin Smelton had to strike. It was the only real opportunity not already proscribed by the gospel accounts of Jesus' last night.

As they returned, the denial of Jesus had begun in earnest. The same faces that had smiled as Jesus walked toward the garden now turned away from him. Dogs shrank back into alleys to growl. Wicked children ran up and smacked his legs with sticks. Mothers called their children to come away as if Jesus was a leper; and in any real political sense, that was exactly what he had become.

The high priest's palace would have seemed humble

measured against other buildings that bore that description, but in Jerusalem it was a grand building, a strong one, hinting at authority without challenging it. Caiaphas, as much a politician as he was a religious leader, had the sense not to invite the Romans to imagine he was a rebel. The palace's appointments remained modest, as did the high priest's robe.

Perry crouched at the back of the main hall, hidden in the shadows of a pillar, as the high priest and his counselors questioned Jesus. He couldn't hear what was being said, but hardly needed to. Caiaphas became increasingly angry. The crowd around Jesus gesticulated wildly, stamped their feet, and screamed at him. And yet, in the midst of that storm, Jesus remained serene, his answers delivered in a voice so quiet, the violence around him had to ebb so he could be heard. Then it kicked up again, growing in intensity until Caiaphas tore his own robe from throat to navel and backhanded Jesus.

The others joined in, more primates than men, yelling, hitting, spitting and cuffing. Jesus made no pretense at protecting himself, though some of the blows spun him around. He careened about within the circle, until one heavy clout dropped him to his knees and blood dripped from a split lip.

The sight of blood dripping seemed to shock Caiaphas. With a hand he summoned those who had brought Jesus from the garden. They led him off, and Perry with him, down a narrow stairway to the building's subterranean chambers. A wooden door swung open on squeaky hinges, then rough hands propelled Perry into a dark pit strewn with sour straw. Moonlight poured in through a narrow window high in the outside wall, transfiguring Jesus' face as he lay there dazed.

Perry rose and moved to check him, but a shadow rose in the cell's far corner. A filthy, naked youth launched himself at the fallen man, a rock clutched in a raised hand. Kevin Smelton, his eyes wide, his teeth bared, roared inhumanly. "Jesus!"

Without thinking, Perry tackled Kevin, smashing him into the cell's uneven stone wall. Kevin hit hard and wetly. The boy gurgled, the stone hitting the ground only seconds before he did. His body shuddered and his breath came in ragged, rasping gulps.

Perry rolled him onto his back. "Damn it!" The young man had a dent in his head over his temple. One pupil looked normal, the other was dilated so almost no color was left. *Depressed skull fracture.* "No, this isn't what was supposed to happen."

"It often is, alas, when fragile bone strikes rock." Jesus came up on a knee and pressed a hand to Kevin's wound. The boy convulsed, and then his breath came evenly and quietly.

Smiling, Jesus sat down, crossing his legs. "He'll be good as new, unless . . . was there something wrong with him before?"

Perry blinked. "You're speaking English."

"I should hope so. I majored in dead languages at university. I may be a bit rusty, however. Been speaking Aramaic for the past three years." Jesus lifted one of Kevin's eyelids, and then brushed a hand over his damp forehead. He rubbed his thumb over his forefingers, smearing blood mixed with sweat. "Let's see, residual traces of antipsychotic drugs. Schizophrenia?"

Perry nodded. "That's what I was told."

"Excellent. Have that fixed up in a jiffy." Jesus placed both hands on Kevin's head, bowed his own, and then smiled. "He'll be right as rain. A little DNA splicing, some code rewritten, and he'll be just fine. All this will be a bad dream."

"You majored in dead languages? At university?"

"That's right." Jesus frowned for a moment. "How do you like working for Timeshares?"

"What?"

"Oh, dear boy, you are confused, aren't you?" Jesus hugged his knees to his chest. "I work for Meantime. We acquired Timeshares in a hostile takeover about, well, doesn't really matter how long after you worked for them. The stories that came down through the files were very impressive. We still follow some of the procedures, like not allowing tourists at some of these critical junctures in time."

Perry sat back, his head hitting the wall. He didn't mind the pain, save that it told him he wasn't dreaming. "But you're Jesus and you're from the future? You can't be. I saw you die."

Jesus scratched at the back of his neck. "If you saw me die, then I know who you are. I read your report. So here's the thing of it. Up the line our equipment is a bit more sophisticated than the duct tape and zip ties you were using to hold things together. Certain perturbations started hitting us. We figured out that we had a bit of a crisis as concerned Christianity. We'd relied on your report about what happened, but back-timed someone in your wake, and what we found was that, basically, there was no historical Jesus. We had to lock it down, so here I am."

"But . . ." Words caught in Perry's throat. If there actually *had* been a historical Jesus, there'd be no need for the man sitting before him to be here. "But how could you come in after what I'd seen . . ."

"Look, even in your time you know that time is elastic. Your little friend here, what did he do? Kill me?"

Perry nodded.

"Well then, that created a new outcome, but you were able to cut back in here and prevent it. That same sort of elasticity of time allowed us to predate you. Time can be pretty forgiving—you're here, now, with me, and a younger you is out there somewhere angling for a good seat to see me scourged tomorrow."

"But you're telling me that the first time around, there was no historical Jesus."

"There didn't need to be a historical Jesus. This whole gospel of peace, it was a coming thing. The Buddhists already had it figured out. And the Essenes, there are thousands of them within fifty kilometers of us right now. They've got their own millennialist gospel of peace. We are pretty sure that the first time around this is what Peter and the others based their teachings on. Someone did a book of sayings—like the Gospel of Thomas and that type of book from the era. They tagged it with a name so the Romans could hunt for their 'leader' all they wanted, but since he didn't exist, he couldn't be found. The teachings got popular, so did the teacher. Miracle stories got grafted onto things. Since the Romans respected antiquity, folks also inserted stories that fulfilled Jewish prophecies. That makes the new religion legitimate in the eyes of the Romans. Then Paul got a hold of it and, well, perfect product met perfect salesman.

"It was a brilliant piece of social programming that actually did succeed in changing the world." Jesus smiled. "The message didn't need the man."

"But you're saying it's all a lie."

"No. What I'm saying is that a beautiful picture doesn't need a frame. And it *is* a very beautiful picture." Jesus brought his hands together. "You've seen, down through history, how the Christian philosophy has moved people toward peace and love. Critics will point out that plenty of men have gone to war in the name of God, but the peace movements all flow from that same spring, and they're more powerful. A bit after your time, after you clean up that global warming mess, you get the next great awakening—like the Renaissance, only better. The nanobots I used to take care of your friend and reattach that ear, they come from that time. Rather old-school now, but they still work splendidly."

Perry started shivering, and it had nothing to do with the night's chill. He stared at his hand, bloodstained and trembling. "But I believed in you. I believed what I saw in your eyes."

Jesus came over and took Perry's hands in his. "You know what you saw in my eyes?"

Perry shook his head, unable to meet the man's gaze.

"You saw my belief that if I failed, mankind would be lost. Maybe the Essenes would have risen. Maybe Buddhism would have come on sooner and harder, but Christianity was our best bet."

Perry looked up. "I truly thought you were the Son of God. What I saw changed my life. I tried so much to be like you."

"But that was never the point, was it?"

Perry frowned. "I'm not sure I understand."

"The whole point of Christianity is not to become like Jesus. He was God and Man. An impossible task. All anyone was ever asked to do was to become his best self and to live in love for all others." Jesus shook his head. "Too many Christians become sheep and a few others wolves; so very rare are the shepherds."

Perry chewed his lower lip. "Because of you I changed my life."

"No. You changed your life because you knew it was wrong. You were not happy. I became—your *idealization* of Jesus became—a catalyst for change." Jesus released Perry's hands. "But are you happy now, or have you so pulled away from who you were that you don't recognize yourself anymore?"

Jacobsen's remark echoed back through Perry's mind. "You wouldn't have liked who I was before."

Jesus shrugged. "Who am I to sit in judgment?"

Perry arched an eyebrow.

"Sorry joke, I know. Just among the crew..." He sighed. "The question is, do *you* like you now?"

I used to be a wolf, now I'm a sheep. "No."

"Then be who you are. Be the best you possible." Jesus stood and offered Perry a hand. "That's all anyone can ask of us."

Perry pulled himself to his feet. "Are you ... are you actually going to die?"

"The answer to that question is not really one your time is ready to hear." Jesus shook his hand. "Thank you for saving me. You came here through the Mark 14:51–52 loophole?"

Perry nodded.

"You know what the other half of that is then?"

Again, Perry nodded.

"You'll have to decide if that's part of who you are." Jesus gestured and Kevin Smelton's unconscious form vanished. "My way will be easier on him. I'll send you back, too."

Perry caught the man's wrist. "Do you really know what you're doing?"

Jesus hesitated, then gave him a bit of a smile. "No, but I know *why*. That makes all the difference." He slipped his wrist from Perry's grasp, then gestured, and Perry found himself sucked back through time.

Rolf Jacobsen got up from his desk and walked to the sideboard. He poured himself three fingers of a very old scotch. "I don't know what to say, Perry. Jesus is a time traveler from our future. Are you sure?"

Perry nodded. "Absolutely. I'm back and my retrieval device wasn't used. How else would I get back here?"

Jacobsen took a healthy swallow of the amber liquid, and then pointed the glass toward Perry. "Well, a divine being . . ."

"No, he was as human as you or I."

"Perry, if what you saw got out . . ."

Perry scratched at his beard, suddenly anxious to get rid of it. "Wouldn't matter. Religious Christianity has too much power. It would be labeled as nonsense. I'd be branded an atheist lunatic and the backlash against Timeshares would destroy the business."

Jacobsen half smiled. "Well, we do have a grateful senator on our side."

"No, you don't." Perry stood up, crossed over to Jacobsen, and poured himself a glass, but only sipped. The scent, all peaty and smoky, filled his head and burned the back of his throat. "If you tell him his son was healed by Jesus, he has proof of the divinity of Christ. He won't keep that a secret, and that will strengthen the theological side of Christianity. That would destroy our future, too."

Jacobsen returned to his desk. "Well, these are not problems for you to be concerned about, Perry."

Time to be me again. The best me. "You're wrong."

"What?"

"You're going to tell me that decisions like this are made above my pay grade, but that's what created this mess in the first place. Your responsibility is to Timeshares, I get that, but this isn't about your company." Perry drank more, and then smiled. "So, what you're going to do is to tell the senator that I caught Kevin, I forced his meds into him, and then brought him back. We left during a thunderstorm, with lightning strikes nearby. As near as we can tell, the time stream flux combined with the drugs and lightning to create a permanent time-release situation with his meds. Kevin will be fine from now on, just a freaky chance side effect of his vacation."

Jacobson laughed aloud. "You can't fool a senator with such nonsense."

"Jake, this is a guy who thinks the world was born in 4000 B.C. Science is not his strong suit." Perry's eyes hardened. "What was his cover story for the time he'd be away?"

Jacobsen sat down and hit a few keys on his computer. "He and his son were taking a fishing trip in the wilds of Maine."

"Good. Get depositions from folks saying he was never there. Have a look-alike actor holographed out celebrating with an escort or three. Senator Smelton begins to talk, that will distract him enough so you pop and drop someone into the recent past to plant solid evidence on him and destroy his career and credibility."

The Timeshares CEO's head slowly swiveled around. "Who are you and what did you do with Perry?"

"You asked if the old me would have recognized the new me. The answer was no. But the old me *would* recognize who I am now, you think? You remember how I was back then? Ask yourself how much closer to the old me do you want me to get?"

Jacobsen held his hands up. "I see your point. But, as long as we're talking extortion ..."

"What do I want?"

"I'll make a list."

"No more lepers. I want back on the payroll, commanding the Stopwatches. And you have to send me back, one more time."

"Really, to say good-bye?"

Perry shook his head. "To finish the job."

By the when Perry arrived, the stone had already been rolled away from the tomb and the guards had run off. Ducking his head, Perry entered and checked. *No shroud, another mystery solved.* He didn't know if Jesus had opened the tomb, or the rest of his crew had done it, but it really didn't matter.

He'd come in using two verses from Mark's Gospel, and scholars had linked them with another. *Mark 16:5– 8.* Perry smiled, and seated himself on the stone shelf where Jesus' body had lain.

Mary Magdalene and another woman hurried to the mouth of the tomb. They stopped, horror on their faces when they saw him.

He calmly raised a hand. The philosophy of Jesus would save the world, but without being clothed as religion, it would die aborning.

Perry smiled. "Be not afraid. The one you seek is gone. Go tell Peter and the others this joyous news. He has died, he has risen, and he has saved us all."

Spoilers
Linda P. Baker

Linda P. Baker's novels *The Irda* and *Tears of the Night Sky*, cowritten with Nancy Varian Berberick, have been published internationally. Linda has short stories in more than a dozen anthologies, including *Pandora's Closet* and *Spells of the City*. In addition to writing fiction, she also writes and edits brochures and Web sites and loves doing research. The Baker pack—Linda, her husband, Larry, and their Airedale terrier/dragon, Grady—live in Mobile, Alabama. Linda dedicates her story to Grady, who has taught her to live in the now, to enjoy the wind in her hair, and to greet every day with an arrrooooo . . .

I did it for the mysteries.

—S. J. Cameroon

"I can get you what you need."

The leader of the Angels of Time, the Reverend John J. Something-or-other, had a shiny slick look that made me want to pick up the handful of change that lay on one of Rick's crates and stuff it deep into my pocket.

He stood in the middle of Rick's squat, in what had once been an upscale apartment building with cavernous lofts, but now was just junk space that nobody wanted. He was beautifully dressed in a dark gray suit and a blinding white shirt, and he pretended a jolly friendliness. But he looked around out of the corners of his eyes, and his nostrils flared as if he smelled something rotten.

Not that I could blame him. Rick's squat wasn't nice and it wasn't clean. It had a tattered old sofa and a couple of wooden crates for furniture. And a sleeping bag for a bed and a chair with only three legs for a nightstand. Propping it up was a stack of old books, probably scavenged from the library where Rick had worked. There wasn't much call for history books anymore, not since Timeshares.

Rick's space wasn't even the nicest the building had to offer. That's why it annoyed me for some jerk to be so obvious with his disdain.

Rick always let others have the best of what was available. He'd done it when he had his dream job, assistant librarian at the university, and he did it now that he had no job and no place of his own. The way he had cared for the books, he now looked after the homeless kids and the crazy old ladies and the men like him, anachronisms in a world without mystery.

But still, there must have been something to the way Rick lived. Even with the library gone, he was once the happiest person I knew. Or he had been, until he won the Time Lotto.

And that's why we were now standing in Rick's room with Reverend John, who reached into the inside pocket of his shiny suit and pulled out the tiniest e-phone I'd ever seen. He thumbed it on, punched a couple of buttons, and then handed it to Rick.

Duane, who had been lurking in the shadows of the

far corner, shuffled forward to look over Rick's shoulder. Duane was the one who'd set up the meeting. He had once been an Angel of Time, before he'd decided he liked things, like drugs and sex, that just weren't all that angelic.

On the screen was a document with a long list of explosives and components. The writing was so tiny I had to squint to see it. Ballistite, guncotton, mercury fulminate, Trinitrotoluene TNT, RDX. The names meant nothing to me.

"Old style C4?" Rick handed the phone back without looking at the list. "Can you get C4 without heavy metals in it?"

The reverend straightened his shoulders as if he was proud of what he was doing. "Yes."

That bothered me. None of us were proud of our plans. We just couldn't think of anything else to do.

"It has to be metal free," Rick insisted.

"Yes," the reverend repeated. "I can get it. You don't need to worry about that."

"We'll decide what we need to worry about," I snapped.

Rick put a hand on my arm. "Good stuff? Not something somebody cooked up in their basement last week? And without metals. We won't make it past the first floor if it triggers the alarms."

The reverend nodded.

Rick looked from me to Duane.

Reluctantly, I nodded. Not so reluctantly, Duane nodded. To my mind, Duane liked the idea of blowing things up a bit too much.

"Okay," Rick said to the reverend. "What's it going to cost?"

"There's no charge."

All three of us were immediately on guard. "No charge?" we said in unison.

"My price is simple. When it's done, the Angels of Time will get credit."

"Credit!" Duane turned very red. "We're not going to risk our lives for—"

Rick put his hand out to stop Duane. "That's fine," he said, and he held out his hand to the reverend to shake.

Before they could agree, I said, "We'll need a weapon, too. A gun with no metal parts."

The man hesitated for just a fraction of a second, and then he gave a brisk nod and shook Rick's hand. "I can have everything within a week or so."

"Duane will contact you about where to drop it off," Rick said.

I walked behind the reverend to the door and watched him. As he walked down the hallway, he pulled a handkerchief out of his pocket. He was wiping his hands when he disappeared down the stairwell.

The air seemed a bit easier to breathe with all that shine gone. "He's gone."

Duane whirled on Rick. "I'm not risking my—"

"Duane. Take it easy." Rick smiled, calm and cool as could be, like always. "All I agreed to was that he could claim credit for the Angels. I didn't say anything about who else might claim credit."

Duane whooped and slapped Rick on the back.

I couldn't meet Rick's gaze. I liked him. And I knew I was going to double-cross him.

A week later we had our explosives, and I had my plastic gun. It felt like a toy in my hand.

My friend Larry came back from his scouting trip and told me who built Stonehenge. Of course, he swore me to secrecy first, because he was expecting to make a big splash on the history reality shows. I couldn't look at him after that.

A week after that, we had our plan.

Dina, a friend who worked at the local coffee shop, took her Timeshares trip and didn't come back. Of course, Timeshares wouldn't have admitted that if anyone had asked.

There was failsafe on top of failsafe. Supposedly, no one could travel back and not return, the same way nobody could go back in time and change anything. The pretrip hypnotic programming prevented tampering. Supposedly it also prevented you from smashing your monitoring devices so they couldn't activate and bring you home. I guess Dina found a way around that.

Dina had wanted to see the world before it was spoiled. She had wanted to see the earth before it was overpopulated by humans and polluted by corporate greed. Now she was living in a green world without pollution, without crowding, without war or hatred, without Timeshares.

I was envious.

The night, *the* night, we used a van Duane had "found" in another part of town.

As we drove past Timeshares, past the elegant, U-shaped drive with its fountains splashing water from Lourdes, I tried to look at it as a first time visitor would, but I couldn't. The expensive, glittering elegance had turned lurid and gaudy for me. The lights were too bright, and the stained glass windows, imported directly from medieval England, were over the top. The Timeshares Travel Agency logo, supposedly painted with pigments from Lascaux, looked faded and tired.

We parked and Jo, Lu, and two others dispersed in different directions to find possible getaway cars and sit tight until they were needed.

Duane, Rick, and I headed toward Timeshares. We were dressed in silvery gray so that at first glance we looked like Timeshares employees.

As we walked, I thought about Rick. He and I were the only two of the group who'd been on a time trip.

There had been such an outcry when the company rolled out the red carpet for its zillionaire clientele, such fury that something like that was only available to the very rich, that a lottery system had been started. Every month, five were chosen out of the millions who'd signed up.

Rick had been one of the first TimeLotto winners. And one of the few people who'd chosen to go forward in time instead of someplace in the past.

It was surprising how most people wanted to go back in time. And it wasn't just a safety issue, though I was sure that played into it. Timeshares sent people back to scout in the past, but who could ever be sure of the future? Going forward was a crap shoot. What someone scouted yesterday and found safe could be completely changed by the events of today.

Plus, Timeshares wouldn't let anyone go just a few years forward. They claimed there was a mental health issue involved in traveling to a time in which you were still alive, though that was crap. I knew that after any important business decision had been made, one of the Timeshares execs traveled a few years forward to make sure they'd made the right decision.

Rick said I was the only one he'd told about what he'd seen of the future. What he'd seen was the reason he was walking beside me wearing a backpack with enough C4 in it to blow up a city block. It was the reason I was walking beside him.

As we approached the city block that housed Time-shares, Duane gave us a grinning thumbs-up and angled off toward one of the visitor parking lots.

Rick checked his watch. It was an old-fashioned one with hands that swept around and around, pointing to the minutes and hours.

I turned aside to look at mine, shielding it from him. My watch was a Timeshares Digital that showed time, date, temperature, and could be programmed to show the same information for five different continents. Or five different centuries.

Rick took a deep breath and blew it out. He gave a tiny nod and walked away toward the back of Timeshares.

I watched to make sure he turned the corner before I started off toward the front of the building. We were supposed to reconnoiter, then rendezvous on the opposite side of the block, near the delivery and service entrance. That's where Rick and Duane thought we were going to break in, after Duane's diversion had everybody's attention, after we'd called in a bomb threat for the building.

My plan was simpler.

At the employee entrance, halfway down the block, I stopped and took out the things I'd stuffed into my pockets—my Timeshares Security badge and my ID.

I held my badge up to the reader, then typed in my PIN.

The wrought iron gate, built by a famous gunslinger/ blacksmith during the period called the Old West, slid open.

I went through to a door that let me into a brightly lit hallway lined with walls of one-way glass. I could see the grounds outside, and the glittering lights from the fountain. The air was dry and overprocessed. The guard post was empty.

The door at the other end of the hall opened, and

a guard came trudging toward me. Then he recognized me, and he straightened and quickstepped the rest of the distance.

"You need to send some guards along the fence," I snapped. "I saw a couple of people dressed in black walking toward the delivery gate."

He thumbed the headset in his ear and relayed my message.

A half dozen guards, all straightening their uniforms, came hustling down the hall. They breezed past me and jogged along the fence.

My guard made an officious pretense of scrutinizing the photo on my ID, then me, then the ID again.

When the explosion came, I started even though I was expecting it. The loud boom rattled the glass walls.

The guard jumped like the C4 had been set off in his pants.

Behind me, some time traveler's car went up in flames. The night sky lit up like sunrise. The reflection of red flames danced in the windows.

The guard rushed out the door, through the gate, and down the sidewalk, yelling for back-up as he went.

Another bomb went off, farther back in the parking lot, then another. That one was closer, but smaller, just like Duane had promised it would be.

I stepped outside. The smell of burning metal and synthetic fuel washed over me.

More guards poured out of the building and ran to the parking lot.

I walked back to the gate as Rick came running up. He'd made good time circling the block. "What are you doing here? What happened?"

Then he saw me. *Really* saw me. With my Timeshares Security badge and my glittering holographic Time-shares Security ID hanging from my collar.

I tugged my Timeshares cap out of my back pocket and pulled it on.

His face, so ruddy from running and from the reflection of the fire, went pale. "What—?"

"Give me the backpack."

"What—?" His mouth worked. He looked like a fish staring out through the glass of a watery prison.

"Give me the backpack. Now. Or I'll call the guards."

The hurt in his face was almost more than I could stand.

I had met Rick after the university had tossed out most of its books and made the library into a virtual theater showing vids of the past, before he won the Time Lotto. I'd heard him talking to a small group of people at a university vid premiere one night, and his voice had drawn me in. It was deep and smooth as caramel. It was a voice made for reading sonnets and poetry, not for recruiting people like Duane and me.

But maybe Rick would live to read sonnets again and make women sigh with his amazing voice. I knew if I stood there much longer, I'd try to explain everything that I was thinking, and I didn't have time for that. "Now!"

He slipped his backpack off.

I took it and slipped it on. The C4 in it was a lumpy weight in the bottom of the cloth bag. It felt like a rock against my spine.

"I'm sorry, Rick," I said. I handed him a custodian's ID that I'd pilfered. "Put this on. Walk like you're tired, but glad to be heading home. They won't pay you any attention."

I turned to go, and Rick pulled me back by my sleeve.

For a second, I thought he was going to try to stop me, but all he said was, "Why are you doing this?" His voice broke my heart. "I told you what I saw!"

I tried to smile at him, but I couldn't make my mouth move. "I mailed you a letter explaining everything."

If I was successful, the letter wouldn't make any sense, but I owed him an explanation. I whispered, "Forgive me," and I gave him a quick kiss on the cheek. Before he could protest, I shut the gate and walked back in.

The first floor was in an uproar. Guards were running to man the huge lobby with its rows upon rows of stained glass and its original, ancient Persian rugs. I had to go through a double line of guards around the main elevator system, but none of them questioned my presence. They expected to see one of the Captains of Security on a night when bombs had exploded nearby.

I got on the restricted elevator, pushed the button for the lowest level, and stepped up to the retina reader when prompted. The computer recognized me. It scanned me and found no metal, nothing it would think of as dangerous. I could feel the gun digging into my hip, the weight of the plastique against my back.

The elevator went down so smoothly I barely felt movement at all.

I stepped out into a white hallway that had come straight from a nightmare. That's all there was, as far as I could see. Shivering white. Just white, disappearing into the distance. It was the most disconcerting thing I'd ever seen, and it hadn't gotten better with familiarity.

The walls were solid if you touched them, but there was a trick to the surface that made them look like they wavered and wobbled. There were no doors visible until you actually touched the entry to the lab you wanted to enter. That, it had seemed to Timeshares' corporate officers, was the best way to protect their priceless time travel equipment. No one could even find it unless they knew how to get there in the first place.

I knew how to get there.

I'd been working for Timeshares since I'd graduated from college, when I'd signed up, all eager and starry-eyed, with my brand new history degree. I'd started out as a tech, then graduated to scout.

Then Timeshares had developed the technology to make vids, and I'd become a vidhistorian, traveling into the past to film history for the virtual libraries. I'd loved it, and I'd been good at it. I'd been the best at capturing not just the pictures of the past, but the essence of the past, the smells and sights and sounds, the spirit of it. That was what I'd thought I would spend my life doing.

But then I'd met Rick. Then he'd told me what the world of the past was making of the world of the future. The week after he came back from his time trip, I'd made a lateral move into Security.

All I'd needed to complete my plans was to find someone who could help me get the C4, once called plastique, and create enough of a distraction that I could enter the bottom floor with it. The elevator scanners would have picked up any of today's metallic-based explosives. And I couldn't go into the past and bring it back myself. The scanners would have caught me coming out with contraband.

I didn't know how Reverend John's people had done it. I was fairly sure his C4 was from the past, not that it mattered. Duane's explosions had shown that the C4 worked. That's all I cared about.

I walked the required number of steps, and put out my hand. I pressed my face to the wall and tried not to blink as the computer scanned my eyes. The door appeared under my hand and slid open.

No matter how many times I saw it, the time machine took my breath away.

Even on this side that visitors never saw, it was sleek

and shiny, but not shiny like the reverend's suit. Shiny like a spaceship and crackling with blue static electricity. It was art as much as it was machine. And it was the worst thing that had ever happened to humanity.

The tech's expression was slack and bored. On the commercial side, the operators had a variety of travelers to keep them occupied. They had costumes to check, and they had to search whatever was brought back, which I'd always thought was one of the most interesting jobs in the building, because you could never predict what someone would pick up and try to bring back.

But on the employee side, there was nothing to do but check authorizations and push buttons.

"What's going on topside?" he asked, as he scanned my retinas and my fingerprints.

"Nothing really. Somebody blew up a car in the visitor lot."

I took off my ID and my badge and put them into a safety basket. The laser field around it wouldn't let anyone but me take them back out.

"Oh." He seemed as disinterested, as lackadaisical, as the security guard had been. "Haven't seen you take a trip in a while, Captain. Where you off to tonight?"

I handed him the gold square with my destination encoded in it. He fed it into the reader, checked the authorization, then the picture that came up on the screen, and gave my clothes a quick once over to make sure I looked appropriate for the time period.

Then, with a yawn, he double-checked everything. He didn't even seem impressed that my destination was such a rare one. He did a desultory check with a metal detecting wand, then checked to see that my implant was still under the skin on the back of my neck.

"Step in when you're ready."

My heart thumped and started to race. Heat rose up

my neck. I'd traveled hundreds of times, but I was more scared than I'd been the first time.

I guess that was why I fell as I materialized in another time. I stayed there on my hands and knees retching for several minutes. My tongue was coated with a taste so sweet it felt thick.

Bill, the PR guy who'd done the original advertising campaign for Timeshares, had told me he tasted vinegar. I'd have traded vinegar for this taste any day. It was like I'd taken a drink of perfume.

I wiped my mouth, wiped my tongue on my sleeve, and I still couldn't get rid of it. This had never happened before, but I'd never gone into the past so close to my own time.

Timeshares claimed that they restricted traveling into the immediate past because of the physical stress it caused. But they also said no one could disable the equipment and stay back in time. I thought of Dina, walking sometime, somewhere, in a pristine forest, breathing in air that had never been through a processor. Would what I was about to do send her back to our time? Or make it like she'd never been there at all?

The paradoxes of time travel, even after all the years I'd done it, could make you crazy if you started trying to follow the twists and turns.

I climbed to my feet and looked around. I'd seen this building so often, on posters in the Timeshares gift shop, in books, that I knew it as if I'd lived here. It was night, and the building was dark, but I only had to retrace my steps once to find the lab.

I eased through the door. The lab looked just like it did in Timeshares' orientation video. It had old-fashioned metal tabletops that looked like autopsy tables. Long lightbulbs cast a greenish-blue light over everything. Every surface was messy with books and papers and charts and snips of computer boards and pieces of oddly shaped metal. That kind of chaos would never be allowed in a Timeshares lab today.

And sitting there, bent over his work in concentration, was the man who'd started it all. The creator of the time travel technology, Dr. Ken Campbell.

I let the backpack slide off my shoulders and pulled the gun out of my waistband. Even though it was made completely of plastic, it pinched the flesh between my thumb and forefinger when I slid the mechanism back and let it go. A shiver of pain went through my thumb.

Dr. Campbell jumped and turned around. "Who are you? How did you get in here?"

I must have been a sight, holding a trembling gun pointed at him with one hand while I sucked my wounded hand to ease the sting.

He said it again as we stared at each other, and I realized I didn't know what to say to him. How do you tell someone they helped you ruin the world?

"You don't know what you did." My voice was all winded and croaky.

His gaze darted between my face and the wobbly gun pointing at his gut. He opened his mouth like he was going to call for help.

I found my voice. "Don't yell. If you do, I'll just have to kill you before I tell you why."

His gaze darted from the gun to the door, but his curiosity got the best of him.

It was exactly what I expected from the genius who created the time machine—more curiosity than sense. "You ruined everything. You and your machine."

I shook the gun toward the guts of the machine he was working on. "You ruined history!"

I paused, trying to find words, and when I did, they boiled out, running over each other and doubling back.

"First, it was only rich people who could afford to time travel, so they started a lottery so that everybody had a chance. More and more people went back, and then the colleges and universities got into it. And more and more historical mysteries were solved. It became a race, a contest. Who built Stonehenge, where the Anasazi went, what the world was like before pollution and over-crowding. How they built the pyramids and why children suddenly started living longer in the 1300s. Who really invented the lightbulb first and whether Lizzie Borden really killed her family. Why Petra was abandoned and where the Maya went. How their calendars worked and why the world didn't end in 2012. Where the Hope diamond went and who stole the Liberty Bell. Who Mona Lisa really was. Why the *Victory* sank and where Atlantis is. Who King Arthur was and what the Druids were really like. Why the Greeks never discovered zero."

My voice sounded mad, even to me. Crazy and shrill. I swallowed and made an attempt to slow down. "Harvard found Hitler's body. Cambridge solved the extinction of the dinosaurs. MIT discovered how the pyramids were built. The University of North Carolina discovered what happened to the lost colony of Roanoke. And a pissant southern college with only a couple of thousand students debunked King Solomon's Mines and took pictures of the creation of the Nazca Lines."

I could see the hunger grow in his eyes, the questions, and the desire to know the answers to all the things I was talking about. It was like watching what had happened to my world in microcosm etched in his face.

I'd forgotten that he had only lived to make one short time trip. He'd died before he could really experience his own creation.

Maybe because of me. I shook my head. *Don't go there. Don't get tied up in time knots.*

"In the future, I—somebody—will come back with a film of Jesus. At first, Timeshares won't distribute it. But, then, someone will get greedy, or just stupid, and they will. And that will start a race for more information on all the religions.

"Except—except everybody sees their gods their own way. The vids won't be the wonders they were intended to be. Not everybody will agree that they're accurate. Not everybody will agree that it's Jesus or the Buddha, or their version of Jesus or the Buddha. So somebody else will go back to debunk the first film. And somebody else will try to debunk the debunker's film.

"And some people won't stop at arguing their points of view. Somebody will kill the person who blasphemed their god. And somebody else will kill that person. And pretty soon the whole world will be at war. Killing each other because they don't like the other person's version of the past.

"The world Rick saw ..." I stopped. I could hear Rick's voice in my head. Rick's beautiful, rich velvet voice, twisted with the darkness of what he'd seen in the future.

My stomach churned. I could still taste the perfume of Campbell's time. And somewhere in the middle of my rant, I'd lowered the gun.

He'd been too transfixed to notice. "Tell me more," he breathed. He stood there, in the middle of his lab, with the last piece of the puzzle in his hand.

I knew the shape and size of it as well as I knew a spoon or a key. Or the gun in my hand.

On this day, he'd made an intellectual leap and discovered the last component that would make his time machine work. Today, he'd changed history.

"It's like the whole world is starving, and all they want to eat is the past. And one of these days, they'll hate other people's versions of the past so much, they'll destroy the future."

But he was ravenous, too. I could see it in his eyes. He was like everyone else in my time. He'd heard everything I'd said, and the wrongness of it, the horror, didn't even occur to him. He just wanted to know more.

The gun wasn't heavy, but my arm came up as if I was in slow motion.

I pulled the trigger. It was as loud as a metal gun, but the sound was flatter.

The bullet hit him in the chest. His eyes went wide and round as a red stain grew on his lab coat. He fell back slowly. Slowly. He crumpled to the floor, and he died with the heart of the time machine clutched to his own heart.

Someone would come, a guard or somebody working late in one of the other labs. But I couldn't move until I took a couple of deep breaths, until I offered up a prayer for forgiveness.

Then I took the component from his fingers. It was sticky and warm with his blood.

I put it in on the table with all the other bits and pieces and shoved them together. On the top, I put his notebook.

I knew that notebook. I'd seen it every day for most of my adult life. It was proudly displayed in the lobby of Timeshares, and every morning, the CEO, wearing white gloves, turned a page of it, so that if you were willing to come by every day for more than three months, you could see all Dr. Campbell's handwritten notes. Except that reading was a dying art.

I opened the backpack and took out two blocks of C4.

I shoved the detonator into it, the way Rick had shown me, and I put it on top of things on the table.

And then I put the rest of the C4 into the belly of the time machine. It didn't look like the flashy thing that sat guarded and worshipped in my time. This first version was just a square gray ugly box of machinery with a transporter that looked like one of the old shower stalls in Rick's abandoned building.

The guards came before I had time to push the button.

There were two of them, older men clad in blue uniforms with shiny brass buttons that winked at me. They crashed through the door and slid to a stop when they saw Dr. Campbell's body.

I could have shot them. I pointed the gun at them. But I hadn't come back here to kill innocent people.

One man drew his gun, but the other one forgot to unhook his holster flap. He fumbled at with it. His eyes were tight with fear.

The faster of the two shot me.

It felt . . . odd.

There was a sound like a meaty punch. My chest went numb, and I fell back against the time machine. And then a fiery pain blossomed, right over my heart.

So this was what dying felt like.

I'd thought I would be afraid, but instead I was so calm.

Everything had slowed to half speed.

I forced myself up. My blood smeared the time machine.

I staggered and dragged my hand up so that the two men could see what I held in it.

Rick had built the trigger in a cute little box that had a red, blinking button like something from a child's game.

They understood exactly what I was showing them. They ran.

I looked down at myself. From my breasts down, my silver gray uniform was bright red and wet. Shiny.

I was going to die shiny. It made me smile.

I pushed the button.

Rick stumbled into his apartment, dropped his satchel, and flipped on the lights. His dog, Grady, danced around his feet, glad to see him, but Rick had to sit down to catch his breath.

He'd obviously run up the stairs instead of taking the elevator, but he couldn't remember why.

The library books in his satchel had to weigh fifty pounds. He could have killed himself running with all that extra weight. His heart felt like it was going to jump out of his chest, and his breath was so rasping that it hurt his throat.

When his breathing had eased, he bent down to pat Grady.

Something in his shirt pocket crackled. The mail he'd picked up before his dash up the stairs, he guessed. He pulled out a letter, addressed to him with way too much postage stuck in the corner.

He opened it and pulled out a single sheet of paper so thick and fine that it felt like something from another time. The logo on it was for something called Timeshares Travel Agency. He'd never heard of it.

The note was written in a neat script.

> *Rick,*
> *If I'm successful, I don't think this note will make any sense to you.*
> *But if you read it in time, please forgive me. Forgive me for making your beautiful voice dark. Forgive me for lying to you. But if I'd let you blow up the machine of today, they'd have just built another*

one. And all that would have accomplished was to delay the inevitable. I had to take out the very first one.

There are so many reasons why I've done what I did. It was for the Anasazi, and Newgrange and Stonehenge and the Mona Lisa. For the books and the libraries. But, mostly, it was for the future.

I did it for the mysteries. And for the children. Everyone deserves the right to grow up unspoiled, not knowing.

Sarah Jane

ABOUT THE EDITORS

Jean Rabe is the author of two dozen books and more than four dozen short stories. She primarily writes fantasy, but dabbles in the science fiction, military, and horror genres when given the opportunity. A former newspaper reporter and news bureau chief, she's also edited anthologies, gaming magazines, and newsletters. When not writing, Jean works on her growing to-be-read stack of books, plays roleplaying and board games, visits museums, and fiercely tugs on old socks with her three dogs. Visit her Web site at: www.jeanrabe.com.

Martin H. Greenberg is the CEO of Tekno Books and its predecessor companies, now the largest book developer of commercial fiction and nonfiction in the world, with over two thousand published books, including more than one thousand anthologies, that have been translated into thirty-three languages. He is the recipient of an unprecedented four Lifetime Achievement Awards in the science fiction, mystery, and supernatural horror genres, the Milford and Solstice awards in science fiction, the Bram Stoker award in horror, and the Ellery Queen award in mystery—the only person in publishing history to have received all three awards.

RM Meluch

The Tour of the Merrimack

"An action-packed space opera. For readers who like romps through outer space, lots of battles with gooey horrific insects, and character sexplotation, *The Myriad* delivers..."   —*SciFi.com*

"Like *The Myriad*, this one is grand space opera. You will enjoy it."   —*Analog*

"This is grand old-fashioned space opera, so toss your disbelief out the nearest airlock and dive in."

—*Publishers Weekly* (Starred Review)

THE MYRIAD   0-7564-0320-1
WOLF STAR   0-7564-0383-6
THE SAGITTARIUS COMMAND
                        978-0-7564-0490-1
STRENGTH AND HONOR
                        978-0-7564-0578-6

To Order Call: 1-800-788-6262
www.dawbooks.com

DAW 48

CJ Cherryh
Complete Classic Novels in Omnibus Editions

To Order Call: 1-800-788-6262
www.dawbooks.com

CJ Cherryh
The Foreigner Novels

"Serious space opera at its very best by one of the leading SF writers in the field today." —*Publishers Weekly*

"Her world building, aliens, and suspense rank among the strongest in the whole SF field. May those strengths be sustained indefinitely, or at least until the end of *Foreigner*." —*Booklist*

To Order Call: 1-800-788-6262
www.dawbooks.com

DAW 8

Tanya Huff

The Confederation Novels

"As a heroine, Kerr shines. She is cut from the same mold as Ellen Ripley of the *Aliens* films. Like her heroine, Huff delivers the goods." —*SF Weekly*

A CONFEDERATION OF VALOR
Omnibus Edition
(Valor's Choice, The Better Part of Valor)
978-0-7564-0399-7

THE HEART OF VALOR
978-0-7564-0481-9

VALOR'S TRIAL
978-0-7564-0479-6

To Order Call: 1-800-788-6262
www.dawbooks.com

S. Andrew Swann

OTHERLAND

Tad Williams

"The Otherland books are a major accomplishment."—*Publishers Weekly*

"It will captivate you."
—*Cinescape*

In many ways it is humankind's most stunning achievement. This most exclusive of places is also one of the world's best-kept secrets, but somehow, bit by bit, it is claiming Earth's most valuable resource: its children.

CITY OF GOLDEN SHADOW (Vol. One)
978-0-88677-763-0

RIVER OF BLUE FIRE (Vol. Two)
978-0-88677-844-6

MOUNTAIN OF BLACK GLASS (Vol. Three)
978-0-88677-906-1

SEA OF SILVER LIGHT (Vol. Four)
978-0-75640-0030-9

To Order Call: 1-800-788-6262
www.dawbooks.com

DAW 44

PO #: 4500301709